Don't Play With Fyre

Don't Play With Fyre

JUDI FLANAGAN

authorHOUSE®

AuthorHouse™
1663 Liberty Drive
Bloomington, IN 47403
www.authorhouse.com
Phone: 1-800-839-8640

First published by AuthorHouse   09/07/2011

ISBN: 978-1-4634-4733-5 (sc)
ISBN: 978-1-4634-4734-2 (hc)
ISBN: 978-1-4634-4735-9 (ebk)

Library of Congress Control Number: 2011914009

Printed in the United States of America

Any people depicted in stock imagery provided by Thinkstock are models, and such images are being used for illustrative purposes only.
Certain stock imagery © Thinkstock.

This book is printed on acid-free paper.

For My Children and Grandchildren

May you always be adventurous.
May you always know who you are.

The bells were ringing in the dale
And men looked up with faces pale;
The dragon's ire more fierce than fire
Laid low their towers and houses frail.

The Hobbit
J.R.R. Tolkien

What lies behind us and what lies before us
are tiny matters compared to what lies within us.

Emerson

Chapter 1

Today is my twentieth birthday and I, Molly Fyre, am becoming an immortal.

I suppose that sounds strange to you, but the society in which I live gives us the choice of becoming immortal once we reached eighteen years old. Since both my parents were immortals I've decided it was time to take the Elixir and complete my transformation; two years late, but I'll explain.

I never knew my father, who disappeared after I was born; Mom had never talked much about him, the subject being taboo in our house. Two years ago, right before my eighteenth birthday, I tragically lost her in a car accident; I miss her terribly.

My grief has forced me to wait this long to make up my mind. With no siblings, I was all alone except for Eric whom I'd met about a year ago when he was some kind of consultant for Arnos, a friend of my family, who had kindly taken me in. Eric was my savior. We've been inseparable since.

I quit my job at an insurance company two weeks ago when Arnos told me I wouldn't need a job anymore. He told me he had something important for me to do and since he has been a friend I trust his judgment. We came here to Arnos' for my transformation because he is the Keeper of the Elixir for our sector.

Here is my story.

"The Elixir is forever, Molly, there's no turning back," he said. "Are you sure?"

I looked into Eric's anxious eyes. We were alone in a small room in Arnos' house. There was only a bed, a tall ornate wooden chest in the corner and a couple of chairs. The walls were painted a rich red; a small window let in very little light.

"I know. Arnos explained the whole procedure to me in detail. This is my decision, Eric. Mother told me years ago to expect this. I've grieved long enough so let's do it."

He looked at me with those steel-blue eyes, so intense, so worried. He'd gone through this himself four years ago. It wasn't pleasant; you go to sleep for three days dreaming horrible nightmares. Some made it through okay, some didn't.

Was I afraid? Sure, who wouldn't enjoy three days of horrific nightmares? Why couldn't the Elixir make this pleasant . . . maybe sunny skies and soft breezes?

Somehow I was confident everything would be all right. After all, I had Eric to come back to.

Eric told me to sit down on the bed while he went to the cabinet in the corner of the room and removed the crystal chalice and the golden bottle of Elixir. As he held the bottle up to the light I was amazed at how it glowed.

My heart started beating madly. *Don't chicken out now.*

He brought the chalice and Elixir to the bedside with a reverence I had never seen in him before.

"Would you like me to mix the Elixir with some wine? It's kind of bitter tasting."

"Yes, please," I said, my voice quivering.

I watched him as he poured the Elixir into the chalice and added the wine. This was it. No turning back.

Eric knelt down beside the bed and handed me the chalice with shaky hands.

As I peered wide-eyed into the chalice I noticed the fluid was bubbling. I began to have second thoughts. What if this didn't work and I ended up a zombie or . . . dead?

I'd thought long and hard about this, pondering what my life would be like to live forever or at the very least a long, long time. My mother would never see how I'd turned out; would never see me happy with Eric.

Oh, what the hell, I was Molly Fyre and committed now. I gripped the chalice with both hands and lifted it to my lips. The first gulp was awful and burned my throat. I chugged the rest and lay down cautiously on the bed.

"How do you feel?" Eric said after a few minutes, looking as worried as I did.

"I'm not sure," I said, because I really wasn't feeling anything out of the ordinary.

"Shouldn't I be feeling something by now?"

"Maybe the effects are different for you. I felt drowsy almost immediately. But that was me," he said. We looked at each other with dread.

"What if . . . ." I whispered but I didn't get to finish my sentence. "Wait, here it comes. Oh, boy, this is so weird. I feel like the room is spinning!"

My eyes closed slowly as Eric's beautiful face gradually faded and the darkness swept me away.

Chapter 2

"**I**s she awake yet?" said a tiny voice close to my face.

"I can't tell. Get out of the way." This one sounded older.

I tried to open my eyes, but they seemed to be stuck together and who was talking? It sounded like children but my hearing wasn't at its best yet.

"Stop pushing!" said voice number one. "You always get to see more than me Pete. It's not fair!"

What a feisty kid, I thought. *Reminds me of a younger me.*

A door opened quietly to my left and someone spoke in a whisper. "What are you two doing in here? You know that Arnos said no one was to disturb Molly right now. Scat!"

The voice sounded familiar but I couldn't place it. What was wrong with my brain? I vaguely remember going to sleep and dreaming some pretty awful dreams. Boy, were they awful! Dragons and fire breathing people. Wait. Maybe it was the other way around. I think I'd like to wake up now.

Whoever was in the room didn't make much noise. They just sat very quietly in the corner. I opened my eyes and gazed around the room. The sun was setting, the light dim through the window. Eric was sitting there looking at a magazine and lifted his eyes when he heard me stir.

"Hey, you're awake. How do you feel?"

"Well, to tell you the truth I feel a little spaced out right now, but otherwise not too bad." I sat up carefully on the edge of the bed and shook my head to get the cobwebs out.

Eric stood up and came and sat down next to me. He was so gorgeous. Two years older than me, he stood six feet two with broad shoulders and narrow hips. His sandy brown hair was cut short and spiked up. I'd always thought he was good looking but somehow he seemed more so right now. His blue eyes were gazing at me with affection. I set my emerald green eyes on his and smiled.

"It worked didn't it?" I said a bit breathlessly. "I can't believe it!"

"Yes. That foggy feeling will clear up soon. You'll need to take it slow for a bit." He put a hand on my arm. "Arnos is outside waiting to see you. Can he come in?"

"Wow, yeah, I have a thousand questions for him," I said, shaking my head some more. "By the way, were there kids in here before?"

"That's Sophie and Peter, Arnos' kids," Eric informed me as he went to open the door to let Arnos come in. "They're very curious about everything. And they fight all the time to see which one gets to see first."

"Wow, I didn't know Arnos had children. How old are they?" My head was starting to feel better, clearer.

"Sophie is ten years old and Peter is fourteen," he said peering out the door. "Arnos, please come in." Eric stepped aside to let Arnos pass through the door.

Arnos Barger entered the room and stood at the foot of the bed. He's very handsome, standing less than six feet tall, dark hair flowing down his back and the greenest eyes I have ever seen, except for mine. He is dressed all in black with his signature long, black coat flowing behind him. His voice is deep and commanding, except for today.

"How are you feeling Molly Fyre?" he said very quietly.

"Quite well, thank you!" I said, maybe a wee bit too enthusiastically. "So, now what happens?"

Arnos looked at me like my own personal Gandalf. "Good. Now we start your training. You have a great deal to learn, Molly. You have been chosen to lead an expedition to vanquish an old enemy of ours. It's not going to be easy and extremely dangerous. Are you up to the task?"

After hearing that I was beginning to wonder if this was such a good idea. A quest of epic proportions to kill someone. Sounds yummy! What was I thinking?

"I'll do my best as always. Who is this enemy and why do I have to get rid of him?" I asked. "And please tell me what to expect with my immortality now that I've taken the leap." Eric came closer to the bed and took my hand.

"His name is Dax. He holds a sacred artifact that belongs to me, the Krystal of Carolan. This relic was used in ancient rituals before my time and as the Keeper I must have the Krystal to complete certain ceremonies. You are the only one who can bring back the Krystal safely.

"As for your immortality, you will maintain your mortal functions and the one thing you will gain is certain powers and skills as you already know. Your senses of hearing, smell and sight will heighten and you will develop one or more special abilities which should reveal themselves in the next few days during your training. I expect that your strength will increase and you'll be able to leap tall buildings in a single bound, so to speak." He paused to look at me closely and then added something I didn't expect.

"Perhaps your dream will come true," he said seriously.

I found it strange he would say that; did he know about my dreams while I made the transition? I'm guessing I'll find out soon enough. My questions continued.

"So this guy Dax has the Krystal and won't give it back. Why hasn't anyone else tried to bring it home? Is he held up somewhere secure where nobody can touch him? And how am I supposed to get the job done alone?" I quizzed. There was a hint of a smile on Arnos' face.

"So many questions!" he cried his voice booming. "I'll answer them all after you've eaten and rested. Eric will bring you to dinner shortly." He turned and left the room in a quick flourish. The interview was over.

I told Eric I'd like to clean up first. Three days was a long time to go without toiletries. He showed me to my room and left me alone to take care of my needs. I showered quickly and dried my long red hair with the convenient hair dryer. It felt good to be spiffed up. After dressing in fresh clothes I joined Eric on the stairs and we went down to the dining room.

Dinner was lively with everyone chattering away, especially the kids. We ate in a large dining room with rich brown mahogany walls and tapestries hanging everywhere. It was quite medieval. The table was set with beautiful china and a super white table cloth. There were goblets of crystal for our wine. The food was great and I was so hungry I could have eaten a horse. I had never seen so much food before. My family had eaten well, but not like this. Each dish was passed around by a servant. Arnos really lived well and from the looks of this spread, much better than I had thought.

"Now, Molly Fyre, what questions do you have for me?" Arnos said as dessert was served.

"I'd like to know a little bit more about this Dax and why we are going after him. Why is he holding this Krystal and how did he obtain it to begin with? And, why me? Couldn't someone else go instead? Why am I so important to your quest?" I blurted out in one big breath as I watched Arnos. His cool green eyes vacantly looked at the table cloth. I wondered if he was even listening to me.

Arnos finally lifted his eyes to meet mine in a steady gaze. He took a sip of wine, set it down and sighed.

"Dax and I grew up as boys in the old country. We were like brothers, doing everything together. As we got older though, our paths took on different directions. His, unfortunately, took a much sinister path and we ended up parting ways on very bad terms. My destiny was to become a Keeper, one who maintains balance in our world. Dax chose to be a warrior, a champion of justice." His lip curled up into a sneer.

"He disappeared a few years ago and no one seems to be able to find him. With him he has a great army and the Krystal of Carolan, which he stole from the Keepers. So, Molly Fyre, you have been chosen to lead this expedition. You are the only one who is capable of finding him and bringing him to justice. You'll find out why in due time." He gave another great sigh and waited for my reaction.

It took me some time to absorb all this information. Was I crazy to agree to this? Maybe. I gazed around the table at all the faces looking intently at me and waiting for my response.

It seemed like they were all holding their breath and Eric had a strange expression on his face I couldn't decipher. It was almost a grin but not quite. He knew me so well.

I cleared my throat. I loved a challenge.

"Well, when do we get started? I don't think I want to waste time sitting here in discussion one minute more. Let's get this party going!" I said with such determination even I couldn't believe I'd said it. "When do I start my training?" There was a collective exhale from the rest of the table.

Arnos leaned toward me and smiled. "Tomorrow morning will be soon enough. Get a good night's rest. Goodnight everyone. Come children." And with that he rose and left the table, the children scrambling after him.

Eric and I looked at each other. "How about a stroll in the garden, I'm really not tired yet," Eric said. I nodded and took his hand as we walked out of the dining room into the hallway.

"You'll like the garden. It has your favorite flowers, peonies," Eric remarked as we exited through a set of French doors at the end of the hall.

The night air was cool and fragrant with the scent of flowers and pine trees. The moon was full and lit up the garden like I remembered back home. It reminded me of my mother and I guess I looked a little sad because I suddenly found myself surrounded by Eric's arms. I snuggled into his chest and inhaled. He smelled so good of musk and maleness.

"What's wrong Moll?" he said, kissing the top of my head when I shivered.

"I had a vision before I woke up. It was frightening. Lots of fighting and evil vibes." My face felt contorted with the memory.

"Just one of the Elixir nightmares, nothing to worry about." Eric took my cold hand in his warm one.

"No, Eric, it was more vivid than a nightmare. It was like I was there as it happened. And I remember the whole thing clearly. Something isn't right. I can feel it." He pulled me tighter to his chest. Maybe I wasn't as strong as I thought.

"I'll protect you, always. Tomorrow we'll start training and you'll find out what special skills you have. We can do this together, Molly. You'll see." He pulled away from me to look in my eyes.

"I'm afraid, but not sure what to be afraid of," I murmured. "I still can't understand why I'm the one to lead this quest. Surely there are more qualified people Arnos knows who are better suited to this task." I stepped away from Eric and walked to the edge of the garden. He didn't follow. When I turned around he was looking into the darkness beyond me.

"Is there something you're not telling me?" He wouldn't look at me. I just stared at him, confused.

"Arnos picked you because you're a key player in his drama. He has no other way to obtain the Krystal. It's not that I don't want to tell you, I just can't. There isn't enough information yet." He raked his hands through his hair and turned away from me. I could see he was wrestling with his loyalty to Arnos and my need to know.

Eric McGuire and I had known each other for over a year and were close friends. He brought me comfort when I was grieving over my mother's death and I shall be eternally grateful to him. We could have become lovers, but somehow it never happened. Neither of us had said 'I love you', but somehow we always knew there was something there on the fringes of our relationship that bordered on true love. We had always been honest about our feelings and thoughts. Until now. Now I felt he was keeping secrets, and I was beginning to wonder why. I felt at this moment that I didn't know him as well as I thought.

I suddenly felt very tired. "I can see you're torn," I said wearily. "Let's just see what tomorrow brings. I'm going up to bed now. See you in the morning." I kissed him lightly on the cheek and left him standing there in the moonlight and went inside.

In my own room I sat down on the bed and tried to figure out what was going on. What did he mean by 'you're a key player'? Sounded to me that I had been chosen a long time ago, without my knowledge. And what information did he need? I needed to get to the bottom of this before too long. The vision was troubling me as well. I'd started having them before my transition and they were scarier and more complex each time. What did they mean?

There obviously wasn't going to be a resolution tonight so I got ready for bed and lay down on the softest bed I had ever been in. I snuggled down into the soft sheets and closed my eyes. Sleep took over quickly despite my worries.

Chapter 3

I *found myself standing in a small clearing in the forest. How I got here I couldn't remember. The sun shone through the canopy of trees in streams of pale light; the shadows were deep and dark. Suddenly a man's voice said my name.*

"Molly," it said softly.

"Who are you?" I questioned searching the tree line.

"Someone from your past," it replied. He stayed in the shadows.

"Come out where I can see you," I demanded to the darkness.

The figure started to advance toward me. All of a sudden there was a brilliant flash of light so bright I had to shield my eyes. When I could see again, I gasped—as a huge red dragon with glowing emerald green eyes emerged from the dark.

I awoke with a start and quickly remembered where I was. I was covered in sweat and trembling. It took a moment before I could catch my breath. Okay . . . that was creepy. I got out of bed and went into the very luxurious bathroom, and splashed some cold water on my face. I looked at my twin in the mirror. These visions/nightmares were getting worse or at least more vivid. Was this part of the transition or did I eat some bad food? I decided I had better take another long hot shower.

I washed my hair with the very expensive shampoo on the counter, blew it dry and pulled it into a loose pony. I had a closet full of clothes provided for me, and if I do say so myself, the most beautiful selection I had ever seen.

I selected a pair of black skinny jeans and a light blue sweater that hugged my body. A pair of knee high boots in black Italian leather and my ensemble was complete. I admired my double in the mirror. I was HOT! Didn't even need makeup.

Someone knocked softly on my door. When I opened the door, Sophie was standing there. She was dressed in a pink sweater, pink leggings and tall pink boots. "Oh, goodie, you're awake. Breakfast is on the table. We don't want it to get cold!" she exclaimed. "By the way, you look fabulous!"

"Thank you, Sophie. So do you. Let's boogey on down to the dining room then." We left the room and went downstairs to find everyone already helping themselves to the buffet. I noticed some new faces and went to stand in line behind Eric.

"Hey," I said to his back.

He turned around and smiled. "Hi, how did you sleep?"

"Quite well, considering." I said a bit sarcastically and averted my eyes, pretending to look at the food on the buffet table.

"I'm sorry about last night. I wasn't trying to keep anything from you. Can we talk about this after breakfast, I'm famished." He turned back to the buffet.

I sighed. I could see I wasn't going to get anything out of him right now, so I started loading up my plate with scrambled eggs, bacon and toast.

We walked to the table in silence and sat down with some of the new faces. A server brought us coffee and juice.

There were five people sitting at the table that I didn't know. Eric introduced them as my quest team that would be accompanying us on our journey.

Hector Stram was a tall, muscular fellow with a handsome, rough-hewn face and a wide smile. He had long dark hair and his dark eyes were deep set, mysterious, with a playful dance to them. He was an immortal with powers of strength and agility . . . according to him. He joked around quite easily. It looked to me like he could take on anybody in a battle with ease.

Next to him sat Jonni Hale, another tall guy with a bald head, a triangular patch of beard on his chin and a peculiar look about him. His eyes were a silvery blue and he didn't look at me directly but gazed past us at something across the room. He explained that as a child he had been cursed by a witch who hated his family. During the daylight hours he was blind, but at night he had super night vision. It didn't seem to bother him at all so I said "pleased to meet you" to acknowledge him. He grinned at me.

At the end of the table sat a tiny woman with a long, blonde ponytail and the palest blue eyes I had ever seen. She was dressed in a black bodysuit and tall black boots. Naomi Pitts was a Dark Angel. DA's could be a trusted ally or a dangerous foe. One never knew where their loyalty would be. She was staring at me intently. I felt a little uncomfortable but gave her a smile and a slight nod. She didn't return it. Her face remained impassive and unreadable.

The last two guys that sat across from me were my trainers, the twins Jeff and Farn Duggan. Their hair was bright blue, spiked up into tall Mohawks. Both were short and muscular, had green eyes and were very animated. I marveled at how good looking the two men were the kind you couldn't take your eyes off.

This was going to be a very interesting journey indeed, I thought to myself. I proceeded to gobble down my food as I watched them interact. Naomi never took her eyes off me for more than a few seconds. This was getting very creepy.

Arnos glided into the room.

"I see you've met your team, Molly. What do you think?" said Arnos as he sat down next to Naomi. She moved away from him ever so slightly. Was that a grimace I saw her make? It didn't look like he noticed.

I had to swallow the bite of food already in my mouth before I could answer him.

"I was just thinking what an interesting journey this will be with these fine folks you've chosen for me, Arnos. I assume we'll all be training together?" I said, watching for his reaction.

He had a slight smile on his face as he answered. "I felt they were a perfect match for you. And, yes, you'll all be training together. I feel this should be a cohesive group that trusts each other's skills. Would you want it any other way?" He cut into the ham slice on his plate and took a bite.

"Probably not. Time will tell, though. My skills are still not developed yet, but I feel some changes taking place already. I've had visions while sleeping that have been quite upsetting to me. Maybe they're nightmares, but they were so vivid I felt I was there as they happened. Some showed dragons fighting. I wake up in a cold sweat and my heart pounding. It gets worse every time. What do you think is happening, Arnos?"

"I'm not sure but as I recall, your mother had visions also. Is that correct, Molly?" He had suddenly become serious.

A flood of memories started within me and I could feel the tears welling up in my eyes. "Yes, she could predict things from her dreams," I whispered my voice thick with emotion.

Eric put his arm around my shoulder. The tears came suddenly and I buried my face in his chest. I hadn't thought about my mother for a while and the memories of her death were still fresh in my mind. She'd been gone for two years but I still grieved as if it was that very day. We had such a strong bond. I could see now how strong that was. I had her skill and it scared me—a *lot*.

"I'm sorry. It was not my intention to upset you. I knew your mother quite well and respected her abilities. She would be very proud of you, Molly Fyre," Arnos said quietly.

I looked up, dabbing my eyes with a tissue and gazed at the people at the table.

I sat up straight and said confidently, "This is all so overwhelming right now. With your help I feel this journey can be successful and I hope to be an able leader and expect you to tell me if I've made a bad decision. Let's get to work." I rose from the table and grabbed Eric's hand.

"Which way to the training room?" I asked. He smiled and led the way out into the hallway and down a flight of stairs to the basement. The whole group, including Arnos and the kids, followed behind us.

Chapter 4

The training room was huge and I would guess at least half a football field long. The ceiling was high with bright lighting. There were no windows. At one end was the exercise equipment, enough for several people to use at once. What looked like the entrance to a locker room stood open at that end as well.

In the middle was enough room for an army to have a battle. Mats were placed close together on the floor for some activity I was afraid to think about. An area with hay targets caught my eye off to the side. At the other end were numerous racks and stands with an impressive array of weapons—crossbows, knives of all sizes, spears, guns and some weird looking things I couldn't even begin to describe. I think there was even an area to make explosive devices.

Arnos and the children stood off to the side watching my amazed face.

All I could utter was "WOW!" Eric started to laugh.

"So, what do you think?" he whispered in my ear.

"WOW! OK, this is awesome. Where do we start?" I was having trouble taking it all in.

Naomi and Hector were already geared up with knives and spears in the middle of the floor.

"Just so you know Pitts, I've been practicing," Hector shouted in her direction. "How about you?"

Naomi eyed him with a look that would melt steel. "Okay Stram, you're on. But be forewarned, I bite. Hard.

"Bring it on, Baby," he growled, circling the area with the meanest knives I had ever seen.

I watched intently as the others picked weapons from the racks.

Jonni was off by himself twirling around with two large swords. He was so graceful; it was hard to believe he was blind right now. It was mesmerizing. I must have had a look of wonderment on my face because Farn glided over to me.

"He's magnificent, isn't he?" he announced proudly. "All of his other senses are heightened to the point of ridiculous. I once tried to sneak up on him just to see what he would do and he nearly cut my head off with one of those things!"

I couldn't help but laugh at him.

"Are we using real weapons for practice? Isn't that a little dangerous?" I asked with a cringe as Hector ran full tilt toward Naomi. She easily dodged out of his way and countered with a graceful flip to his left, just missing his arm with her knife.

Eric looked at me with a curious expression. "You do realize you're immortal? You'll heal fast." His voice sounded flat. And without a backward glance he turned and trotted over to the weapons cache.

I nodded and sighed. "Hmmm, yeah, I forgot about that," I muttered to myself. Could he be any more annoying? I hurried after him.

"Are these mood swings of yours temporary or should I expect them to continue, because right now I'm really confused?" I asked when I caught up to him.

He didn't look at me as he chose an evil looking crossbow from the rack.

"Tell me what's going on," I demanded. He still wouldn't look at me. "Tell me," I said more insistent. My patience was running thin.

"This isn't the place or time for this conversation," he hissed at me, whirling around. His eyes met mine and they were so angry I had to take a step back. This was not Eric.

I swallowed hard. "Okay, when would be the right time and place? This abrupt change in personality is frightening me. What is going on with you?" My voice was as icy as I could get it, but my eyes were blazing. I suddenly started to feel warm all over. His expression softened and he shook his head as his gaze fell to the floor.

A pained look crossed his face. I could see I'd hurt him. "Molly . . . I . . . , he stammered. Then his expression changed abruptly when he looked at me again.

He didn't get the chance to finish because at that moment Jeff and Farn strolled over. "So, shall we begin?"

I turned to look at them, the fire still in my eyes. Odd, my eyes felt really warm. And my hands were tingling too. Stranger yet. Jeff and Farn looked wide-eyed at me.

"You're glowing, Molly!" exclaimed Jeff. Your eyes are on fire—a brilliant green glow!"

I had to take several deep breaths to calm down. The warmth subsided. Everyone had amazed looks on their faces.

"What. Was. That?" Hector said quietly. It was unusual to hear him speak so calmly.

"I wish I knew," I said, staring at my hands. "My body started to feel warm as I was talking to Eric." I suddenly felt a little sheepish and gave Eric a quick glance. He was staring at me his eyebrows raised. No one was moving.

Naomi was the first to speak. "How did you do that?"

"I have no idea. The fact was I was angry at Eric and it just happened. This is really freaky. Maybe it's a power I'm developing."

Hector came over to me and put his arm around my shoulder. "Let's see if you can make it happen again." We walked to the center of the room. "Now, think about what you were doing when it started and try to duplicate it." I stole another look at Eric. For some dumb reason he was grinning. I started to blush.

Jeff came to stand by us. Seems he's the expert on powers. "He's right Molly; let's see what you can do. Close your eyes and concentrate," he said, taking hold of my hands, my palms up.

"OK," I muttered to myself and closed my eyes. I started to think about how much anger I was feeling toward Eric at the time and how frustrating the whole issue was to me. Soon I could feel my hands getting warm, my eyes burning. Jeff felt it too, because he jerked a little at the feeling.

"Molly, I want you try and project that warmth a bit further than your hands." He said as he let go of me. "That's it! Keep going." His voice got very excited. "Now, open your eyes."

As I opened my eyes I did not believe what I was seeing. Each of my hands was holding a bright red ball of fire. I gasped and everyone else did the same.

"Amazing, your eyes are that brilliant green again," Farn whispered. "Like they're lit from inside. Does anything hurt?"

"No, my body feels warm. My eyes burn a bit, nothing I can't handle." I moved my hands around in a circle, the glow held steady.

Hector came and stood in front of me shaking his head. "Well, I guess we know what to work on now."

I couldn't stop playing with the fire in my hands. "This is kinda fun," I giggled. I gave my right hand a flick and threw a ball of fire over his shoulder. He gave me a nasty look as he ducked. I smiled my sweetest smile. "Sorry."

Jeff and I worked on my skills. I think I might have singed his eyebrows once or twice when my fire balls went astray. Surprisingly he never complained.

We worked with the fire for most of the morning until I could smell some delicious aromas in the air as my stomach started to grumble. It was lunch time.

The servants were bringing us lunch on huge serving carts. After the workout Jeff had put me through, I was ravenous and ran to be first in line. Naomi was at my side in a flash of movement.

"You did really well today, Molly," she whispered in my ear. I looked at her, shocked. She was talking to me. Had she actually given me a compliment? I didn't know what to say.

"Uh, thanks," I muttered and grabbed a turkey sandwich on rye. After I took two bags of chips and a soda I went and sat next to the wall. Eric came and sat next to me and we actually had a civil conversation while we ate.

It was late afternoon before we finished in the training room. Everyone went their separate ways, including Eric. He must have disappeared quickly because I never noticed him leave. I was getting annoyed again at his avoidance of our discussion and wasn't about to forget it. So typical of me, persistence, wanting to bring an end to this madness.

I decided to wander around the mansion to calm myself and admire the home's décor. I'd only seen some of the rooms since arriving and was fascinated by all the antiques and paintings. Besides, Arnos never said I couldn't explore.

I wandered down the first floor hall toward the sound of angry voices. Light spilled out of one of the rooms into the hallway.

Chapter 5

The door to what I guessed was Arnos' study stood ajar. The conversation was very heated. I crept close to the door to listen.

"I can't do this anymore, Arnos," Eric complained tightly. I pictured his teeth clenched together.

"Oh, but you have to, dear boy." Arnos' voice sounded like syrup. "Remember our agreement."

"How can I forget? Where are they?" Eric said heatedly. I could feel the anger and frustration building in him. I wondered who 'they' were.

"Safe. For the time being," Arnos answered, unconcerned with Eric's anger. "You will continue to be nice to her and direct her on the right course or you won't see them again! Court her, win her confidence back. But get the job done. The mission must be completed before the blue moon is full. Is that clear?"

My breath caught in my throat. Surely they weren't talking about me? This would certainly explain Eric's erratic behavior lately. Was I really a pawn in some sick game of Arnos' creation? Poor Eric.

I needed to get to the bottom of this tonight.

Eric didn't make a sound and since I couldn't see what was happening, I could only imagine what Eric looked like right now. I heard him move closer to the door and say, "*Very* clear. This isn't over!"

I looked around for a hiding place before Eric saw me. His footsteps came closer, the door opened and he stormed out of the room. I was safely hidden in a side hall. As his footsteps faded away in the other direction, I peeked around the corner. I didn't want Arnos to see me backtrack behind Eric. The coast seemed clear so I nonchalantly walked past the study and hurried to the stairs. I needed to talk to Eric as soon as possible.

A crazy idea crossed my mind as I ran to my room. What if our rooms were bugged? Don't ask me why I would think that, but I planned to check out my room when I got there. Arnos certainly was not the benevolent man I had known all these years. I took the stairs two at a time.

As I entered my room I had no idea what I should look for in the way of bugging devices. I surveyed the furnishings. I checked under the lampshades and the bottom of each lamp. Nothing showed up there. There was no phone in the room so that was out. The furniture was mostly overstuffed chairs, an ornate desk, a chest of drawers and the bed, a four-postered monster. I noticed some pictures and a tapestry on the walls so I started to look behind each one.

When I got to the last picture which hung over the bed, there it was! Just a small silver disc the size of a dime stuck to the back of it. I ripped it from the backing and looked around for something to smash it. I couldn't see anything that would do the job . . . only one thing to do. I walked across the room to the balcony door and tossed the offensive thing over the railing. I hoped whoever might be listening got an earful of hurt.

I sat down at the desk and jotted down some notes. Eric's room was close to mine so I peeked out my door to make sure no one was in the hall and quickly walked three doors down and knocked softly. I wasn't sure if he was even in his room when the door opened and there he was. My heart thumped. I held two fingers to my lips to shush him before he could speak. I motioned for us to go inside and he stepped aside to let me in.

I showed him the notes I had made.

DON'T TALK
ROOM MAY BE BUGGED
MINE WAS

He gave me a quizzical look and nodded his head. '*Where*', he mouthed.

'*Behind a picture*', I mouthed back. We started searching his room.

Yup, there it was, under a table between two chairs exactly like the one in my room. Eric angrily tossed it out the window unceremoniously. Every piece of furniture was checked before we attempted to talk freely.

"OK, what's going on, Eric? We need to resolve this issue right here and now." I could feel my eyes getting warm. *Gotta calm down.*

"I don't know what to say, Molly. This has gotten so twisted. You have to understand," he said, his voice shaky. His eyes were actually fearful.

"Understand what? That you're playing me for Arnos' sick pleasure? I'm sorry but I heard your conversation with Arnos downstairs. What were you planning, dinner and a movie?" My voice raised an octave as I paced back and forth furiously.

His face was contorted into a grimace and he looked like he might cry.

"It's not like that, Moll. It's bigger." Tears started to well up in his sad eyes. "Arnos is not the person you thought he was. He's evil and self-serving. The Krystal isn't for good. It's a powerful weapon and Dax is protecting it . . . from Arnos!" He dropped his head into his hands. "I never meant to hurt you, Molly." He paused. "*I love you.*"

My pacing stopped abruptly and I looked at him, stunned, tears stinging my eyes. Had I heard him right? Had h*e* said the words I've waited so long to hear? I couldn't speak and struggled to compose myself.

"Who is Arnos holding hostage?" I finally asked.

"My family. And he won't release them until we return with the Krystal. I have no idea where they are."

That stopped me cold; my attitude softened. "Oh, Eric, I'm so sorry. No wonder you've been acting so strangely. It must be awful for you. We can't let him get away with this," I said angrily. "What can I do?"

I walked over to him and put my arms around him. He hugged me tightly and kissed my hair. I pulled back and looked up into his watery eyes.

"Just so you know . . . I love you, too." He smiled and leaned in ever so slowly and pressed his lips softly to mine. I'd been waiting so long for this; I could feel my heart beating loudly in my chest.

He ran his fingers lightly down my cheek. "I suspected," he whispered in my ear. "I've waited a long time to hear that." Chills ran down my back.

A loud rapping on the door made us both jump.

"What?" Eric shouted.

"Hey, you coming to dinner? And do you know where Molly is? Is she with you?" It was Hector on the other side of the door.

"She's here," Eric replied, not opening the door. "We'll be down in a sec," he said. "Or maybe not," he whispered, turning to look at me with a soft smile. I could feel my cheeks getting red and glanced at the floor to compose myself.

"OK, but just so you know, we're having lobster tonight," Hector said with a chuckle. I could hear his heavy boots go down the hall.

We stood there staring at each other for a long time. Neither one of us wanted to move out of this moment. I had to speak.

"Eric, what are we going to do? We need to make a plan of action before this gets out of hand. I can't go on this journey knowing I might lead my team into a battle we can't win. Dax must know we're coming. I think my dream last night was about him. He said he was from my past but I have no idea who he is."

Eric paced around the room in deep concentration for a few minutes apparently thinking about what I'd said. I wasn't sure if I should say anything else when he suddenly stopped and spoke.

"What do we know so far?" he queried. "Arnos isn't playing fair. Dax may not be the villain we thought. And why are the rooms bugged? Is Arnos afraid of something? Are we in danger here in his house and *definitely* . . . who can we trust?" he said rapidly, his face a torrent of emotions.

"Do you know the rest of the team well? Is there any one of them you personally don't trust?" I asked.

Eric went to the window and stood still as a statue for the longest time. I wanted to go to him and comfort him; he seemed to be in so much distress over his family and now this. He finally turned to me.

"I've worked with Hector and Jonni before. They're very trustworthy and honorable and I believe I could persuade them to follow us. Naomi is new and I've heard she can be fickle with her alliances. It would be tricky getting her on our side. She's a great fighter and I'd hate to lose her to Arnos." He stopped and sighed. I had to put my two cents in.

"In just the short time I've known these people I think I have a small sense of who they are. I agree with you about Hector and Jonni. We'll have to see what they think. What about Jeff and Farn? If they're going with us we need to find out their thoughts as well. Naomi is another matter. She creeps me out, Eric. I find her staring at me all the time." I shivered and wrapped my arms around myself.

Eric smiled and shook his head. "She's different all right. Maybe you should work on her yourself. You know . . . woman to woman. Maybe she'll be your buddy," he said with a smirk. I gave him an incredulous glare. "Or maybe not."

Yeah, like that's going to happen.

"What do we do about Arnos and his sinister plan? And what is his plan, to take over the world? What is it he wants with the Krystal? God, I don't know why I agreed to this. Things are getting more than a little complicated now," I muttered to myself.

Perhaps I could just leave and go home. Get my old boring job back and lead a normal life. Not gonna happen, Molly. Get over it.

All at once Eric was at my side. His eyes were opened wide and he had a determined look on his face.

"Molly, here's what we're going to do." I looked at him expectedly. "We're going down to dinner and act like nothing's wrong. Arnos wants me to make nice with you and gain your confidence. So let's make him believe it. What do you say?"

"Hmmm, kiss me again and I'll let you know," I said, lifting my eyes to his and smiling coyly.

His lips met mine with unexpected urgency and we stayed lip-locked for a long time. When we finally pulled away I sensed we were done with the old us. I wondered what tonight would bring.

Chapter 6

We walked downstairs holding hands and smiling. Play acting was so much fun, except I wasn't. There were more people at the table than had been at the other meals. A lot more! I saw our quest team, but wow, there were at least twenty extra burly guys sitting at the table tonight. Things were getting slightly crowded. I plastered on a cheery face.

"Hey, everybody, how's it going?" So . . . maybe I was a bit too cheery. Arnos was giving us the once over with his usual quizzical expression. I ignored him. Eric and I took the seats to his right. Everyone else was eating already and the servants brought us our salads. I smiled weakly at Arnos and his mouth gave a slight twitch as if he wasn't sure if he should return it or not.

"Glad you decided to join us," he said a little too sweetly for my liking. Did he know about our debugging escapade? I was feeling paranoid now and hoped it didn't show on my face. I glanced at Eric and took a bite of my salad. He raised his eyebrows and did the same.

Arnos continued. "We were discussing your amazing ability, Molly. Quite extraordinary. You must learn to control it and use it wisely."

"I'm feeling very comfortable with it now," I remarked. "Jeff will be working with me again in the morning and perhaps you could watch me when we go outside. I believe he said I would be practicing with targets so I don't burn the house down." I glanced around the table with an amused expression.

Several people laughed softly. Arnos' expression never changed. "Perhaps I will," he said coolly.

"Where are Peter and Sophie? Aren't they eating with us tonight?" I asked as the main course was served, lobster, garlic mashed potatoes and grilled veggies.

Arnos glanced at the two men sitting on his left. "They're eating in their rooms tonight," he said quickly. The two men snickered and Arnos gave them a warning look.

I looked at them curiously. They put their heads down and started to eat furiously. They acted suspiciously like children. What a weird bunch of people we have here. I nudged Eric under the table and continued to eat.

The rest of the meal went quickly, thank goodness. It didn't seem like anyone was into much conversation, which for my team was saying a lot. They loved to talk. The extra men at the table made me a bit uneasy and I could see my team was too by all the eyebrow flicking going on. I'm sure they were all wondering, as I was, who these men were. Arnos certainly wasn't introducing them and although I was tempted I sure wasn't going to ask.

After dessert was finished Arnos nodded at the men and they all left the table at once, including the odd couple who were sitting next to him.

As I looked at Eric, he frowned and then wiggled his eyebrows. We were doing a lot of that tonight. We needed to add this to our list of odd happenings.

I stood up and turned to leave the room when Arnos spoke.

"Leaving so soon? I thought perhaps we could chat a bit about your upcoming journey. Training should be completed by the end of the week so you can all be on your way. By the way, the men you saw tonight are your army backup who will travel with you. I thought it best if you had some protection even though it seems you all are well equipped to defend yourselves." He idly folded his napkin and placed it on the table.

"And who is in command of all these men?" I asked facing him with my hands on my hips. "If I am the leader of this quest do I have any say in this matter?" My gaze was as steady as

Arnos'. I knew I had to take charge here and now. There was no giving him the upper hand. I waited for his answer.

His eyes lowered as he rubbed his hand along the edge of the table. It looked like he was trying to control his temper. Had I hit a nerve? *Goody.*

"There will be someone in their ranks to control them for you, but yes you will be in charge," he answered very slowly. He made eye contact with me and I glared back at him, my green eyes blazing. He got a brief startled look on his face, then composing himself quickly, rose from the table and without a word left the room.

Someone gave a soft whistle and I looked around at the others.

"Way to thump him, Molly!" said Hector. "He probably hasn't been talked to like that in centuries." He was grinning ear to ear.

Jeff and Farn just stared at me in amazement.

Naomi was hiding a smile behind her hands. Looks like she's not fond of him either. Maybe I will talk to her.

Jonni was more cautious when he said, "Be careful how you push him. Arnos is very powerful and you don't want to get on his bad side." His eyes were looking straight at me as he said it. I guessed his night vision was kicking in.

"Don't worry; I know what I'm doing. He doesn't scare me anymore," I said confidently turning to leave. "So, who's up for a little hand to hand work tonight?"

Eric shook his head and grinned. I guess he thinks I'm totally nuts now. Maybe I am.

There was a lot of murmuring from the gang as they jumped up from the table and we filed downstairs to the training room en masse. I wanted to kick some Hector butt tonight.

Chapter 7

The session tonight was very interesting. Hector and I did a lot of hand to hand with the long knives and I must say with all honesty, I was awesome. We sparred around the mats like two jungle cats. He came at me with such force I wondered if I could avoid getting skewered. My reflexes were at their best as I leaped out of his way a number of times just as he came close to slicing my arm. I flipped in all directions with an ease I never had before. It was intoxicating.

"Molly, I do believe you've bested me tonight," he shouted as I did another back somersault over the top of him.

"You think?" I said breathlessly. "You haven't seen all that I can do yet." Eric sauntered over after having a go at Jonni. I noticed blood on his left sleeve and paused my next parry long enough to make sure he was all right. He noticed me staring at his arm.

"I'm fine, just a scratch. I heal fast." He grinned at me as he leaped over Hector and took a swipe at his arm. Of course, Hector was ready for him and ducked just in time.

"Aha! Thought you had me didn't you McGuire? Never gonna happen," he laughed still in a crouch. "What do you say we take a break and talk a bit? We've been at this for two hours now." He put his swords down on the floor and headed for the refreshment table. We followed willingly.

I grabbed an iced tea and went to sit on the floor next to Hector and Eric. Jonni and Naomi continued to play fight on the mats. It was almost midnight and I was feeling a bit tired.

Hector took a long draft of his cola and sighed. After a moment he looked in my direction with a serious look on his face.

"He knows," was all he said. I don't know why, but the way he said it gave me the chills.

"Who are you talking about? And what does *he* know?" I asked nonchalantly, not wanting to hear the answer.

"Arnos. He knows something about you that's very important to your mission. I can't tell yet what it is but I can sense he isn't going to reveal this information." He paused to take another drink. "Just so you're aware, I have other abilities that allow me to sense things others can't. I'm getting some weird vibes from him. Be careful."

I stared at my tea. Could there be anything else go wrong? I caught Eric's eye and tilted my head toward Hector. He cleared his throat.

"Hector, we've got to tell you something and I want you to hear us out before you answer." He took a deep breath. "Our rooms are bugged. Molly and I found the devices in our rooms and got rid of them but there might be one in your room as well. We have reason to suspect that Arnos is not telling us the whole truth about this mission, as he calls it. What if Dax isn't the bad guy here and Arnos wants to get rid of him with our help? In addition, Arnos has kidnapped my family and won't release them until we return with the Krystal." His voice became shaky so I took over.

"Hector, we need your support. I'm aware that you don't know me as well as you know Eric, but we both want to make sure this isn't a suicide mission for all of us involved. And this army Arnos has gathered, how do we deal with that? Can we count on you to join us?" It was hard to gauge his response because he leaped up and started to pace around. When he finally turned to me his face had a big grin on it.

"I've been watching you these last few days and I must say you are a unique woman, Molly. I admire your courage to take on this 'mission' without any forewarning. Arnos was no fool putting you in charge. He knows what will happen and *we* can't let that happen. Hell, yes, I'm in." He paused and chuckled. "I suppose I'll have to get the bug spray and search my room when

I get back." I guess my mouth was open in response to his reply because Eric gave me the *close your mouth* sign with his hand.

"Thank you," both of us said in unison.

"Have you spoken to Jonni or Naomi yet?" he asked as he picked up his swords where he had left them.

"No, we started with you," I replied and yawned at the same time.

"OK, I can talk to Jonni. He and I go way back and I know for a fact that he doesn't trust Arnos very much. Molly you need to talk to Naomi. She's new to this sort of thing and maybe a woman can be more convincing. Looks like it will be tomorrow from the way you're yawning. Go get some sleep and we'll get together in the morning." He turned to Eric.

"Eric, I'm sorry about your family. I can't even imagine what you're going through right now but believe me when I say I will do everything I can to get them home safely. Let me deal with the 'army'. I used to be in one and they can be influenced with a little finesse."

He turned and strolled over to where Naomi and Jonni were finishing their practice. I noticed he put his arm around Jonni's shoulder and took him off to the side.

It was comforting to know we had Hector on our side. There was hope that this mess would turn out better than I'd thought it would. I took a sideways glance at Eric. His face was passive and it was hard to tell if it was fatigue or sadness or maybe relief.

"Are you OK?" I said.

"Yeah." He paused to look at the two men across the room. "I didn't think it would be so easy, but Hector's a good guy." He ran his hand over his face and I could see the fatigue catching up to him.

"We should get some sleep. I need to be at my best if I have to tackle a talk with Naomi in the morning." I started for the door. Eric took my hand gently.

"Stay with me tonight. Nothing else, just sleep." His eyes pleaded with me. A tingle went through my body.

"Yeah, that would be nice," I breathed. How could I refuse with all that's happened so far? We both needed the comfort and closeness and oh, I so wanted to lie next to him tonight.

Tomorrow was going to be a bitch.

The sun was shining dimly through the curtains as I slowly awakened nestled against Eric's body. The clock said seven. I could feel his arm across my waist and marveled at how cozy and warm I was and the fact that I'd had no visions last night. What a relief! He stirred next to me and I wished this moment could last forever. There was a reason we met and call me crazy, but I was not going to let this man go. I couldn't help smiling like an idiot.

"Good morning," he said stifling a yawn. "How did you sleep?" He kissed the back of my neck. There were those chills again!

"Wonderful. No visions, no nightmares. You are my own personal sleep aid." I felt his breath on my neck as he gave a soft chuckle.

"I had a dream about you," he whispered, nuzzling my neck.

"Really? Was it a good one? I could use good right about now." I turned my head to look at him. He was frowning. "What. I didn't do something stupid did I?" I whined. His expression slowly changed to a smile.

"No, actually it was quite . . . how shall I put this . . . well, erotic comes to mind. Unfortunately I woke up before we got to the good part and that's why I was frowning."

My face went magenta and I turned and pulled the sheet over my head. Being a virgin stunk. I wondered how many women he had made love to.

The sheet was slowly pulled away from my head and I could feel him looking at me. Suddenly I felt very bold.

"We could remedy that right now, you know," I said as I rolled over to face him eye to eye.

His surprised expression became softer as he raised his hand and stroked my cheek.

"Are you sure about this?"

"Yes, very."

"You're not afraid?"

"Of course not."

There was a slight hesitation before his lips met mine with determination as he pulled me closer. I could hardly breathe as his hand slid down to my hip.

Thank you. Thank you. Thank you.

A pounding on the door woke us up. I glanced at the clock; it was ten.

"Eric, breakfast is over and training starts in twenty minutes. Rise and shine," Hector bellowed from the hall.

"Damn, can't they just leave us alone," Eric muttered into my hair. He didn't move.

I sighed deeply. That had been amazing. Not a virgin anymore! I raised myself on one elbow.

"I am so happy right now. It was so worth the wait; but right now we have to get our behinds in gear." I kissed his nose and threw the covers off and walked into the bathroom. Eric groaned and then came in behind me in all his naked glory. "How about we shower together and save water?" His eyebrows wiggled up and down. I reached in and turned on the water, never taking my eyes off his. This gets better all the time!

After toweling each other off, we dressed and Eric opened the bedroom door. Wouldn't you know it; Hector was lurking against the opposite wall with his arms crossed on his chest.

"Well, well, well. Aren't you two cozy." He had a smarmy grin on his face like—gotcha!

We glanced at each other and walked right past him with big Cheshire grins of our own. As we headed for the stairs Hector came running behind us.

"What's on the agenda for today?" he said poking me in the back. I ignored him.

"Not now H, we need to do something first. Am I going to have to cuff you right here and now?" Eric said over his shoulder. Hector stopped and put his hands up in defeat mode. We took to the stairs and descended to the foyer.

Instead of going left to the training room, we went right. I pulled at his arm.

"Aren't we going in the wrong direction?" I asked.

"We need fuel. The kitchen is this way," he said pushing open a swinging door. The smells coming out were divine and my stomach growled in agreement. The kitchen staff started to rush around furiously, cooking up a sumptuous meal which they served right at their huge table in the middle of the room.

When we were finished and I could not eat another bite, the kitchen workers cleared away the dishes and we just sat there letting our food digest.

"You know Hector is going to tell everyone about our night?" Eric muttered, taking a sip of coffee.

"Let him have his fun. I'll figure a way to get back at him. Today I get to throw fire outside with Jeff. Maybe I'll misdirect one. You know, my aim is still a bit off sometimes." I smiled sweetly over my cup. Eric chuckled and shook his head.

Chapter 8

As we entered the training area I braced myself for the 'talk' with Naomi. She was off by herself doing some Tai Chi moves. Very impressive. Smooth, fluid, and focused. I waited until she was finished before approaching her.

As I walked over to her she glanced up from wiping her face with a towel she had around her neck. She nodded my way and I acknowledged by smiling and nodding back.

"Hey, Naomi, some nice moves there. Maybe you could show me a few sometime." I sat down on the mat and invited her to do the same. She regarded me with wary eyes as she sank to the mat.

"They're quite easy once you learn the basics. It helps to keep me calm and focused." She paused and took a swig of water. "What are we doing today? I thought you were going outside with Jeff for your fireball practice."

I smiled and took a moment to collect my thoughts staring at my hands. No need to rush this. Take a deep breath. *OK, now you're stalling,* I told myself. I looked up to see her gazing intently at me.

"Naomi, I need to talk to you about something important and vital to our mission. Eric has informed me that Arnos is holding his family hostage until we return with the Krystal and it's tearing him apart. I want to make this right but I need all of you in my camp. Eric says the Krystal is a weapon and who knows what Arnos is planning to use it for. This Dax that Arnos says stole it may not be the bad guy after all. We also found bugging devices in our rooms. So what I need to know is will you support us when we need it? I understand your nature is to choose your allies carefully." Phew! I paused. "We would like you to choose the team."

Her facial expression never wavered while listening to me. She stood up and wandered around in a circle for a few minutes. It was hard to tell what she was thinking. My panic intensified. I looked over at Eric and saw him shrug his shoulders.

"You're right; I do choose my allies with care," she said finally. "What you've said makes a lot of sense. A couple of nights ago I was in the garden and overheard Arnos speaking to someone. When I got a look at who it was, I was surprised to see the children with him but he wasn't talking to them like kids. They were speaking as adult to adult." She tipped her water bottle up and took another drink . . . watching me.

"What . . . ?" I motioned for Eric to come over. He brought Jonni and Hector with him.

"Things just got a little more complicated guys. Naomi, tell them what you saw." She related the information and I saw Hector's eyes narrow to slits.

"Remember those two guys who sat next to Arnos at dinner last night? Could they have been the kids in some kind of disguise?" I asked, a bit afraid of the answer.

"Shape-shifters," Hector said. "They can change form to whatever they want. I can only guess, but they're probably meant as spies on our journey. I can't believe that Arnos would stoop to this."

Jonni was shaking his head. "I would. He hasn't exactly been forthcoming with info, has he?"

Eric started that infernal pacing again. We definitely needed to do something now. "Look, we need to meet tonight to figure out a strategy. My room, eight o'clock. I'll search for listening devices before then," he said. "Meanwhile we have to keep up our practice drills. Molly, you need to find Jeff and throw some fireballs. Naomi, you and I haven't sparred too much so could we go at it today?"

Naomi nodded her head in response and headed for the mats. I headed for the door to go outside and looked back at Eric as he too went to the mats.

Boy, he was sexy when he took charge. My man, oh yeah.

Hector and Jonni followed me outside. As my boots crunched along the stone path, I thought about how far I'd come in just a few days. Who'd have thought I'd become an immortal, the leader of a suicide mission, and lose my virginity all in less than a week's time? Not me. Eric mattered the most to me right now. I don't know how I would cope without him and to tell you the truth, my mind was so confused right now I could scream. My release was just a few feet away.

"Are you okay?" Hector asked.

"Yeah, I'm great," I answered over my shoulder as I continued walking.

"I see you have the targets ready, Jeff. Do you want me to start pitching a bunch or do you have a pattern in mind?" I said as I approached his side.

"Why don't you start by trying to hit one?" He quickly stepped aside as I concentrated and fired up my glowing hands.

I lobbed a red ball of fire at the farthest target and hit it dead on, exploding it into fiery splinters. I must have had a smug look on my face because Jeff breathed out, "Oookay, very . . . accurate. Now do some quick shots at all of them. Let's see if you can maintain an even firing speed." Hector gave a loud chuckle behind me.

As my concentration increased, I sent every target to oblivion and whirling around I let one fly at Hector. His startled reaction was priceless as he ducked to avoid getting roasted. Payback was a bitch.

"My word, aren't we annoyed!" he shouted. "Are you out to get me good and toasty?" Jonni and Jeff were roaring with laughter behind us.

"No, just thought a human target would be better practice," I said primly as I walked toward him. "Did I singe your hair much?"

"You're getting pretty gutsy, young lady. Is it something I said?" he said checking his hair. I ambled over to him and put my arms around his waist and hugged him hard. It probably surprised the hell out him because I could feel his body tense. When I pulled away I smiled.

"I will never do that again, I promise." I assured him. "Only the enemy gets toasted; if you promise not to reveal what you've seen upstairs." He looked at me quizzically and then laughed as he realized what I was talking about.

"Oh, thanks. That makes me feel so much better," he muttered. "Care to try that again? I could run around a little to give you a moving target." He saw the frown on my face. "Don't worry; I don't intend to get fried. And . . . I'll never tell." He grinned wickedly and proceeded to run in wide circles and I wondered if this was a good idea.

"I don't want to hurt you," I shouted at him.

"Just do it already."

So I did. My aim was spot on but he was fast, even when he didn't see one coming. Amazing. I was feeling a definite heat throughout my body; a kind of tearing sensation, like I was transforming into something else entirely. A quick glance down at myself told me I was still me. After about thirty minutes of this craziness I shouted, "Enough. Let's eat lunch. I'm starving!" He ran back to me in a rush. Jeff and Jonni came over all smiles.

"Good job, Molly Fyre. Let's go." We all hiked back up to house and met the others in the dining room.

Arnos and the 'kids' were already seated and waiting for us. Our wary glances must have been a red flag to Arnos; I could see him tense up as we sat down.

"I trust your practice went well," he said tightly. "I saw how you performed outside this morning, Molly. Very impressive indeed," he said unfolding his napkin into his lap. "It looks like you should be ready to go very soon. We'll need some time to discuss your route and figure out what supplies you'll take. "Tomorrow morning sound all right?" He had that wicked glint in his eye again . . . like a wolf.

"Sure, that sounds good. I think I can speak for us all when I say we are very anxious to get started." I saw all heads nod in agreement. "I would also like to thank you for your hospitality and the use of your facilities. I certainly feel stronger and more confident since coming here." I could see some quizzical looks from my teammates but I ignored them.

I needed to keep him off balance.

"Thank you for that, Molly. I shall miss you all until your return. Now, shall we eat? Roland, you may serve."

"I'll miss you too," murmured 'Sophie'. I looked at her sadly. It was too bad she wasn't what she seemed, a cute little girl. I wondered what her exact form was. Maybe this was her true self. One could only hope.

The rest of the afternoon saw us all outside working on battle strategies, if they were ever needed. I practiced some more with my fire and was really getting good at throwing them accurately. Eric and Naomi even let me target them. Boy, are they fast. I prayed that any enemies we met were not as speedy.

We all went to dinner exhausted.

Chapter 9

After dinner we all went our separate ways to relax. By *relax,* I really mean go to our respective rooms and think about the plan we needed to make for the journey. I for one wondered how I was going to keep a straight face in our meeting with Arnos tomorrow. For all the years he was our family friend I never suspected he would resort to something like this to gain power. How could my own mother not see this coming? Or had she, and not done anything about it. Had he held some kind of control over her I wasn't able to see? Perhaps my recent visions were in some way a continuation of my mother's and the truth would become clear to me in the near future.

I was getting a headache thinking about this so I lay down on the bed and stared at the ceiling. I must have dozed off.

A loud knocking on my door woke me. "I'm up," I mumbled. As I dragged my body to the door the rapping kept up. "What!" I shouted over the din. "Who the hell is it?" This was getting really annoying now.

I ripped open the door and wouldn't you know it, there was Hector, his Cheshire cat grin beaming. In his hands he held a bouquet of flowers.

"What's this, a piece offering?" I said rubbing my eyes. He held them out for me to take. I didn't and walked back into the room.

"Yeah, I've been giving you so much grief lately I was hoping you wouldn't try to singe my hair anymore. Friends?"

I couldn't help but laugh at him, this big lug of a guy. I took the flowers and gave him a big hug. "Thanks for being my friend."

There was a beautiful blue vase on the table so I filled it with water and placed the flowers in it and set it on the same table. Hector sat down on one of the chairs and stared at me.

"What?" I asked. "Enough with the staring." I went and sat on the bed and absently looked out the window for a few minutes.

"Do you believe in fate, Hector?" I mused.

"I think things happen for a reason. Call that fate or kismet or whatever. Take for instance you as the choice to lead us. Who would have thought you were capable? But I've seen you mature in just these few days and you've proven yourself a strong warrior. Forget what other people think. Take charge," he said.

"You're very kind to say those things." I looked at him and he was regarding me thoughtfully. "But what if I'm not the leader material everyone thinks I am?" He shifted in his chair and leaned forward.

"Your true test will be when we finally get out of here and on our way. You have good instincts. You'll know when to use them, trust me."

Hector was such an amazing man; kind and crazy funny all at the same time. Not bad to look at. He loved a good joke and I admired his strength and agility. So this next question was really hard to get out.

"Have you ever killed anyone, Hector?" I idly fingered the hem of my shirt, my eyes averted.

He didn't answer right away but walked over to the window and stood there staring out into the darkness, I suppose to gather his thoughts.

"Yes . . . many times," he said softly. "Though one stands out from all the rest. It shouldn't have happened."

"Oh . . ." I breathed looking up. His reflection in the glass was pure sadness. I wanted to cry.

He went on. "It was in a country far away from here. We had been sent to bring back a rogue Keeper who was making an immortal army. When we finally found him he was ready to fight and so a clash ensued. My group had him cornered but he wasn't giving up without a battle. His army was quickly defeated despite its strength and he fled across the countryside."

I heard him sigh deeply. "It was never my intention to kill him. When I found him I tried to talk him into surrendering but he would have nothing of that. We argued and then he pulled out his sword and proceeded to wave it around. I unsheathed mine and we began to fight. He was no match for me unfortunately . . . and I killed him." He paused and sighed again.

"He was my brother."

Tears welled up in my eyes. I didn't know what to say to him. When he turned around his eyes were misted. "I miss him still," was all he said.

A soft rapping on the door brought us both to attention. I wiped the tears from my eyes and opened the door to find Eric standing there. He looked from me to Hector with a frown.

"Is everything OK?" he said.

"Fine. Hector was telling me a sad story. What's up?" I stood back to let him in. His eyes tightened on Hector. He didn't go very far from my side.

"It's nearly eight. The rest of the group is in my room already. I came to see if you were asleep or what."

"What about Jeff and Farn, are they there as well? If they're going they need to be included." I said. Eric kept looking from me to Hector and scowling. Hector took the hint.

"Don't worry, she's not my type, just friends," he said heading for the door and giving me a wink. He put his hand on Eric's shoulder. "Be good to her." He pushed past Eric and left the room.

I regarded Eric with narrowed eyes. "Don't tell me you're jealous. I can't deal with that now. So . . . are Jeff and Farn included?"

"Yes, they're there. And no I'm not jealous." He turned to the door.

"Coulda fooled me," I said to his retreating back. MEN!

As we entered Eric's room, all eyes turned to us. I could feel the tension in the room; it hung like a heavy mist on a foggy day. I wondered what I could say or do to relieve it. Before I could do anything Eric started to speak.

"We are here . . ." he began.

"Wait," I interrupted. "I just want to say, anything we say here tonight is not to leave this room. Sorry Eric, this is my team and I'll conduct this." He shrugged and gave me a 'go ahead' gesture and sat down next to Jonni. Hector gave me another wink and a smile.

I cleared my throat and gazed around at my team. "I'm glad you're here. We have a dilemma on our hands that needs to be resolved soon and I need everyone to be on board. Know that you're all free to back out at any time. I just want you to know I trust each of you and hope you'll feel comfortable with me in command."

I paused when I saw each of them look around at the others. Hector and Naomi spoke at the same time.

"I'm in," and then pointed at each other and laughed. That seemed to ease the tension a bit and everyone relaxed. Jeff and Farn looked a little confused so I continued with a condensed explanation of the situation since they didn't have a clue.

"Damn, I didn't think it was so bad," said Farn, fidgeting in his chair. "What can we do?" He glanced at Jeff sitting next to him. His eyes were big as saucers.

"Our biggest problem right now is Arnos' deceit. He hasn't told us what to expect but perhaps we'll hear this tomorrow night when we get our instructions. Some of you know the situation Eric is in. Jeff, Farn . . . Eric's parents are being held against their will by Arnos and he doesn't intend to release them until we bring back the Krystal. As I explained, the Krystal isn't the benign object he claims it is." I stopped to take a breath.

"What is it then?" said Jeff. "Do we have to kill someone to get it? I don't know if I could do that." He grimaced and he shut his eyes.

"It's a weapon," Eric said flatly. I glared at his bluntness.

"No one is going to get killed, Jeff. We do have to be cautious, though. Eric and I think this guy Dax is not the bad one here.

We're not sure what his role is but I sure as hell want to find out . . . but not with violence if possible." I went to stand next to Eric. He took my hand and squeezed it gently.

Hector and Jonni had been very quiet this whole time and I was wondering what was going through their minds when Jonni stood up and spoke, his silver-blue eyes focused on mine.

"I've known Arnos a long time. Centuries, in fact. Yes, I'm that old, Molly. We were warriors together in many immortal wars. Like you I always thought he was a noble man, one who would fight for the good of our race. It's only in the last couple of decades that I've begun to doubt that loyalty. He's changed and not for the good. I haven't said anything before because I felt you needed to figure this out for yourself and indeed you have. Know this . . . I will wholeheartedly support anything you do to bring this affair to its conclusion safely."

I wanted to hug him but all I could manage was a hoarse, "Thank you." There was nothing but silence in the room for several seconds that seemed like hours.

Finally Hector coughed. "Well, I guess we all need to get some shuteye and finish our training in the morning. I'm going down for a snack. Anybody care to join me?" With no one making a move he went for the door but before he exited I saw him peer into the hall. "Just making sure the coast is clear," he said looking around at me and grinning. I just shook my head and smiled back. Bless his crazy heart.

As each person left the room they gave me a slight nod. I wasn't sure how I felt. I had their support but I still sensed a foreboding I could not shake. Something big was about to happen and I was in the middle of it . . . with both feet. As I moved forward to go to my room, I felt Eric's hand on my shoulder.

"Wait, where are you going?" he whispered as I turned around. He had that *look* in his eye. My frown must have been a surprise because he took his hand back slowly.

"I need to be alone for a while. I can't think straight when we're . . . you know," I stammered, kissing his cheek and walking away reluctantly.

"I'll be here when you're ready," he called after me.

I know.

Chapter 10

The trip to my room was agonizing. I wanted to be in that bed with Eric tonight more than anything, but I also had to have time to process what we needed to do about Arnos. I wasn't sure what he already undoubtedly knew about our meeting tonight; what with all the spyware he had lurking around. For all I knew one of the chairs could have been a shape shifter in disguise. My whole body shook at the thought. Ugh! My head was in a tailspin by this point and I knew I'd better de-stress before it exploded.

I walked into the bathroom and looked into the mirror. *Is this the face of a leader?* On a whim I raised my hands into claws and growled like a tiger and had to laugh at my childishness. I gazed at myself again and decided, yes, I am!

Just as I made up my mind to take a long, hot shower, I heard a knock on my door. Who the heck was this?

"Who is it?" I called out the bathroom door.

"It's Naomi. Can I come in and talk to you a minute?"

Crap.

I dragged myself to the door and let her in. I wasn't sure what this was about, but it better be quick.

"So, what's up?" I said as I sat down in the nearest chair. She made herself comfortable in the chair next to me, drawing her legs up to sit cross legged.

"Remember when I told you about the conversation I overheard in the garden between Arnos and the *kids*?" I nodded. "I know a little bit about where he's sending us."

OK, she had my attention. "And you know this . . . how?" I said leaning forward in my chair.

Naomi didn't seem like the type to mince words and she didn't disappoint me.

Very quickly she said, "I've been there before. And believe me it's three days ride through some weird territory."

I shifted in my seat and thought about this. "So how long ago were you there? And most importantly why were you there?"

"Last year I was visiting a relative." She started fidgeting in her chair and it was clear there was more to this trip than she was telling me.

"I can see you're nervous." This was highly unusual for Naomi. "If there's something important I need to know, get it out now. This relative . . . anyone I know?"

She leaned toward me and whispered, "Not yet. It's a secret."

WHAT THE . . . ! I thought.

"Excuse me? Did I hear you right . . . a secret?" I sat up straight in my chair and gave her an incredulous look. "You must be kidding."

"I'll tell you what I know about the terrain, the forests and the wildlife, but no more. The rest you have to find out for yourself." With that said she sat back with a smug expression and a smile.

The back of my neck tingled and was that a red glow I saw surrounding her? I had to blink a couple times. Yup, it's still there. If I had known a week ago things were going to be like this . . . I need to get back to reality!

"Look, I don't know what this is all about, but right now I really do not like it." *At. All.*

"I'm sorry, that's all I can tell you," she answered shrugging. "And don't worry. I am not on Arnos' side. He gives me the creeps."

That makes two of us.

Alrighty then, let's review. Naomi has been to our destination. She knows the whys and wherefores of the place. She was hiding something and was not going to reveal it. Great! Now I really am confused.

I felt like pulling my hair out strand by strand. Did she think I was stupid?

"Since I'm obviously not getting any pertinent information from you, how about telling me what you can? That at least will be something." She leaned forward and started talking.

Our conversation lasted two hours. I took notes so I wouldn't forget. Naomi just chattered on about the kind of terrain we'd encounter, the animals we might see and how the forests change. That one was strange. I wondered how a forest could change as abruptly as she described it. But somehow it didn't scare me as much as I thought it would. Nothing about this journey surprises me anymore. She concluded by giving me a piece of advice.

"Don't underestimate anything you see or hear. It may not be what you think it is," she whispered conspiratorially.

OK, disturbed just doesn't describe what I feel right now. This girl is just plain weird!

"Look, I need to get some sleep. Thanks for the talk and I'll see you in the morning," I said as I hustled her out of my room. I closed the door and leaned against it to calm myself. After a moment I decided I needed that shower right now so I ran for the bathroom, turned on the water to warm it up and jumped in before anyone else showed up with their advice.

The bed felt wonderful but I lay awake for some time pondering every little bit of information I had and aching to be with Eric. Eventually I drifted off to sleep without any clue as to what to do next.

The forest shadows hid many secrets. I stepped into the middle of the clearing and suddenly sensed a presence nearby. As I looked around at the trees, a lone figure emerged from those shadows. It was a slight woman, dressed all in black her long blond hair swinging in the breeze. She smiled at me and pointed at the opposite side of the clearing and then vanished into thin air. I whirled around to see a red dragon with glowing green eyes staring at me. Amazingly I wasn't afraid and I just stared back until it, too, disappeared. In its place stood a hooded figure.

Chapter 11

Huh, I thought as I sat up in bed. The sun was just starting to rise and peak in through the window. A vague recollection of a vision popped into my mind. That clearing has got to have some significance because all of the visions I've experienced have taken place there.

I needed to talk to Eric.

Dressing quickly I ambled down the hall to his room, knocking softly. Another knock later and he opened the door with a towel wrapped around his waist. I believe drool was hanging off my mouth at the sight of him.

"Hey, beautiful, good morning," he said cheerily as he stepped aside to let me in. Oh, how I wanted to tear that towel off and . . . . *control yourself, Molly.* Instead I started babbling on about my vision concerns and how I didn't know what they meant. He smiled and pulled me into his arms where I melted like ice cream on a hot day.

"Let me get dressed and we can talk about this." He pulled away and sat me in a chair while he dressed.

"Do you need any help?" I offered. I heard him chuckle from the bathroom.

"Now you know where that might lead?" he said.

"Uh, huh." More chuckling.

When he finally came out of the bathroom he was dressed in light colored slacks and a navy blue silk shirt. Was I drooling again? My heart was racing as I gazed at his perfect form.

"Now, what's this dream you were concerned about?"

"I keep having the same vision with the same people in it but I can't make out who they are or what they are doing there in the clearing. One man turns into a really large dragon. I can't help but feel this has some significance to our journey," I said as we approached the door.

"Sounds like your visions are getting more involved. Are any of the team there with you in the clearing?" He stopped and left the door closed.

I lowered my eyes as I thought about that. "No, I think I was alone in each one. Do you think I'm seeing the future? If I am, we'll need to remember this. I don't want to be alone and vulnerable at any time."

"I'll make sure that doesn't happen, Moll. We'll all protect you."

"Thanks, Eric," I said. He opened the door and stepped into the hall.

"Ready?" he said. I nodded my head in response. He held my hand as we walked downstairs. I could hear the others talking quietly behind us and turned around to say hi.

Jonni was in front his hand on Naomi's arm, his eyes shining their silver blue. He gave me a big grin. It was freaky because I knew he couldn't see me.

As the others caught up and we were in our little pack, I said, "Since I haven't a clue as to what we'll find out there except what Naomi has told me, we can't go in blind. Arnos has to give us more information. Are we all agreed?"

"Good luck with that," I heard Hector mutter. "We'll be lucky if he tells us anything useful."

"I'm trying to be positive here, H," I whispered. "So here we go." We were outside Arnos' office.

As I walked into the room I wondered what I was going to say and how I'd react to his 'instructions'. God knows I had trusted him as a child and he was always kind to my mother and me; there was never any hint of treachery or deceit. But I had been a child and what did I know? He had even comforted me and took me in when Mom died.

We piled into his office and sat down, me next to Eric on the plush sofa, some stood, and some sat on the floor. There were several of the soldiers there as well, standing on the periphery of the room like they were on guard. The sight of them made me nervous but I did my best not to show it.

And there was Arnos sitting behind his desk like King Tut, his hands steepled in front of him.

"Nice to see you all rested and ready to go. I have but a few things to say before you go for breakfast." He leaned forward and placed his elbows on his desk.

I sat quietly listening to him blather on for an hour about the obstacles we would meet and how it was so important to overcome them—blah, blah, blah. Our goal was to retrieve, intact, this Krystal he needed so badly, pack it up a certain way and transport it to him personally. He failed to mention that it was a weapon of epic proportions. Or that we might die searching for it. Just a little oversight there. Nothing to worry about.

Hector snickered quietly a couple of times. I could see Naomi off to my left rolling her eyes. Jonni and Eric sat passively. I couldn't take it anymore and smiled to myself as I stood up. No more Miss Nice Girl.

"Let me get this straight, Arnos." Pause for effect. "You want us to risk our lives to bring back this Krystal from God knows where for you to use for . . . whatever. So, how come you haven't gone after it yourself? You have your army to protect you."

I swept my arm around to indicate the soldiers and stood with my arms across my chest in what I thought was an intimidating stance. That nice warm glow was starting and my eyes burned.

Arnos' eyes widened so much I expected them to pop out. The soldiers came to attention, but he waved them back. Hector, Naomi and Eric stood to surround me as the room shook with his fury.

I stood my ground.

"How dare you speak to me like that?" he roared. I barely flinched.

As calmly as he could Hector said, "Arnos, you need to calm down."

Arnos' face was almost purple and his hands were clenched in fists in front of him. His eyes were turning red.

Then suddenly his demeanor changed abruptly to a controlled anger. He took a couple of deep breaths. The vibrations stopped.

"You have no right to question me," he said tightly. He placed his hands palm down on the desk as if he was going to stand.

"Oh, but I do," I said, my face a mask. I wasn't giving him any inkling of how scared I was right now. My hands were beginning to shake but I willed them to stop. I started walking back and forth in front of his desk and stopped and slapped my hands on the edge of it facing him.

"You've made me the leader of this group and I intend for all of us to get back safely. It's become apparent you haven't given us enough information about Dax and his stronghold. For instance, how big is this army he has? Where the Krystal is located and is it guarded? Is there magic surrounding it?" I fluttered my hand around. "Little things like that."

He tried to stare me down and didn't say a word for several minutes. I could sense movement behind me but wasn't going to turn around to see who it was. Finally that annoying smirk came out and I wanted to smack him.

"You've certainly found your wings young lady. The truth is I don't have that information or I would certainly have given it to you," he said smugly, settling back into his chair.

We were playing a game of chess. *My move.* I stood up straight. What he didn't know was I had the ace. Oh, wait . . . that was poker. I needed to play it.

"I happen to have a reliable source who knows the area well."

"Really. And who is this reliable source?"

"You needn't worry about that. I'd like to speak to my team alone, if you don't mind." I didn't wait for an answer, turned and left the room with my group surrounding me like a rock star's entourage. My knees were becoming jelly as I reached the hall. I stopped for a moment to gain my balance, Eric at my side.

We ran up the stairs and by the time we reached Eric's room I was hyperventilating. I felt like there was a tight band constricting my breathing. My head was spinning like a top and I was sure I'd pass out when Eric grabbed me around the waist.

"Whoa, Molly, take slow breathes, darling."

"Let's get her to sit down and lower her head," said Hector, opening the door.

"Get her a glass of water, Naomi, in my bathroom." Eric sat me in a chair and pushed my head to my knees. After a few minutes I began to feel better and sat up to take a sip of water.

"Oh my God, that was awful," I gasped. I could hear chuckling from behind me.

"Molly, you were magnificent. I don't believe I've ever heard anyone speak to Arnos like that and live to tell the story," said Jonni. He put his hand on my shoulder and squeezed gently.

"I don't know what came over me in there. It was like a different person took over my mind."

Hector was laughing softly. "You kick butt, baby."

I smiled at him and took another sip of water. After a few more minutes I announced, "This may sound strange, but I really need to eat." I stood, still feeling a little shaky. Eric was by my side in a flash.

"How about we take breakfast outside on the terrace where we can relax before the real work begins?" said Hector.

"After that rush I need to calm down. Let's go," I said.

We all nodded in agreement and walked to the dining room. I still needed to have that talk with them; it would have to wait.

Chapter 12

The rest of the morning and early afternoon was spent loading our weapons and supplies for the journey. Five large, black SUVs had been waiting in back of the mansion, plus a small panel truck; we all started hauling and loading after breakfast.

I was exhausted. The confrontation with Arnos had drained me so bad I could have curled up in one of the SUVs and fallen asleep instantly. Eric looked over from where he was packing an SUV and smiled at me. It took all my strength to give him a wan smile back. He crossed the parking lot to where I stood.

"What's the matter, Moll?" he said putting his hands on my shoulders. His concerned expression brought me to tears. I leaned against his chest and sobbed. Eric wrapped his arms around me and gently rubbed my back. "It'll be all right, Moll. I think you need some sleep."

He picked me up, carried me into the house and up to my room where he gently laid me on the bed. I felt the covers come over me and Eric kissed me on the cheek. That was the last thing I remember before drifting off to La La Land.

I awoke three hours later. I figured it must be close to dinner time because my stomach was rumbling; I went into the bathroom and splashed some water on my face.

There was something different about me when I looked in the mirror at my reflection. My dull red hair was now flaming red; my eyes were more green and glowed steadily. I took a step back and noticed my skin was clear, not a blemish in sight.

Being immortal was great. What had happened to me while I slept? Obviously a vast improvement over the old me. I also felt stronger, like I'd been doing some serious weight lifting. I needed to try something that Arnos had mentioned after my transformation.

I stood at the doorway of the bathroom and started to run as fast as I could toward the balcony. In one big leap I was up and over the edge and sailing into the air. I felt exhilarated.

My landing on the ground was perfect. Then it hit me . . . I just jumped down two stories . . . and I'm still alive! Awesome!

I was like a kid with a new toy. Now I wondered if I could get back up as easily. I looked up to the balcony. Easy as pie. Backing up a few more feet, I ran and kicking off the ground I soared and landed lightly on my balcony.

Okay, able to leap tall buildings . . . check. Throw fire . . . check. See the future . . . well, maybe. That part remained to be seen. I needed to tell somebody about my new skill.

I ran down the hall to Eric's room and knocked. And knocked again. And again. Where was he? I tried the others and none of them seemed to be in their rooms either. What was going on?

I decided to go downstairs and see if they'd gone to dinner without me. As I started toward the dining room I could hear Arnos' angry words coming from his study. I tiptoed down the hall and stood outside the door.

"You were supposed to keep her under control," he said heatedly.

"As you can see she isn't the naïve little girl you thought she was. I doubt she'll ever be again. I love her and support her and nothing you can say will change that. She's getting stronger every day and knows her mind. Tomorrow we leave and we'll bring back your precious Krystal and you *will* release my family or I will personally come and kill you."

"Don't threaten me, McGuire."

Oh my God, it was Eric. I needed to do something and quick. There's no telling what Arnos might do to him. Without giving it much thought I burst into the room and walked over to stand next to Eric.

"Molly, what are you doing?" he said stiffly. I ignored him and put my whole attention on Arnos.

I just stared at him for a couple of seconds to gather my thoughts; I was really winging it. I could feel the vibrations start again and I wasn't letting him do that.

"Don't you dare throw out your energy. I can feel it building up inside you."

Well now, that was new! I can feel emotions?

Eric tried to step in front of me but I pushed him back. "I can handle this. He won't hurt me, Eric, he needs me," I said, leveling my stare at Arnos again. "Don't you?"

I really surprised Arnos with that one because he immediately toned it down to a slow boil.

"There now, that's better, isn't it?" I purred. "Eric is right; I've become much stronger since coming here in both mind and body. As a matter of fact, I just jumped off my balcony and landed quite nicely on the grass. And then . . . I leaped back up." I said smugly.

They were both gaping at me as if my hair were on fire. Well with my new appearance it probably seemed that way.

"Do you guys like my new look? Kinda sexy, huh." I did a little twirl. Arnos was glaring at me intently.

"It seems your transformation is almost complete, my dear," he said icily.

"Yes, you might say that," I said flatly. "Stop threatening us or we just might forget this whole mission and go our separate ways. I for one would like to see a little normalcy again."

Eric stiffened at my side. I guess he didn't think I should be talking to the almighty Arnos like this. I was glad he wasn't saying anything, I was focused; this was between Arnos and me. Right now I felt I had him by the jewels and he knew it. And I didn't care.

"You're getting pretty bold, Molly. I don't think you realize what power I have." He was leaning back and smiling that exasperating smile again.

I sighed and shook my head. I was getting tired of this game.

"Let's cut the crap, Arnos. You and I both know you could cut me down in an instant. But you can't, because I'm valuable to you. So how about we call a truce and get this done."

He nodded but said nothing more. I wondered if this was a good or bad gesture. My trust in him had expired long ago.

I went to leave but turned around as I thought of one more thing. "By the way, tell the kids to come as they are, whatever shape they might be. I know what they are now." As I turned on my heel I thought I heard him grumble something unintelligible.

My smile was huge as I exited his office into the hall.

Eric and I hurried back to his room and collapsed on the bed. He propped himself on his elbow and started playing with my hair. My eyes were closed but I could feel him getting closer and then he was kissing me.

"Do you even know how wonderful you are?" he whispered against my lips. He pulled back. "And what's this about you leaping out a window? You are so crazy."

I smiled and kissed him back. Gosh his lips were soft. I hadn't paid much attention to that before.

"I felt . . . powerful after I woke up from my nap. My hair is so red now and my eyes blaze greener. How could I not take a leap of faith? It was totally absurd I know to jump out a window without thinking but it made me feel as if I could do anything." I ruffled his hair. "Besides, you like me as a super hero, right?"

He nuzzled into my neck and laughed. "Right. We'd better see if there's any food left Super Girl and then tonight . . . ."

"I have to meet with everyone and finalize our plans. But then . . . ," I teased.

He groaned and leaped off the bed and grabbed my hand and lifted me effortlessly off the bed to go downstairs.

Chapter 13

Naturally, everyone was at the dinner table having a riotous conversation about which knife was the deadliest. Eric and I sat down next to Naomi after filling our plates at the buffet.

"Hector seems to think the long knife is best in a fight but I say the short Galley knife is best for in-close combat. What do you think, Molly?" she asked winking at me.

"I don't know, Naomi. The Galley offers a much sharper edge. That would be my choice; but the long one sure would leave more room for maneuvering. It's more a personal preference I think. Besides, that long one is too heavy for my taste," I said, cutting a piece of steak and popping it into my mouth. I purposely looked at Hector and grinned.

Hector was ignoring our teasing. He kept on eating as if he hadn't eaten for a week. Naomi was laughing.

"I think he's mad at us," she said.

"No, I'm not," he said with a mouthful. "Just keep pushing the right buttons, girl and see what happens."

"You should have seen how Molly pushed Arnos a few minutes ago. She really gave him an earful. Did you know she leaped out her window this afternoon?" Eric said smiling at me.

Everyone's eyes were on me in an instant.

"Really? Out a window? To the ground?" Jeff said amazed. "Good grief, Molly, you could have been killed."

I glanced at him with an amused look on my face. "Have a little faith. Notice anything different about me today?" I said tossing my hair.

He looked at me intently and then his eyes got big as saucers. "Good gosh, your hair is . . . redder and your eyes are glowing greener. Wow!"

Everyone else had to make their comments as well especially Hector. I was a rock star all right, but I wasn't going to let it go to my head.

"Okay, you guys, I'm really flattered and all, but we need to discuss the journey tonight. Come to Eric's room after dinner," I said briefly. I could see Arnos coming into the room out of the corner of my eye. He didn't look at me or anyone else for that matter. His soldiers were nowhere in sight.

He sat at the far end of the table away from us. It was hard to tell his mood from looking at him, but I could sense his uneasiness. My new skill was paying off. I wondered why I couldn't pick up on the others and concentrated hard on Hector. He would be an easy read.

Nothing. Hmmmm. I tried the others. Still nothing.

There has to be some connection here but I just could not see it. I must have had an absorbed look on my face because Eric leaned in and whispered, "What is it?"

I leaned closer to him. "Remember in Arnos' study when I told him not to throw out his power? Eric, I could feel it. Right now I can feel his inner turmoil, but . . . I can't seem to read anyone else," I whispered back, indicating the others with my knife. "That's just plain weird."

"All these new skills take time to develop. Maybe this one will take a little longer," he said. "And his emotions are stronger right now; stronger than any of us."

I considered this possibility.

"Yeah, maybe you're right." I shrugged and went back to eating.

Later we gathered in Eric's room and I mapped out some of the obstacles and creatures we might encounter on this journey.

"Naomi tells me there are animals with secretive ways in some of the forests. They can hide in the unlikeliest places, so be alert at all times. Part of the way will involve going on foot so we'll need to stay close together. We don't have communication devices so if someone gets lost we may not find you." I paused to bring out the crude maps Naomi and I had made of the terrain. Everyone crowded around the table to see.

"What are these?" said Hector pointing at some red marks.

"Those are phantom gates we must go through from one region to another," Naomi said. "There are three such gates that are maintained by a guardian race called the Halin. They have strict rules for entry to the next region but I doubt we'll have much trouble getting through."

"You hope," Hector muttered. Jonni, Jeff and Farn nodded their heads.

"I've been through them. They weren't hard," she said flippantly. "Thing is, they change the rules every now and then to confuse their enemies." She turned away from the table and sat down.

"Oh, wonderful," Hector said shaking his head.

"Quit fussing, H. We'll be fine," I said reassuringly. He grunted.

I rolled up the map and stuffed it into my backpack.

"Now, what are we going to do about this army? Do you think they'll be helpful or what? There's no telling who the shifters are and who are not. If anyone sees something strange about them, let me know. We're kind of outnumbered here. I've spoken to the leader, Nolin, and he seems to be a decent fellow. I don't trust Arnos, so be alert."

"We haven't seen much of them lately. Where do they hang out?" said Farn.

"They have a barracks they stay in between duties. It's somewhere out back of the house. Should we scope it out?" Jonni questioned.

"No, let's not. But if someone wants to snoop, go ahead. I can't stop you." I looked at Hector. He was smirking. "So, I guess that's it. Tomorrow we roll. Any questions?"

Nobody offered any so they said goodnight and filed to the door. Eric opened it and let everyone out; he quietly closed the door, locked it and turned around.

Without saying a word he approached me slowly, unbuttoning his shirt, keeping his gaze on me. I got that warm all over feeling and started to lift my T-shirt.

"Wait, let me do that," he said quietly. God, he was beautiful. His chest muscles rippled as he pulled the T over my head. I put my hands on his chest and he pulled me closer for a long passionate kiss. My insides melted like molten lava.

It might be the last time we would be together like this for some time. We melded together like two pieces of a puzzle. I wanted it to go on forever, but all I would get was tonight . . . for now.

Chapter 14

J ournal entry—Day One,

Our journey begins today to find Dax and the Krystal. I can't say I'm thrilled with all that's happened so far as Arnos wasn't a fountain of information and he proved to be sinister and untrustworthy as hell. But I have complete confidence in my team of warriors. Not so sure about the soldiers Arnos is sending with us, but we'll deal with them as needed.

Eric has become my rock. He is my friend, my lover and I don't know what I would do without him.

I'm missing my mother terribly and could really use her wisdom about now. Maybe she could explain my visions to me and give me guidance. I can't think about that now and focus on the task we have taken on.

I shall try to write as often as I can to chronicle what happens as we travel.

The morning was sunny but cool. A light breeze blew my hair around like dancing fairies as I stood on the balcony of Eric's room. Having spent the night with Eric in divine bliss, I was in good spirits. I couldn't help but smile.

The rest of my team was happy but reserved this morning, a bit unusual for them. There wasn't a lot of joking around you'd normally hear at breakfast.

"Hey, guys . . . here's to a safe and profitable journey," I said raising my glass of orange juice. They all did the same and we clinked glasses all around. I would give my life for any of them and know in my heart they would do the same for me. I had to blink and lower my eyes to control the tears I felt coming.

Afterward Eric and I went to my room where I finished packing what I'd need. I'm not your typical woman who packs three suitcases for a week. Nope . . . three pairs of jeans, six shirts, socks, undies and an extra pair of hiking boots and done. Eric watched me in amusement.

"What?" I said. "I pack light." It all went into my duffel bag along with two coats, one light, one heavy and some essential toiletries.

"I'm ready," I said hoisting the duffel onto my shoulder. "What about you?"

"Already in the vehicle," he chuckled. "After you, noble leader." He was bowing and gesturing with his arm out.

I socked him in the arm as I passed him.

Outside we checked our supplies and weapons one more time and loaded into the vehicles. Eric, Hector, Naomi and I were in the first SUV; Jeff, Farn and Jonni were in the next. The soldiers occupied the other three SUVs and the truck, twenty in all. I wondered which ones were the 'kids' in disguise. Nolin gave me a thumb up and Eric started the engine and pulled out of the driveway onto the main road.

I glanced up to the house and noticed Arnos peering out a window on the second floor. He didn't look happy. I couldn't care less.

A million thoughts raced through my head as I gazed out the window. We were traveling through the small town outside Arnos' compound and this was the main drag, nothing but small stores, a restaurant, and a church. Funny, I'd never noticed how small the town was until now. It didn't take long to get through it and we were soon zipping along in the countryside.

Thoughts of my mother danced around in my head. We'd been very close and losing her had been a real shock. Not having siblings to turn to had made me feel very lonely. Arnos had comforted me in the beginning and even took me into his home where I'd met Eric.

I hadn't seen much of Arnos these last few days which was fine with me. Having found out in just a week how ambitious and conniving he had become, I knew he was dangerous. It made me nervous. Even though I'd stood up to him and something about me scared him, I didn't think for a minute that this 'quest' he's sending us on was just about the Krystal.

It was personal.

And I had the feeling we would see him again real soon. I had a buzzing in my head as if he was very near.

I noticed Eric peering over at me and smiling.

"You're lost in thought," he observed.

I nodded weakly. "Just thinking about my mother and some of her visions. I think she may have predicted her own death," I said sadly, turning to stare out the window.

"Really," he said frowning. "How so?"

"I don't know. Something she said a few weeks before the accident, about how life was going to change in an unusual manner and I would find my own way. Could this be it?"

He was looking straight ahead and didn't speak for a few moments.

"Your life has certainly changed in some dramatic ways lately. I've seen you mature before my eyes. Who you were then is not who you are now, Molly," he said with conviction.

I closed my eyes and didn't say anything for a long while. The landscape flew by in a blur and there was no time to enjoy it right now.

We passed through several small towns and began to climb into the mountains. In time we left the main road behind and turned onto a two-lane going east. The vista changed to stands of pines and birches; I could see wildlife roaming amongst the trees. Large birds flew overhead. It looked peaceful and serene with the sun dappling through the trees.

I glanced back at Hector and Naomi who were playing a game. Looking out the back window I could see the other SUVs right behind us with the truck not far behind them.

"How long do you think this will take, Eric?" I said turning back around.

"The first gate should be one or two days from here. After we pass through that one the terrain gets pretty rough," said Naomi from the back seat.

"So, what, we go four wheeling then. I hope the truck can keep up," Eric said.

"We may have to abandon the vehicles at some point after the second gate and go on foot," Naomi added.

"So are we talking a week or two?" Eric asked, looking at her in the rear-view mirror.

She just nodded, absorbed in the game.

He paused to look at me. I was deep in thought again. "You okay?" he said reaching over to touch my arm.

I shook my head. "Do you think Arnos will follow us? I can't believe he'd sit at home waiting patiently for us to return with his precious Krystal. He's probably had GPS units attached to the vehicles before we left. I can picture him jumping in his 4x4 and trailing us," I rambled on quickly. I was hell bent on hysteria right about now.

"If he does, we'll deal with it," I heard Hector say from behind me. I tried to be comforted but somehow . . . .

As we traveled along at a good pace, I somehow thought the day would go slower. Before I realized it the sky was turning dark and we were pulling into the parking lot of a small motel called *Harry's Comfort Inn and Campground*. Naomi had made reservations for the team to spend tonight in the motel and the soldiers would rough it in the camping area. I thought a little comfort would be real nice.

The rooms were neat and clean and had two queen size beds in each. Naomi and I were bunking together while the boys divided up the rest of the rooms. Eric ended up in a room by himself; I stared longingly at him as he opened his door.

Naomi looked at me as we entered our room. "Go ahead. I don't mind being by myself." She tilted her head toward the door and threw her bag on the bed.

"Are you sure?" I said sheepishly.

She nodded and smiled.

"Thanks. See you in the morning." I walked quickly to Eric's room. He had the door open before I got there and pulled me into his arms and closed the door.

Chapter 15

J*ournal entry-Day Three*

We've traveled over a hundred miles and will be approaching the first gate today. I can't say I'm very excited to finally make progress. The trip so far has been quite ordinary and we haven't run into anything dangerous or even threatening . . . so far.

Everyone is in good spirits and we joke around from time to time. Hector has some fabulous stories to tell about his adventures long ago. Hector likes to tell outrageous jokes and we are obliged to laugh at them. Mostly we sit quietly, each with their private thoughts.

Naomi, the dark angel has finally opened up about herself a little more. Although I suspect she isn't telling the important parts, but at least I've got a better picture of who she is even if it is contrived.

Eric and I have had some quiet moments alone when we've stopped for gas. We can't wait for this to be over so we can figure out what direction to take our relationship.

Jonni doesn't say much so I don't know what's on his mind until he speaks. When he does say something you can bet it's very important.

The rest of the team, Jeff and Farn are just too hilarious for words. They love to play tricks on us. The rest of us are going to get back at them as soon as we figure out how.

The soldiers mostly keep to themselves.

Our arrival at the entrance to the first gate was quite sudden. One minute it wasn't to be seen and the next thing we knew, there it was in front of us. It didn't look as impressive as I'd thought it would be; just a rusty old gate.

"Whoa, that was weird," said Eric as he slammed on the brakes.

"Yeah, what's going on?" I turned around to Naomi who just shrugged her shoulders. "Are we in the right place?"

"Beats me. Must be one of their new changes," she said leaning forward for a better look. "Let's get out and see. If the Halin are here they'll show themselves pretty quickly."

We piled out of the vehicles and so did the rest of our entourage. I went to approach the gate and all of a sudden there were three red-cloaked figures in front of me with their hands out in front of them in the universal 'stop' signal.

One of the figures stepped forward and said crisply, "Your credentials, if you please." At least he was polite.

"Credentials? We weren't told we needed any," I said turning to Naomi. She shook her head and made a face.

The Guardians sighed heavily. "Then you will need to answer three questions."

I nodded my agreement trying not to smile.

"Who are you?" they said in unison.

Well, that seemed easy. Maybe too easy. I thought about this for a few seconds. I wasn't sure if my answer should be long and complicated or short and sweet. I chose short.

"We are Arnos' quest team and I am Molly Fyre, the leader," I said smiling confidently.

"Where are you going?

"We are going to an area called Carolan."

"What do you seek?"

"We seek the Krystal of Carolan." I hoped I'd answered correctly because they gave no indication whether I had or not.

They conferred amongst themselves for several minutes in a language I couldn't understand. We all just stood there and shook our heads at this nonsense.

The three of them finally faced us and nodded their heads in unison. "You may pass. Safe journey."

Okaaay.

The gate opened spontaneously and we hopped back into the SUVs and drove through what seemed like an enormous bubble into a completely different kind of forest. Naomi had been right about the forests changing. This was a bit disorienting.

This forest was ancient with gigantic trees that stood so high we couldn't see the tops. Great lengths of green ferns hung down from the branches. It was dark and dank and dangerous looking. There didn't seem to be any birds or animals around. No other sounds were evident but our engines. The silence was palpable. The road was only a wide path through the trees and I wondered if our truck would make it.

We stopped the vehicles and got out to look around. There was something sinister about this place. I called to Nolin and he jogged over to where I stood.

"Do you hear anything?" I said. My voice seemed to echo in the air.

"No, nothing," he said looking around nervously.

As we stood there pondering the atmosphere I sensed other beings watching us. Hector gave me the indication that he sensed it too. We stared at each other frowning.

"Back in the vehicles!" I shouted . . . too late. They were upon us in an instant, surrounding the vehicles in an unusually non-threatening way.

For a moment they just stood there gazing intently at the bunch of us. Then one of them I assumed to be the leader came forward and stood in front of me. He was dressed in a dark blue cloak, the others in forest green. His eyes were like a cat's with black slits inside the blue. He spoke in a strange language also.

"I'm sorry, I don't understand," I said quietly. I didn't want to be impolite. "We just need to pass through to the next gate."

He looked back to another individual who walked over and conferred with him. The man in green turned to me.

"Our master, Dagan, wishes to know what you are doing here," he said politely. At least we weren't being attacked.

"As I've said, we are only interested in traveling to the next gate on our way to the area known as Carolan."

He conveyed this to his master.

"You have soldiers. Why?" he asked softly.

"Only to protect us in the event of an attack," I said just as gently. "May I ask who you are?"

"We are the Fresnah who occupy this forest and protect the creatures that dwell here." He spoke quietly to his master again. The leader raised his eyebrows and nodded to his follower. He was very serious.

"My master is curious as to who *you* are."

"My name is Molly Fyre and this is my quest team," I said sweeping my arm around to indicate everyone. I saw the leader's eyes widen and he spoke hastily to his minion.

"My master knows that name. He grants you safe passage. We shall watch your progress."

Hmmm. That was a surprise. I stood silent for a moment.

"We thank you," I finally said, giving a little nod.

The leader nodded back solemnly and with a wave of his hand there immediately was birdsong and insect noise. We all stared in amazement.

In a blink of an eye the Fresnah disappeared into thin air.

"Okay, add that to our list of strange happenings," I said to no one in particular. "Let's get going everyone," I shouted. Nolin jogged back to his vehicle and Eric started forward . . . on a completely paved road! Whoa, didn't expect that. I so liked these people.

Chapter 16

J ournal entry-Day Five

The journey through the ancient forest was largely uneventful thanks to the Fresnah. They provided us with a safe camping sight that night just as it became dark.

We set up camp beside a lake that seemed to go on forever in the dimming light. The air smelled clean with only a slight breeze to ruffle the leaves on the trees. The smell of campfires soon wafted into the night along with the aroma of food cooking.

A low murmur of voices filled my head. There was something else however that caught my attention. It was coming from the soldiers. I couldn't quite put my finger on the source but it came to me as anger and impatience. It was only one mind I heard.

I went and roamed amongst the soldiers, nodding and acknowledging greetings. They were a very friendly bunch and I stopped to talk with some of them when I spied the two shifters who were Sophie and Peter sitting around a campfire talking animatedly. They stopped their conversation at once when I stepped in front of them. The heat of the fire felt good on my rear end.

"Hi there, a little chilly tonight," I said with a big smile. "You guys doing all right?"

"Uh, yeah, fire feels good," the soldier/Peter said cautiously. He glanced around nervously.

I could feel a nearby presence with the anger problem.

I was enjoying this so much. The soldier/Sophie darted her eyes anywhere but at me. I stared at them a few more minutes and decided they'd had enough . . . for now.

"Well, gotta go. Have a good evening," I said cheerily, laughing my ass off inside.

I ambled back to the team's area and saw Jonni sitting in front of his tent on a tiny stool. It looked like he was whittling something out of a chunk of wood. He'd seen the whole encounter and was laughing softly to himself. The rest of them were sitting around our campfire talking and joking quietly. I watched them with amusement. They were so comfortable with each other in a way that made me smile. I was so glad I knew them; they were my family, if only for a short while. Eric caught my eye and smiled.

Jonni's sight was back for the night and he ambled over to me and sat down.

"How are you doing, Molly," he said quietly. He looked at me thoughtfully his silver-blue eyes shining.

I didn't say anything for a few moments as I peered out into the trees in the dimming light. Something was different about them. They weren't as ominous looking now, but more friendly and normal. More changes I guessed.

Jonni was watching me intently. I looked at him and smiled.

"I guess I'm doing okay," I said.

"You're quite a woman," he remarked matter-of-factly.

"So I've been told," I said blandly. "I'm waiting for the other shoe to drop."

"What do you mean?" he asked, frowning.

"Jonni, there's someone here who shouldn't be. I feel their anger and edginess and whoever it is, is cloaked somehow. As I wandered through the soldiers' camp the feeling became quite strong near the shifters that are Sophie and Peter. They were very nervous with me around them," I said.

"Your new found skills are coming in handy. Do you think this person is dangerous?"

"I can't tell that. I wish I could read his mind. It would make it so much easier." My body was restless and I had an idea.

"Excuse me, Jonni," I said quickly and walked over to where Eric was sitting.

"Come with me a minute," I said softly in his ear. He rose and followed me to a quiet area away from everyone else.

"What is . . . ," he started to say until I kissed him. Just then Hector strolled by.

"So, you two sharing a tent? Gonna get cold tonight," he said giving us his best grin. I scowled at him and returned my attention back to Eric.

"Don't say anything else, just listen," I whispered in his ear. "We have to stroll into the soldiers' camp and talk to Nolin. Just two lovers taking a walk."

He nodded and whispered back, "What's going on?"

I looked into his eyes. "I think Arnos is here under disguise. We have to see if Nolin knows anything."

"How do you know this?"

"I've been feeling anger and frustration from someone here in camp. It has Arnos' signature on it. Trust me." I pulled away and grabbed his hand as we took our stroll around the camp. I pretended to see no one but Eric but my mind was concentrating on homing in on the one giving off the bad vibes.

A noisy disturbance up ahead quickly had us on the run to see what was happening. Several of the soldiers were hunched over something in the bushes at the edge of the forest. I pushed my way in to see and stopped dead in my tracks. It was Peter on the ground, he had been stabbed and he had strange burn marks on his body. He was dead.

I turned away weak in the knees, my hand to my mouth. Eric caught me in his arms. I thought I would faint. I had to compose myself and fast.

Nolin came running and pushed his way through the crowd now forming around the body.

"Be quiet! What happened? Did anyone see anything?" he shouted above the din. Everyone shut up and shook their heads.

Just then Sophie came running out of the trees bloody and screaming, "Peter, Peter!" She dropped to the ground beside

Peter's body, rocking and wailing with her hands over her face. It broke my heart.

"Fan out and see if you can find who did this," shouted Nolin at his soldiers. They scattered into the trees in all directions.

I knelt down beside Sophie and put my arms around her. She was shaking, inconsolable. "Sophie, you need to tell us who did this," I said calmly in her ear. She stopped crying long enough to whisper a name, "*Arnos*".

I grimaced and gave Eric a knowing nod. His face became hard and he whirled around to Hector, Naomi and Jonni who had been standing on the periphery of the crowd. Jeff and Farn stood there with stricken faces.

"Come with me," he said quickly and they all ran into the forest after the soldiers, weapons in hand. I stayed with Sophie and Nolin, who covered Peter's body with a sheet.

"Sophie, let's go sit by the fire so I can tend to your wounds," I said gently as I lifted her to stand. She numbly looked down at the corpse of her brother.

"We never thought this would happen," she said miserably. "I fought to get away. Peter told me to run. Why would Arnos do this? We trusted him."

"I don't know. Come along now. There's nothing we can do for him now. We'll find Arnos and he'll pay." I sat her down near the fire in our area and I found the first aid kit in my tent. Her wounds were largely superficial but the emotional wounds I couldn't heal.

A half hour later the soldiers and my team returned empty handed. Eric stomped over to me and sat down, his head in his hands.

"We lost the trail a half mile from here, but it was Arnos all right," he murmured.

Jonni came over looking incredulous. "I guess that other shoe has dropped, Molly," he said breathlessly. "I'm sorry, even my night vision couldn't see him." He had his hands on his thighs breathing hard and shaking his head. I looked up at him sadly.

"I should have gone after him myself. I can sense his emotions," I said to no one in particular.

"It wouldn't have made a difference. He's long gone," said Hector. "Besides, if he had gotten his claws into you, where would we be?"

I looked up and shook my head.

"You think he'd come after me? I thought I was the only one who could get to Dax and the Krystal. No, he's telling me to beware. We need to move ahead." I turned my attention back to Sophie.

"Molly, we've made our pledge to protect you and that's what we'll do. Don't go doing something reckless to prove yourself. Please don't let your emotions dominate your instincts," Eric said.

"Don't presume to know my emotions," I said sharply. "Peter died today because of me." *Revenge was clearly on my mind.*

I packed up the medical supplies and returned them to my tent.

When I came out I saw Nolin running up to us out of the corner of my eye. "I'm putting extra guards out tonight, Molly. What else can we do?"

I thought about it for a moment, looking at each person. It was decision making time.

"I don't think he'll be back tonight. He's made his statement. But the extra guards are a good idea, just in case."

I paused to glance at Sophie. "We'll need to bury Peter's body tonight." Sophie started to weep again and I put my arm around her shoulder. "Can you get a detail together for that Nolin?"

"We'll get it done right away," he said, gently placing a hand on Sophie's head. Her reddened, tear-stained face looked up at him and smiled.

"I . . . I have something I'd like buried with him," she said shakily. She reached in her pocket and brought out a gold locket. "It belonged to our mother. Could I put it around his neck?"

"Of course you can. Come with me." Nolin took her hand and they walked over to where Peter lay.

I had a feeling this was only the beginning of our battle. *Arnos was mine!*

We went to bed tonight with heavy hearts.

Chapter 17

J ournal entry—Day Six

The event of last night left us all anxious and incredibly sad.
I'm keeping Sophie close to me. She wasn't speaking to anyone
but me and I could truly understand how she felt. She did tell me
that they actually were brother and sister and had been rescued
by Arnos' men and recruited by Arnos after their parents had died
in a fire. I now suspected it was Arnos' doing. They were young
and already able to shape shift; a definite asset to him.

We have reached the second gate and approach it with
trepidation. I hope it will be as easy as the first. It seems like the
same guardians are here as well; a very curious thing. They of
course asked the same questions and I gave the same answers.
There was one difference however, they told me we were very
close to the last gate and to beware of the inhabitants of this
sector. When I asked why, they just disappeared. So much for
information. We are going to be extra cautious as we proceed.

This next sector was not just forest. There was a town up
ahead and before we entered I halted the caravan and consulted
with Nolin and my team.

"Naomi, who are these 'inhabitants'?" I asked. She scrunched
up her face and looked like she didn't want to answer.

"As memory serves me they are a race of pig . . . people," she
said, distaste showing on her face.

"Eeeuw. Are they dangerous?" I said wrinkling my nose.
"How should we proceed?"

"Sounds to me like we should avoid them," said Hector, leaning casually against the SUV. "Unless we want pork chops for dinner." Ever the comedian.

"That might be a good idea but is there a way around the town?" Nolin asked Naomi.

She thought for a minute or two, pacing in a circle and pointing her finger this way and that like she was trying to figure something out.

"I believe we can go that way," she said pointing to the west. "And if we head in that direction we can backtrack to another road on the far side of the lake. Yes, that's the way," she said emphatically. "It will take longer but it should keep us well out of their territory."

"You're sure? We don't want to run into an ambush," Eric said.

"Yes, I'm sure," she answered.

"Okay, let's go," I shouted down the line.

We piled back into the vehicles and turned around to find this other road. It was a couple miles until we saw the turnoff on the right. It would be dark in a few hours and we needed to find a safe place to set up camp. I had warned Nolin to have his men be on the alert for danger and I could see them hanging out of the windows their guns visible.

Ten miles later we came to the lake Naomi had mentioned. The forest encroached right up to the water's edge three quarters of the way around, leaving a sandy stretch of beach open on the road side. We stopped and set up camp there for the night near the trees.

The sun would set soon and I needed to get away from everyone for a while, so after camp was set, I wandered into the trees. It smelled damp and musky like the sun never quite warms the place up enough to dry out. It was quiet here as if the whole world was on the other side of a curtain and here I was . . . alone; then I realized I wasn't.

A sudden crack of a twig made me whirl around with my dagger in my hand, crouched ready to strike.

"It's just me," Eric said softly. His body was tensed, his hands in defensive pose. We both eased at once.

"Sorry. You scared me. I think we're all a bit on edge right now." I sheathed my knife and sat down on a large rock. "I just needed some space," I said, my eyes focused on the dirt in front of me.

"I can leave if you want, but I won't be far away if you need me," Eric said. He didn't move and I really didn't want him to go.

"No, stay. Please." I hesitated as my gaze found his. "It's just . . . I needed to think some things through."

"I understand, but this place isn't safe to be here alone." He came a little closer and I could see the worry on his face. He looked like he'd aged since we started.

I looked away and took a breath to calm myself so I could say what I needed to say.

"Two years ago I remember Arnos coming to our house a couple of days before my mother died. I was almost eighteen at the time and didn't think anything of his frequent visits; he was a friend. They argued occasionally about some guy I didn't know; only this day was different. Arnos must have thought my mom knew where he was but she kept telling him she had no idea where to find the man."

I paused as Eric came and sat on a rock near me.

"Anyway, on this particular day he was furious at her, accusing her of keeping her visions from him. I could see my mother was frightened of him but she never gave him any information. He stormed out of the house cursing and threatening her. He didn't know I was listening to all this." I sighed and got up to walk around.

"Eric, I don't think my mother died in an accident. I'm certain she was murdered and I couldn't save her." I stopped in front of Eric, tears choking me. He stood and put his arms around me. I was becoming a real crybaby.

"Molly, we will get him and he'll be punished. He won't get away with any of this," he assured me. I sniffled against his chest.

Just then Hector came running into the clearing.

"Oh, sorry. I don't mean to interrupt your moment but have either of you seen Naomi? I can't find her anywhere," he said.

I wiped the tears from my face. "No, we've been here for a while. Where would she have gone?" I asked. Eric shrugged his shoulders. "She didn't tell anyone she was leaving? You know how she is. Miss Independent," I added.

"She and I were going to do the first watch," Hector said quickly. "We need to find her. These woods are not safe even with an army at the ready." Hector turned to leave us when I caught sight of movement in the trees.

I pointed in that direction. "What was that?" I asked, trying to get a better look.

Hector took out his binoculars and peered into the distance. "Looks like a dog or small wolf," he said. "We have to be careful about even something as ordinary as a dog. Wonder where it came from and what would a stray be doing out here at night all alone? We'd better watch for those pig-people."

I took the binoculars and peered through them. The animal was moving slowly, head moving back and forth, almost like it was patrolling, and probably thinking it wasn't seen.

"All good questions," I said. "I don't know how much more can happen but let's find out if anyone else has a clue. We're still close enough to those pig-people to make me nervous and remember, Arnos is still on the loose. No telling what he can do."

We returned to the camping area together. I felt as if I needed eyes in the back of my head. While I was laughing to myself at that thought, who should come strolling along but Naomi. She acted like she always does . . . unconcerned and distant.

"What's up guys?" she said brightly.

"Where have you been? We were getting worried. There's a dog or wolf roaming around in the woods," said Hector stopping dead in front of her. "We have first watch, remember?"

"I was just taking a look around," she said haughtily, her hands on her hips.

A faint breeze blew from her direction and I lifted my face to sniff the air. I wrinkled my nose. Was that dog I smelled? I drew closer to Naomi and the smell got stronger.

I scowled; she looked at me sheepishly when she saw me sniffing. I pushed Hector aside and faced her.

"Okay, Naomi, spill it. You're a shape-shifter aren't you?"

I saw her flinch. "Amongst other things," she said softly.

I couldn't believe my ears. "Why keep this a secret? Didn't you think this would be an important piece of information for me to have? And what other 'things' are you?" I snapped.

After a moment she murmured, "I'm a healer."

"A healer," I repeated skeptically. "Like you can actually heal people? Could you have healed Peter?"

"No, he was already dead. I can't raise the dead." I saw tears welling up in her eyes. "I wish that I could," she said tearfully. She looked miserable. "I suppose I'll be punished."

"No, no," I said quickly. "Why would I do that? I'm just surprised that's all." I paused and looked around distractedly. "You and Hector better get ready for your watch. You and I will talk later."

She wiped her eyes and gave a sigh of relief and left with Hector. I'm sure she was going to get an earful from him tonight. I couldn't blame him. I think he really adores her . . . a lot and his concern shows. And he teases Eric and I. Oh, the paybacks continue.

I turned to Eric and gave a heavy sigh.

"What do I do now?" I said.

"She is who she is, Moll. We have to give her credit for fessing up. I think you handled that very well." He was rubbing my shoulders. It felt divine. I suddenly felt exhausted and leaned into him. He heaved his own weary sigh and put his arms around me.

"We need some sleep. Tomorrow we meet the last gate and who knows what's in store for us beyond that," he muttered into my hair.

"Naomi says the gate is a good day's ride so we'll have to make camp after entering the next sector. We'll be in Dax's territory then and I'm sure he knows we're coming," I said.

I turned and put my arms around his neck. "I'm going to check on Sophie and then I'll come to your tent, if that's all right with you."

"I'll be waiting," he said as he kissed me.

I walked off to my tent to see if Sophie was all right. She was sitting cross-legged in the middle of the tent looking at some pictures.

"What are you looking at?" I said quietly. I sat down next to her.

She lifted her tear stained face to mine and smiled weakly.

"These are pictures of Peter and me and our parents. We were so happy back then. I don't remember my parents as well as Peter did, I was only four when they died, but he told me all about them. These pictures help," she said sadly.

I couldn't believe these children had been with Arnos for six years—as his lackeys. What else had he done to further his cause? I couldn't wait to find out.

I sat with her for a while until she fell asleep. I covered her with a heavy blanket and stole out of the tent to Eric's. I needed comforting tonight as well.

Tomorrow would be very interesting.

Chapter 18

A shimmering shadow took form a few feet in front of me.

"Mom?" I said, tears welling up in my eyes.

"Hello, Molly," she said adoringly. "It's been so long and just look at you; you've grown into a lovely woman." She smiled at me lovingly, her image just hovering in the air. I wanted to run and embrace her but know it's not possible. It saddened me and I started to cry.

"I miss you so much," I sobbed. "I need your help. What should I do?"

Her image floated in and out of focus.

"I don't have much time, darling, so listen carefully. You've not reached your full potential yet; that will be revealed soon. I know the visions you have are puzzling but all will come into focus and a great surprise awaits you." Her head swiveled to the left and back again.

They're coming," she said quickly. "Farewell, my lovely."

"Wait!" I shouted running toward her as her image slowly dissolved into blue mist. I fell to my knees and my sobs racked my body so hard I could hardly keep upright.

"I love you, mom," I whisper haltingly, burying my face in my hands.

Did I mention that I hadn't had a vision lately? Well, that one was bewildering. That's the first time I've dreamt of my mother and maybe this was another sign. Of what, I couldn't say but it seemed as if she was trying to tell me something. Something to help me. Why did everyone have to speak in riddles? It is so annoying.

I reached behind me and Eric wasn't there and I panicked. It was still dark and as he had told me, this was a dangerous place to be wandering around alone.

I got up and went in search of him. The moon was almost full and I didn't have to go far. I could see him sitting in front of his tent peering into the forest, deep in thought. I walked over as quietly as I could.

"Eric," I whispered. He jumped but when he saw it was me he relaxed and slumped in his chair. "What's wrong?" I went to sit beside him.

"Something has been bothering me, Molly, ever since we left Arnos'." He started drawing circles in the dirt with a stick, his expression flat.

"And you're just now mentioning it?" I said absently.

He heaved a weary sigh. "What happens to us when all this is over?" he muttered.

I wasn't sure I'd heard him right. "What? What are you talking about?"

"My parents are going to need me. That is after we find them. I'll need to go home." He turned to look at me.

I struggled to absorb this latest revelation. I was having a hard time believing this and couldn't quite wrap my head around the idea that even though we loved each other, Eric felt duty bound to stay with his parents. I understood that. Was he telling me we were over or suggesting I join him?

"Are you saying I can't go with you, wherever that may be? Eric, I love you. Nothing can take that away. If you need to be with your parents then I fail to see the problem," I said plaintively, adding, "Are you still under Arnos' spell, is that it?"

He stood to face me. "This started out as an assignment." He hesitated as he gave me a half smile. "Then I fell in love with you, which of course complicated things. I do want to be with you Molly, more than you know. If Arnos dies my father becomes the next Keeper and as his son I have an obligation to be by his side as his protector. That's why Arnos has them hidden away; as incentive for me to finish what we started."

I regarded him in amazement.

"I don't know what to say. Why didn't he just kill them and be done with it? Why make us go on this mission to retrieve a weapon that could destroy us all?" I said, regretting my words already. I hadn't meant to be insensitive.

"He thought I could get you to do what he wanted if he had them hidden where I couldn't find them. Then . . . he would kill them. Arnos has the power to threaten or eliminate anyone who dares to oppose him. My father was on the Keeper's Council until a few weeks ago when he disappeared along with my mother and my sister."

I raised my eyebrows.

"You have a sister? You've never mentioned her in all the time I've known you. Why?" I asked.

"Fran is two years younger than I and has a very special power that Arnos hoped to use. He told me never to tell anyone." He looked me straight in the eye. "She can read and manipulate minds."

I directed my gaze at the ground. "Wow. And Arnos never forced her to use this gift? He would be way ahead of the game and could have brought her along for his own little quest. Seems like a lost opportunity"

"The truth is he's afraid of both Fran and Dax. Since Fran could control his mind she could warn others of his plans and apparently Dax has a certain ability that could destroy Arnos. The only way he can obtain the Krystal is to use you to get to Dax. You are the key." He sat down again, his head in his hands.

The key. I wondered where the lock was; well, I guess that means I'm important or something. I don't have any idea what to do about this but it's too late to turn back and Arnos is out there somewhere just waiting to strike. I was too exhausted to think right now. I stood and kneeled in front of Eric.

"Eric, we can work this out. I want to go wherever you go, to your home with your parents or we can part and go our separate ways; it doesn't matter. But right now we need rest. Come back to the tent with me and we'll talk more tomorrow. We need to finish this."

I didn't know what else to say so I took his hand and led him back to the tent. He was like a robot . . . numb and without emotion as we lay down and I held him close. Sleep gradually closed around us like a glove.

Chapter 19

I gaze out at the forest before me for signs of the travelers. My land borders on the edge of Carolan and the last gate and my castle which I built many years ago sits on a knoll in the middle. I can see anyone coming in any direction. My army guards me well and I reward them handsomely for their loyalty.

The travelers are getting very close now. Soon they will be at the final gate. I feel their presence and their mixed emotions as they grapple with life and death in this hostile land.

There is someone else out there as well . . . my enemy, who lurks in the forest waiting for his opportunity to destroy us all. I cannot allow this. He is powerful but I also possess my own strength. Between us we have two abilities that can wipe each other out in the blink of an eye.

My enemy doesn't value the worth of others as I do. He takes for his own personal gain without conscience. He has already destroyed my first love and has been cruel to the other. I can't give him the chance to harm the rest.

My children have become strong and clever just as I knew they would. They each have their own special gifts. Long ago as I witnessed my oldest child's birth, I got to hold her in my arms for so brief a time and I could sense then what she was to become. I knew I couldn't stay, in order to protect her and her mother.

I loved both mothers and provided for them all as best I could. The mother of my youngest child lives here in the castle with me although we are not together. After her husband found out about the child and knew it wasn't his, he banished her and she came with me for sanctuary. That was eighteen years ago.

I had not seen my oldest child since the birth; this one definitely has my blood circulating in her veins. I have followed her life course closely. Hopefully she will see that my enemy is hers as well and that I mean her no harm. My pride hopes she will join me in my mission to safeguard our world. I deeply regret that her mother will not be here to see her triumph.

My enemy seeks us now to impart his vengeance on me for taking the Krystal into safekeeping. I can feel he is near and I am ready to face him.

For now I can only wait patiently as the time grows near.

Chapter 20

The day dawned grey and cloudy and there was a definite chill in the air. I shivered as I emerged from the tent. I felt grubby and tired and in a not so happy mood after Eric's disclosure last night. I left him sleeping peacefully in his tent as I grabbed a knife, a gun and a heavy coat and started off into the forest.

There wasn't a clear picture in my mind of what I was looking for, but I couldn't feel Arnos right now and needed to walk off my anxiety. I wanted to see if I could flush him out of his hiding place and confront him. This was one of those reckless things Eric had mentioned but there was a burning hatred inside of me and this was one of those times you wake up and the decision has already been made for you. He had killed my mother, I was sure of it, slaughtered Peter, and held Eric's family captive. I needed to make him pay before anyone else suffered.

"If I was Arnos where would I hide?" I mused quietly to myself tapping my finger against my lips. As soon as the words left my mouth I felt another presence nearby. My body went into alert mode.

My eyes flitted back and forth trying to see something . . . anything in the dim light. I had my knife in one hand and my gun in the other. I guess it never dawned on me to call up my fire.

A crackle of footsteps in the underbrush to my left had me running. Too late I realized I was running deeper into the forest. The sound was more like an animal than human but it was coming closer. Turning around to see who my pursuer was I failed to see the obstacle in my way and ran smack dab into something rubbery. As I bounced off of it I felt a stinging sensation on my arm; I went down in a heap on the ground. Then I blacked out.

I awoke on the ground with something licking my face. Oh, not just any old something . . . a dog. And not any old dog either. It was Naomi. I'd know that smell anywhere.

"Now cut that out!" I shouted batting her away.

With difficulty I raised up on my elbows, my thoughts all jumbled in my head. I felt like I'd been hit by lightning. My head swam and I had to lie back down for a moment.

A flash beside me revealed Naomi grinning like a Cheshire cat. The smell of dog was very strong. And her clothes were intact. I suppose everything on her transformed together when she changed. She turned her head and I followed her gaze through the trees. All I could see was a shadowy form in a mist.

"She's awake, Father. Do you want to see her now?" she said to the figure.

"Not yet, daughter," he said wistfully. Then he turned and disappeared into the mist in a flash of light. What's with all this flashing?

The fuzziness in my brain was slowly clearing and I looked at Naomi in wonder. Father . . . daughter? Somehow my mind was having trouble processing this information properly. She had mentioned that she had visited here before. Was it to see her father?

"Who are you?" I asked stupidly.

"You'll find out soon enough," she said, waving her hand over my face. "Sleep now." And I did.

When I finally woke up I could hear my name being called in the distance. I was lying on a pile of pine needles and wondering how I got there. My visions were getting so bizarre. I tried to remember this one but parts were blurry. Unusual, because I could always recall them in vivid detail before.

"Molly, can you hear me?" someone shouted close to me. I focused on the voice and realized it was Eric's.

"Over here," I croaked. My mouth felt like the desert. Eric was at my side before the words were out of my mouth.

"Molly, are you okay? You're not hurt, are you?" he said breathlessly as he knelt down beside me. His hands were waving in the air over me, as if he was afraid to touch me. "She's over here," he shouted into the trees.

"No, I'm fine. A little damp perhaps from lying out here on the ground. I have no idea how I got here, but Eric, I had another vision . . . dream . . . whatever; I'm not sure what it was," I said propping myself up, my head all fuzzy. "What time is it?"

"It's nine. We've been searching for you for an hour. I woke up and you weren't there. What were you thinking going off on your own like that? I've warned you . . ." he chastised.

"I know, I know. I *do not* remember coming out here, let alone falling asleep," I snapped. I noticed my knife and gun were neatly set beside me and I was covered with a blanket.

All at once we were surrounded by the team and several soldiers. Everyone was chattering at once. I held up my hand to silence the din. "I'm all right." I went to get up and Hector grabbed my hand and hoisted me upright in one smooth motion. Eric glared at him.

"Stop," I hissed at him and strode off toward the camp. I was not in the mood for this foolishness.

I observed Naomi standing by herself with a bemused look on her face. Something in my brain triggered a flash of that vision. Had she been there? I shook my head and headed for my tent stomping through the underbrush.

As I walked briskly in that direction I saw Sophie helping the soldiers break camp; we needed to continue on to the last gate today. My last vision kept niggling at the back of my mind as I helped pack the SUVs. I consulted with Nolin about the route we had to take and made sure we hadn't left anything behind.

Sophie walked over to me with a bunch of flowers in her hand. I wondered what this was all about.

"Molly, can we visit Peter's grave before we leave? I found these wildflowers nearby and I'd like to lay them on it," she said with the saddest eyes I'd ever seen.

"Of course we can. It looks like we're ready to go. Let me tell the others and we can all say goodbye together," I said.

"That would be nice," she said quietly. I left her next to our SUV and went to gather the others who were busy loading the last vehicle.

Eric glanced my way with a sullen expression; I suppose I deserved that. I hadn't been very nice this morning and we had a whole day to think about our conversation of last night. How could I be happy about his terms when I didn't even know whether we'd be alive in the next few days?

I had way too many issues to think about.

Everyone looked my way as I marched toward them.

"Are we ready to go?" I said. They nodded their heads. "Good. Before we take off Sophie would like to visit Peter's grave to say goodbye. I thought we could join her and say our own goodbyes." They looked at me silently.

"Arnos treated them badly and they didn't deserve this," said Jonni. "It's the least we can do."

They all murmured agreement. I returned to gather Sophie and I heard their footsteps crunching behind me as we made our way to the gravesite in the forest. Nolin had even erected a wooden cross with Peter's name on it and found some stones to cover the grave.

We gathered around the site and when I looked up I saw the soldiers coming through the trees. It was fitting. Peter had been one of them.

Sophie laid her flowers near the cross and tearfully whispered her goodbye. I don't think there was a dry eye amongst the bunch of us. After a moment of silence and sniffing we walked solemnly back to the vehicles and took off for the last gate.

Where are you Arnos? *I'm coming for you.*

Chapter 21

My men inform me that the travelers will be approaching the last gate very soon. Preparations are being completed for their arrival and I wait with much anticipation. I have had rooms prepared for them as I expect they will be tired and in need of a comfortable bed and food after their long journey. It has been a long time since we have had guests to grace these lonely halls.

My youngest child has visited us so infrequently, seeing her these last few days has been a joy; her mother has been happier than I've ever seen her. She comes to us in another form so as not to be noticed and I worry that someone will mistake her for the wildlife that roams our land. She however is fearless and tells me not to worry.

I do anyway.

Seeing my other child has filled my heart with love. She has grown into a lovely woman who seems to have found her new skills an amusement. She will certainly be in awe of the one ability that hasn't shown itself yet. I will help her develop this skill and together we can fly the skies together.

Tonight I must go and prepare the last obstacle they must cross to reach me. I will be waiting there to greet both my children; and very soon my enemy who I'm sure is making his own preparations at this very moment. It should be a grand fight.

As I get ready to leave I pause to see Ali, my companion, arranging flowers in the front foyer. She is lovely and I wonder about my affection for her. Although we have never felt the need to express our feelings in all the years together, I know she may *have the same ones I do. It makes me smile and she responds in kind.*

I stride out the door and mount my horse where my men are waiting and we ride quickly to the clearing to complete our task.

As I go I reach out to my eldest daughter and hope she sees what we are doing.

Chapter 22

I'm having a vision right now . . . I'm awake. There is a group of men riding along a stream at top speed. The man in front is handsome, tall in his saddle; a striking figure in a flowing black riding coat, sword at his side. He has long red hair that billows out behind him and he glows with a blue light. They are hurrying to complete some very important task. The man turns to look at me and seems to see into my soul.

"Molly, are you all right?" Eric said. I snap out of my trance and turn to him.

"Uh, yeah. I just saw Dax and his men riding to some location . . . I don't know how I know this but it was as if he were speaking to me. In some way I believe he meant this to calm me." I stared out the window. Somehow everything was becoming clearer in my mind.

How could it be? He was long dead. My mother had said so. Suddenly I couldn't breathe.

"Eric, pull over," I said frantically, clawing at the door handle.

He pulled off the road and screeched to a halt just as I jumped out. I gasped for breath, crouching down on the ground my hands over my head.

I could hear Hector and Jonni shouting, "What's wrong!"

"I don't know. She had a vision and then went bonkers," Eric said bewilderedly. "Molly, can I help you in any way?"

He was crouched next to me his hand on my shoulder. I couldn't help it; I started to laugh . . . hysterically.

"Oh, boy, this can't be good," said Naomi.

"I think she saw something really troubling. Molly, what's so funny?" Eric said.

When I finally got myself under control and could talk I told them.

"I just saw my father Eric. He's alive," I blurted. And I started to laugh again. "He's the one in my other visions."

I looked into the faces of my friends who were staring at me with astonishment.

"No, I'm not going crazy. We have to hurry and get to that last gate. I believe my father will be waiting for us. He's not the enemy we thought he was."

"Can we trust your visions to be accurate?" Jonni said.

"My visions have been getting increasingly more involved with glimmers of people I don't know. Until now. Yes, I believe they are accurate. If they are true then we should also see Arnos very soon as well."

I leaned on Eric to stand. He gazed at me skeptically.

"We should still be cautious about this. It could be a trap," he reminded me. His eyes were intent on my face.

"Always," I said smugly. I jumped back into the SUV and stared straight ahead. He was ruining my happy thoughts.

Eric got behind the wheel and started the engine without a word. Off we went in a cloud of dust.

We rode in silence for a while and I guess it was getting to Hector. He began to sing in a very soft voice. Then Sophie added her melodic harmony. I twisted around to look at them in the back seat. Hector grinned at me and glanced at Sophie and they continued to belt out the most romantic song I'd ever heard. They sounded pretty good, too. I couldn't help but smile and shake my head. Naomi just rolled her eyes.

When I turned back Eric was laughing softly. My heart melted. How could I stay mad at him after all we'd been through?

"I'm sorry," I said over Hector's singing.

"What for?" he asked.

"For being such a weirdo back there," I said.

"You managed to figure out something that had bothered you for a long time. That's not being a weirdo. It proves he knows we're coming and he's thinking about you. That alone should make you happy," he said. I saw him take a quick look at me and smile.

"I don't even know him. How can I feel any affection for him when he never made an effort to see me or at least contact me in all these years?" I said. "Still, we seem to have a connection mentally if I can see him so clearly. Remember when you found me in the forest this morning? I think he was there standing in the shadows last night. He left in a flash of light before I fell asleep."

I turned to look at Naomi. We had a silent moment of understanding. She actually gave me a knowing smile, nodded and resumed gazing out the window as if all was right in the world.

Oh. My. God!

I whirled back around in my seat and must have had an astonished expression. Eric looked at me and I think he was ready to pull over again.

"Okay, now what?" he said quickly.

"Nothing. Nothing at all. I'm fine. Let's get to that gate," I said. My thoughts were jumping around in my head like a bunch of bees ready to attack.

Bring it on.

Chapter 23

We reached the last gate by late afternoon. The Guardians must be able to move through dimensions or flash anywhere they pleased because there they were in front of us . . . waiting.

"You have reached the last gate, Molly Fyre. From here on out you must be cautious of the environment. It can be quite unhealthy."

Like we needed to be reminded of the treacherous terrain. They asked the same questions . . . again. And I of course gave the same answers . . . again. I can't tell you how happy I was to get this far with a minimum of difficulty. I wondered if Arnos had passed this way.

"Has Arnos Barger passed through the gates?" I asked the guardians.

"Yes," they said briskly.

Well, that was short and sweet. And answered my question. He was ahead of us no doubt and we still had at least a two to three day trek through the mountains according to my map.

The gate opened silently and I was looking at no sign of a road when I felt Nolin put his hand on my shoulder. He looked at me sadly.

"We were only commissioned to bring you safely to the last gate. I'm afraid this is as far as we go."

"Great. Well, thank you for your help. I'm sure Arnos will reward you handsomely," I said sarcastically.

"I'm sorry, but I no longer serve Arnos. He betrayed you and I can't in good conscience follow someone like that," he said.

"Then continue on with us. We can use your further assistance and I'll make sure you are compensated well." I was getting a little desperate. I didn't know what lay ahead and eighteen soldiers would be a great asset.

"We can't." And he turned and walked off toward his men.

"Then this is goodbye," I said to the air between us. So much for protection; we were on our own now. To say I wasn't scared would be an understatement. I was terrified. My team was good . . . better than good actually, but we had no idea what Dax had planned for us and Arnos had shown us he could be lethal.

The view through the gate was not promising. No road meant we had to hike the rest of the way which could take several days at best. I looked over at my team as they milled around the vehicles. They looked at me expectantly as I approached.

Jeff and Farn walked over to me looking sheepish. "We've decided to return with the soldiers," Jeff said apologetically. "We don't think we can go on after all that's happened."

I gave them a sad look. "We'll miss you," I said giving them both a hug. "Thank you for all your help. Safe journey home." They walked off to join the soldiers.

"So, what do we do now?" Hector said.

"We gather our gear and start walking," I said, picking up my duffel.

"The soldiers aren't coming?" Eric asked taking his pack out of the SUV.

"No," I said wearily. "This is as far as they were told to go." I know I had little expression on my face as I scanned the landscape.

"Where to, Naomi?" I said as she came to my side with her backpack slung across her shoulder. We had another *moment.*

"This way," she said pointing to the north. There before us lay a towering mountain. I sighed. At least the weather had cleared and the sun was peeking through the clouds. One thing in our favor.

Eric took the lead with Naomi on his heels.

After several miles in this forest I could see why the Guardians warned us. There were eerie sounds all around us as we picked our way forward through brambles and thick underbrush. I noticed a curiously large bird soaring high in the sky when there was a break in the trees. It looked familiar but from this distance it was hard to tell what it was. It shown red in the sun and when it looked down its eyes were green and sparkled. I watched it intently as it soared out of sight.

This forest wasn't exactly what I had expected from my father's land. Of course I *knew* it was his land; I could feel his emotions all around me . . . and someone else's.

Arnos was near. I felt a chill run down my spine.

Hector and I walked behind Eric and Naomi a few paces. Jonni and Sophie were behind us; Sophie acting as his guide.

"You look quite preoccupied," Hector said cheerily. I kept my eyes straight ahead, concentrating on the sounds and smells.

"Hmmm," I said absently gazing around. "Do you sense others in the forest? Not us but . . . others?"

"I can feel animals and birds and . . . yes, there's someone else. I can't tell who it is. Can you?" he said.

"My fa . . . um, Dax's emotions are very strong now. The other has to be Arnos. His head is so filled with loathing and vitriol. I have to block him to think straight," I said shivering.

"I know what you're going through," he said matter-of-factly. "My senses were so acute at the beginning; I thought I'd go crazy with all the traffic in my head. I had to install a mental traffic light to deal with it." He paused. "Granted it took me seventy-five years to get it right." He looked at me sideways and gave me his famous grin.

"Great, something to look forward to," I muttered. He chuckled.

I turned to glance at Jonni and Sophie behind us. They were conversing quietly about the animals she had spied in the forest. He was such a private man it was good to see him taking an interest in Sophie. He usually only spoke if he felt the necessity but he was quite animated right now and making Sophie laugh hysterically. I fervently hoped his fighting skills weren't going to be tested out here.

A sudden movement and snap of underbrush had us on alert. I quickly scanned the area around us. Luckily it was only a deer scared by our presence.

I let out a quick breath. Crap. *I'm going to need every ounce of my sanity to get through this.*

When I looked for Eric and Naomi they had turned a bend in the road and were out of sight.

"Eric, where are you?" I called.

"Over here," he answered from off to the right. "We found a cabin."

"A cabin?" I said. Hector and I exchanged raised eyebrows.

We hurried toward the sound of a babbling brook and came to a clearing. Eric and Naomi were standing in front of a large cabin. The stream ran alongside the cabin and meandered into the forest. The area around had been cleared for about twenty yards. The setting sun dappled through the trees.

"Who would build a cabin like this in the middle of the forest?" I pondered out loud.

The air was thick with some kind of magic; it crackled all around me and made the hairs on my arms stand up. At once I felt connected, peaceful. I walked to the steps and ascended them to the porch. The door was unlocked and I stepped through.

The inside had no signs that someone lived here, but everything was clean and tidy as if it had been recently prepared. It was big enough for an army and was stocked with wood and enough food for several days.

The furniture was new and all leather; a few tables and lamps were scattered around. The kitchen area at the back of the room was very modern. An alcove under the stairs had a door that led to who knows where. I wandered over to the massive dining table jutting out from the kitchen. It could easily accommodate ten to twelve people.

I walked over and paused in the center of the great room. *Dax was speaking to me again;* I tilted my head back and forth as if to find better reception. Everyone was gaping at me curiously; they still weren't used to my visions hitting me without warning.

"Moll . . ." Eric started to say.

"Shhh." I put my hand up to stop him.

"This is meant for us," I said slowly. "There's magic surrounding the area to protect us."

"So we stay here tonight," Hector mused clapping his hands together. "Works for me. Seems like there's enough rooms for all of us to be comfy. I wasn't looking forward to sleeping on the ground again." He bounded up the stairs to the second floor bedrooms. "Jonni, want to share again?" he shouted from the first room.

"Right behind you," Jonni said as he deftly strode over to climb the stairs. It always freaked me out when his sight was back and he could navigate without help. Sophie stood beside me with her mouth agape.

"He was cursed as a child so now he has sight at night and is blind during the day," I explained. All she said was "Whoa, cool!"

Naomi ambled over and took Sophie's hand giving her a smile. "What do you say you and I share a room? It'll be like a sleepover," she said brightly.

Sophie lifted her bag and practically dragged Naomi up the stairs. "Cool." They giggled the whole way.

Eric and I just stood staring at each other for a few moments before he put his arm around my shoulders and we slowly ambled up the stairs to find a room. "I need a hot shower and . . . you," he muttered. We disappeared into the room at end of the hall.

I knew we had to make dinner soon, but not right now . . . if you get my drift.

Chapter 24

We must have dozed off after our showers and fun because the next thing I knew my brain registered a familiar smell wafting up from the kitchen.

Stew? Cornbread? Who was cooking?

I dressed, leaving Eric dozing peacefully and went into the hall to the balcony overlooking the kitchen area. Hector was happily humming one of his favorite tunes and setting the table for dinner.

I leaned on the railing and watched him for a few moments.

"You cook? You'll make some woman a great husband someday," I said finally.

He looked up and stopped humming. "Yeah, doesn't every red-blooded male?" he said as he finished laying silverware on the table. "You hungry?"

"Famished. This beats camp food any day. It smells great. Shall I call the others?" I said.

I didn't need to call anyone. Before the words were out of my mouth people started coming out of their rooms, their noses in the air and bounding down the stairs.

"Smells wonderful," Jonni said grabbing a seat at the table.

"Who hired a cook?" Naomi said giving Hector a wink. He smiled back at her warmly. Oh, yeah, they liked each other.

Sophie went to the stove and lifted the lid of the stewpot. She took a long whiff and a look of pleasure crossed her face.

"Smells like home," she sighed, her eyes closed.

Eric stood at my side pulling on a shirt. We went downstairs to join the others.

"So, Stram cooking. That's a first," Eric quipped.

Hector gave him a quick glare as he set the stew, cornbread and a big salad on the table and sat down.

When we were all seated Sophie looked around the table at us all. "Should we say grace?" she asked shyly.

"That would be very nice. Do you know any prayers?" Jonni said in a gentle tone.

"Yes," she replied and quietly said thanks for us. "Okay, dig in," she said gleefully.

We ate until we were stuffed and happy; Hector had made enough food for a small army. Hector's bad jokes made us laugh until we cried and it felt good to share some fun for a change. I thought about Jeff and Farn and hoped they were safe.

We also did some planning for our next move. Outside the wind began to blow across the clearing and I had an uneasy feeling send a shiver down my spine. I didn't want to ruin the good frame of mind we had; after a momentary wince, I plastered a smile on my face to mask my anxiety.

Leave it to Hector to pick up on my mood. When Eric left to use the john, Hector sat next to me on the couch his eyes intent on my face.

"There you go with the staring again," I said squirming in my seat. The smile was pasted on my face.

"You don't fool me with that smile. Something is bothering you," he said calmly and put his arm around my shoulders.

My expression impassive, I looked into my lap to see my hands balled into fists. "I can feel Arnos again," I said through clenched teeth. "It feels like he's very close." I relaxed my hands and looked up to see Hector frown.

"I wish I could fix you and make all this go away," he said switching his gaze upward where Eric was standing at the top of the stairs watching us. Hector removed his arm.

"Thanks, but I'll be all right," I whispered. I glanced up at Eric as he disappeared down the hall. He was not going to like what I had to say later.

Hector jumped up from the couch and announced, "Dish duty. Come on, Molly, I wash, you dry." We quickly cleared the table and set about washing them. Sophie helped by putting the leftovers in the frig and then went to play a game with Naomi and Jonni. Soon they were laughing and calling each other cheat. It was gratifying to see Sophie so happy after the loss of her brother.

After drying the dishes and putting them away I climbed the stairs to talk to Eric. It was getting late and we needed to have this conversation.

When I came into our room Eric was sitting on the floor at the end of the bed. I sat down beside him without a word and we stayed like that for a while in complete silence, both of us staring at the floor.

I finally spoke.

"Eric, I'm not a possession and I don't want to be treated like one. I don't understand what it is about Hector that upsets you so much. He and I are only friends and you have nothing to be jealous about. I love *you*. End of story. Right now I have enough drama in my life without worrying how you might react when he touches me." I stopped to take a breath. His head hung down touching his knees. I could see his jaw clenched and I couldn't decide if I should be angry or hurt.

He raised his head and looked at me, a pained look on his face.

"Molly, I've never thought of you that way. I have no idea what comes over me. It's like I'm another person when I see him around you. I can't help myself. I'm sorry."

I regarded him thoughtfully. I could not read his emotional state no matter how hard I tried, only his face.

"You have nothing to be sorry about, Eric, and nothing to worry about either. How could I possibly be attracted to someone else when I fell in love with you the first time I saw you." My hands went to his face, our eyes locked. "I can prove it to you right now."

I kissed him as passionately as I could. His arms wrapped around me tightly and before I realized it we were lying on the floor in full contact. You can imagine the rest on your own.

Molly, beware. The voice whispered in my mind so softly I wasn't sure I'd really heard it.

I awoke with a start and was instantly alert. It was dark as pitch and rain was pelting the window; the wind howled pitifully. My heart was pounding in my chest as I got out of bed carefully so I wouldn't wake Eric and went to the window to look out.

A flash of lightning made me blink. When I could see again I thought I saw a dark figure standing in the clearing. My improved vision let me see who it was as another flash of light revealed a man in a long coat. There was no mistaking who it was—*Arnos.* He was grinning wickedly at me. My stomach lurched.

I panicked and woke Eric.

"Eric, wake up! Arnos is here . . . outside the house," I cried.

He leaped out of bed and threw the curtain aside.

"I don't see anyone. Are you sure it was him?" he said quickly.

"Yes, it was him," I breathed as I slumped on the bed, shaking.

Eric came and stood in front of me his hand on my shoulder.

"He's only trying to scare you, Moll. Is the magic still strong around the cabin?"

"Yes, he can't get in. Do you think he's causing this storm?" I said almost in tears.

"Who knows. I'll believe anything right now." He sat down on the bed and held me. I clung to him fiercely.

I was suddenly disconnected from everything . . . floating in a mist. The night just got a lot scarier.

Eric broke me out of my reverie. "Molly, I have to go and see if he's still out there." He pushed away from me.

"No, Eric, stay with me. He's too dangerous," I pleaded grabbing his arm.

"I'll wake Hector and Jonni to go with me. We'll be careful. You stay here."

I groaned a protest but there was no stopping him. He jumped into his clothes and went to wake them. I could hear their urgent voices as the men ran down the stairs and out the door. I said a silent prayer.

Over the storm I heard them shouting to each other as they ran around the periphery of the cabin. There was no way I could stay in this room. I put on a robe and hurried down the stairs. Naomi and Sophie were right behind me and we sat huddled on the couch waiting for the guys to come back inside.

A pounding on the door made us all jump.

"Let us in, the door got locked," shouted Eric. I let out a breath and ran to open the door. They came in soaked to the bone.

"We searched all around the cabin but there's no sign of him," said Hector shaking his wet hair.

"I know I saw him," I said wearily.

"Let's just go back to bed. There's nothing we can do tonight and you're sure the magic will keep him out. We still have a long way to go and if this storm doesn't let up by morning, we may be spending another day here," said Jonni.

"I agree," said Hector. He gathered Naomi and Sophie and headed upstairs. Jonni followed them.

Eric turned and put his arms around me.

"This has been frightening for you, love, I know. He's just messing with your mind to keep control. Don't let him," Eric encouraged me.

I nodded and we returned to our room and fell into bed exhausted. Eric fell back to sleep quickly, his arm draped across my body hugging me to him. I lay there thinking for some time, my mind in a jumble, the adrenaline raging. The day was coming when I had to face Arnos. The thought made me tremble and wonder again if I was up to the task. This was ridiculous. I had to pull myself together.

Outside the storm had slowed and the rain was deceptively calming. I drifted off to sleep with a solid plan in my head.

Chapter 25

I'm running for my life through the forest. The air is thick with smoke and energy from some unknown source; I can hardly breathe. A lone figure is behind me throwing streaks of light at my heels. I hurl balls of red flame back at him, missing every time. I run faster but he is rapidly gaining on me. Up ahead I see a misty curtain and head for it with all my strength and reach it just as a bolt of light hits behind my foot. My body heaves forward through the mist and I'm alongside a large body of water . . . alone.

I woke up early to another grey day. When I looked out the window the rain had stopped but everything outside was soggy and dripping. Eric stirred beside me and rolled over on his side away from me. There was only time for a quick shower and I dressed in a hurry. I needed to carry out my new plan before the others woke up. As I tiptoed out the door I blew a kiss at Eric's sleeping form.

Downstairs I took a bottle of water and exited the cabin quietly. Once I was out the door I headed for the middle of the cleared area and set the water on the ground. My eyes closed, I concentrated on my hands and produced two rather large balls of fire and juggled them into the air. I tossed one higher than the other and watched it grow into a gigantic form of a dragon. It dissipated into the air quickly. I tossed the other one higher and it too became the image of a dragon. This one didn't disappear like the other. Instead it raised its head and breathed out a long flame before slowly dissolving.

Okay . . . this was interesting. Now what? There has to be more to this than me tossing fireballs around. *What to do. What to do.*

"Pretty impressive," stated a husky voice behind me. "Should you be out here with Arnos lurking nearby?"

I turned to see Hector standing there with no shirt, muscles bulging. I took a long look, surveying him head to toe; pretty impressive himself. I cleared my throat and gave him an admiring smile.

"He's moved on. I don't feel him," I said, tossing around another fireball. "I was just about to try something else. Wanna help?"

"Sure. What did you have in mind?" He walked closer. "I hope you don't want me to play dodge the fireballs again? Those were pretty big," he said while dodging back and forth in jest.

"No, maybe something a little more dramatic. Did I ever tell you about my visions?"

"Not all of them," he said, intent on my face. He was putting on the shirt he had in his hand.

Oh, darn.

"Well, I've had several that had dragons in them. And sometimes I feel like I'm turning into something else. So, I was curious. I sort of had this plan to see what else I was capable of. As you saw I can turn my fire into dragons . . . fire breathing dragons," I said looking up as I tossed another fireball which turned into an even bigger dragon.

"And your point is . . ." Hector said rolling his hand around in the air.

"That maybe I'm able to morph into a dragon," I replied in one quick breath.

He looked at me with his eyebrows raised almost to his hairline. "Huh."

I wasn't sure what that was supposed to mean so I gave him a '*so is there more*' sign.

"Let's try it," he said stepping back a few paces. "Just don't get the idea of blowing me to cinders if this works."

I just rolled my eyes and shook my head.

"Here goes nothing," I shouted.

I closed my eyes and concentrated on the red dragon with green eyes of my visions. After a few minutes my body started to vibrate slowly and built up in intensity until I sensed myself transforming from my head backward. I looked at Hector. His eyes were as big as saucers and I almost laughed.

I felt a pop as a pair of wings appeared in my peripheral vision. My body followed as a scaly coating covered me and I saw a tail flow out behind me. I stretched my wings, flapping them a few times . . . and took off.

As I flew up and over the cabin I could see Hector running around and punching the air with his fist and shouting.

I soared around him a couple of times and then took off over the forest, my wings flapping gracefully in the wind. My eyes could see for miles and I spied some settlements off in the distance.

The freedom I experienced was so overwhelming I let out a belch of fire and I thought I'd nearly burned down the forest as I headed back. When I looked around I saw I'd only singed the tops of the trees. Thank God.

After about ten minutes I alighted gracefully in the clearing. Hector raced across the grass towards me shouting.

"That was magnificent!" he said, clapping furiously. I noticed he kept his distance; not that I'd even think of hurting him. I lay down on the grass and turned myself back to a human.

Hector ran to me and helped me stand. I marveled at the fact that my clothes had morphed with me. So that's what happens when Naomi changes.

"Whoa, that was so exhilarating," I said breathlessly. "And tiring." I stumbled and Hector caught me in his arms.

"Okay, Super Dragon, let's go inside," he muttered in my ear. I was in complete agreement. We walked slowly to the cabin. Just as we started up the steps, Naomi was coming out with a steaming cup in her hand.

"Well now, what have you two been up to?" she said suspiciously. "Are you all right, Molly?"

"I'm better than all right. I flew . . . over the trees," I announced. Hector plopped me into a chair on the porch.

"You what?" she said, not showing much on her face.

"I transformed into a dragon and flew. Several miles in fact over the trees. And guess what, there's a town or two in the direction we're going." I noticed a nasty smoky taste in my mouth. Must be the fire I blasted out.

"Okay," was all she said. She sat down in the chair next to me and glanced up at Hector who was beaming like a mother hen.

"Kinda puts your dog to shame, doesn't it, sweetheart?" he snorted. She glared at him.

"We all have our purpose," she sneered back.

"All right you two. Truce," I said grinning.

Naomi stood and headed for the door. "Breakfast is ready." She went inside and slammed the door behind her.

"I love that girl," Hector said sighing. He gave me his hand and hoisted me up to go inside. I smiled at him sideways.

Eric was in the kitchen, cooking eggs and bacon. No surprise. Jonni sat at the table with his fork and knife in hand, waiting.

"So, what have you two been up to out there?" Eric said.

"Your girlfriend just became an official shape shifter," Hector said nonchalantly and grabbed a piece of toast.

"I beg your pardon. Did I hear you correctly?" Eric replied, casting a curious glance my way.

"Yup, a shape shifter. A dragon to be exact," Hector said sitting down at the table and helping himself to eggs and bacon.

Eric stood there his mouth open and eyes wide, spatula in midair. After a moment he shook his head.

"Damn . . . and I missed it." I walked up behind him and put my arms around his waist.

"Don't worry. I can do it really easy now. I'll show you all later, after I eat. Changing makes you hungry." I went and filled my plate and proceeded to stuff my face, smiling at them the whole time.

Sophie ambled downstairs and yawned. "What's going on?" she said when she saw their faces staring at me.

Hector laughed and handed her a plate. "We'll show you later. Grab some food."

The quizzical look on her face made us all giggle. "It's not something about me is it?"

"No, darlin', but it is awesome," said Hector.

We sat and ate breakfast, all the time complimenting Eric on his fabulous food. He beamed.

After the kitchen was cleaned we all convened in the clearing for my demonstration. Sophie still had that clueless expression on her face. I walked several feet away from my friends; I could hear Sophie asking Naomi what I was doing. Naomi told her to just wait and watch.

I closed my eyes and started my transformation. A gasp rose from the group as my wings unfurled and I leaped into the air.

Sophie's expression of delight was priceless. As I swooped around I did a few loops. I loved the feel of the wind over my scales; I went higher above the clouds until I felt the sun's warmth on me. I glided along lazily and smiled inwardly, enjoying the freedom. It seemed I hadn't a care in the world.

Silly me.

A unexpected feeling of dread washed over me and I had to dive under the clouds again to where my friends were waiting. Everything seemed okay when I swiveled my head to survey the area. But that feeling wouldn't go away. I swooped down and landed in the clearing circling around searching for the source of that sensation as the group ran to get out my way.

"What's wrong, Molly?" Eric called, ducking under my wing.

I changed quickly so I could talk to them and fell to the ground, my breathing heavy from the effort. It wasn't Arnos I felt. Someone else was coming toward us. Lots of someones.

"We need to get ready for company," I said quickly trying to catch my breath.

"What did you see?" said Eric.

"It's not what I saw but what I felt," I replied. "Someone must have seen me flying around. I'm sure they're pretty superstitious around here. Whoever it is, is full of fear."

"Do you think it's someone from one of the villages you saw?" asked Hector. His gaze was scanning the edge of the forest.

"Perhaps. They seem to be very close." I leaned on Eric to stand. "Let's get into the cabin and be ready."

We ran to the cabin and were through the door in about five seconds. Everyone but Sophie armed themselves and peaked out the windows to watch for intruders. We hid Sophie under a table.

Chapter 26

Out of the woods strode a group of fifteen men. They were carrying nothing but farm implements—hoes, pitchforks, shovels. They looked scared to death and crept across the clearing slowly, all the time gazing around warily. When they spied the cabin they halted, nearly knocking each other over.

I furrowed my brow and walked to the door. I could feel Eric and Hector come to my side.

"What are you doing?" murmured Eric. He grabbed my arm.

"I'm going out to talk to them," I hissed back and opened the door. "I'm sure our weapons can stop them if it becomes necessary." He let go.

The townsmen stood there stunned as I walked onto the porch with a big smile. "Hi there, gentlemen. Something I can do for you?" I called pleasantly.

"Uh, well, have you seen anything unusual around here, miss?" the man closest asked. He looked hesitant about moving closer. I could see his eyes regarding me up and down.

"No, my friends and I have been here only a couple of days and nothing unusual has happened. Are you looking for someone?" I asked politely.

"We've seen a strange bird flying around but we think it may be a . . . dragon." He paused, waiting to see if I had a reaction. I didn't. "We thought we saw it fly in this direction. You should be careful. It could be dangerous."

He glanced around at the other men who were nodding their heads and then back toward the cabin.

"Are you a friend of Dax? I believe this is his cabin." He looked at me suspiciously.

I kept my face placid. "Yes. He let us stay here for a few days while we travel through his land. We'll certainly keep a watch out for any strange birds." I kept up my charade and smiled some more. I wished they would leave.

"How many in your group?" he asked annoyingly.

"There are six of us," I replied curtly. "Is there anything else I can help you with?"

"No, we'll be on our way. Be careful," he said turning to his companions and walking back into the forest. He turned back and looked at me again before disappearing into the trees. I hoped this was the last we'd see of them.

After they were gone I went back inside. The others were still staring out the windows, weapons in hand.

"I don't think they'll be back. I just won't do any flying unless it's necessary and only at night." Eric came to my side.

"That wasn't very smart," he scolded loudly. I glared at him.

"I'm doing what I'm supposed to do, keep us out of trouble," I said, irritated.

"Eric, she handled that very well. Leave her alone," Hector protested. He had crossed the room and was at my side defending me.

Eric was in his face in an instant. They stood nose to nose, toe to toe in front of me. I waited for the first punch. It never came. Hector stood there, jaw tight, but not moving as Eric fumed.

"Don't tell me what to do, Stram!" Eric shouted. His face was livid. Hector didn't move.

"Look you two," I barked with my hands on my hips. "Who's the leader here? Or have you forgotten? Wait, I'll answer that myself . . . ME. So knock off the male posturing and let's figure our next move."

They both turned their heads at the same time and stared at me in disbelief. There. I was boss now.

"Phew, what a spitfire you have for a girlfriend, McGuire," Hector laughed and strode off to the kitchen. "Good luck with that."

I don't think Eric had any fight left in him. He slumped into the nearest chair glowering at the floor. For a moment I just stood in the middle of the room, bewildered by his sullen behavior. Where had this animosity come from? Something needed to be said.

Kneeling down in front of him I looked him in the eye. I kept the tone of my voice quiet.

"Look at me Eric." He tried to avoid my stare. My hand brought him reluctantly back to my face. "I do not want you to get mad anymore when I make a decision. I'm not going to do anything foolish. Promise."

He stared at me coldly. He tapped his fingers on his thigh impatiently. I rambled on, not letting his mood affect me.

"I need your help and I don't think fighting with Hector is the best move right now. *You* are my protector, I get that. However, I'm relying on all of the people in this room to trust my judgment and that includes you." I swept my arm around to include everyone. He huffed out a big breath and shook his head.

It was hard to read his expression as it vacillated between anger, frustration and pain. I argued with myself as to whether I should say anything else or wait for his reply. Hector came back over to where we sat. Eric's face softened abruptly when he saw him. He looked at me, repentant.

"Here I go again, apologizing for my idiotic behavior," he sighed. "It won't happen again, Hector. I'm sorry." He hung his head.

"Already forgotten," Hector replied. "But you and I need to have a talk. What do you say we go outside and chat?"

Eric looked at Hector warily and gave him a shrug as I scooted out of the way to let him stand up. Hector was at the door and the two of them went out to the porch and sat down face to face. They were talking so low I couldn't hear what they were saying, or rather what Hector was saying. He looked pretty stern and animated as he talked. Eric hung on every word Hector had to say and nodded his head every now and then. I suspected he was getting a good chewing out.

I ambled into the kitchen to make some tea. I put the kettle on, grabbed a clean cup from the cupboard and placed a teabag in it. Then I noticed Naomi and Jonni weren't around. I saw Sophie sitting on the couch and I asked her where they had gone.

"I think I saw them go out the back door," she said peering over the book she was reading.

After the water boiled and my tea was steeped, I added sugar and lemon and walked out the back door to find Jonni and Naomi. I saw them down by the stream and sat in one of the chairs on the back porch sipping my tea.

They were standing facing each other; Naomi had her eyes closed and her palms against Jonni's eyes chanting in some language I couldn't understand; I really needed an ancient language dictionary. That was strange enough but Jonni was holding her wrists tightly like he couldn't let go. I sat there mesmerized, wondering what they were doing. I felt like a voyeur sitting on the edge of my chair.

Suddenly Jonni let out a cry and jerked back away from Naomi so fast he almost landed in the water. I stood up knocking the chair over, my first instinct being to run to them, but something told me not to interfere. Jonni had recovered his footing and was blinking quickly as if he had suddenly gotten something in his eyes. I saw him open them and look around in amazement and then he picked Naomi up and twirled her around, half laughing, half crying in joy. It dawned on me in an instant that something amazing had happened.

It was still daylight. And Jonni could see.

I couldn't help myself; I ran to them. "What just happened?" I cried my eyes wide.

Jonni was still whooping and hollering. I'd never seen him so animated. He saw me and before I knew it I was in his arms being whirled around until I was dizzy. He set me on the ground, breathing hard. "Molly, I can see again!" he shouted.

For a moment I couldn't say anything, only gaze into those silver blue eyes. Naomi stood there, a triumphant look on her face, her hands to her mouth.

"You did this?" I said in disbelief, firing my questions at her. "When did you figure this out? How long have you known you could do this?"

"Oh, I've known for a long time," she said sweetly.

If there's one thing you can say about Naomi, she's secretive in a quirky sort of way.

"Why now?" I asked, curious. Jonni was finally composed and sitting on the ground gazing about in wonder. He dipped his huge hand into the stream and watched the water trickle through his fingers. Turning his face upward to the sun he closed his eyes and took a deep breath. He was in heaven.

All she said was, "It was time." She turned and with a serene look on her face, walked over to where Jonni sat and lowered herself beside him. They just gazed at each other for a moment and then together they lay down and kicked their feet in the air, laughing.

I left them to their celebrating and ran inside to find Eric and Hector having a quiet conversation in the kitchen. They stopped when they saw my beaming face.

"What was all that hollering about?" asked Eric.

"Are you guys ready for another surprise?" I said excitedly, clapping my hands and jumping up and down. "Come outside with me right now." I didn't give them a chance to ask questions as I led them to the back door.

Jonni was still sitting by the stream when I practically pushed the two men out the door. He lifted his head and looked at them with his eyes shining.

"What's up Jonni?" Hector called. Jonni jumped up and ran over to Hector and grabbed him in a bear hug. When he finally let him go and looked him in the eye, Hector waved his hand in front of Jonni's face and watched him blink.

"What the hell. You can see? How did this happen?" He couldn't contain his wonder. His hand flashed in Jonni's face again.

"Okay, you can cut that out now," Jonni said, batting the annoying hand away. "Naomi is a miracle worker." He glanced down at her lovingly, his arm around her shoulders. "She and I have been talking about this for some time now and thought we'd try today. I wasn't sure her magic would work at first but she convinced me to at least try. You're going to need my expertise on the next part of this journey and I expect most of the action will be during the daylight."

"Well, I'm dazzled by your talents, Naomi," Hector purred.

"Don't get all mushy on me, Stram," she said with a twinkle in her eye. "It's not at all flattering."

"You'll never see me mushy, girl," he retorted. He gave her a wink. I think she blushed.

"This is a wonderful day," said Eric as he shook hands with Jonni and gave him a man hug.

"All right people, I hate to interrupt this fabulous mood but we need to have a meeting and then start packing for what I hope is the last part of this quest," I announced brightly. I herded everyone into the cabin for a quick lunch first and we ate sitting around the table chatting about Jonni's miracle.

Sophie sat next to Jonni and kept peering into his face until he said "BOO!" at her, making her burst into giggles.

"I'm so glad I won't have to lead you around like a puppy anymore," she gushed.

We had a good laugh over that comment. I silently said a prayer that our journey would come to successful conclusion and that we would go home safely. I still had that feeling that something was going to happen and soon; it needed to be tucked away for now.

Chapter 27

After the table was cleared I spread out the crude map and we huddled around it like vultures. It was good to have Jonni at the table actually seeing for a change. Sophie sat on the couch reading her book, uninterested in our plans. She was coming with us no matter what. Every now and then she would look up and smile at Jonni as he flirted with her.

"Now, we have to go from here to . . . here," I said pointing to the two spots on the map. "Naomi says the quickest and easiest route is through this valley, here." I indicated the area. "What are we likely to encounter along the way?" I asked her.

"There are two settlements of humans a few miles apart. They were friendly the last time I traveled through; that was some time ago however," she answered, polishing an apple on her jeans.

"You traveled all by yourself?" asked Hector, concern in his voice. I noted with interest that he was standing very close to Naomi. She didn't seem to mind his proximity.

"Yeah. I don't mind a little challenge. Most of the time I travel as my dog. Everyone likes dogs and they don't bother me," she retorted smugly, biting noisily into her fruit.

"Uh, huh," Hector breathed out lightly making her hair flutter. He closed his eyes and the corners of his mouth curled up slightly. *Was he sniffing her hair?* I stifled a smile. Shifting my gaze I took a breath and focused on the map.

"And there are no more barriers or obstacles?" I continued. I felt Eric put his arm around my waist and lean in closer.

"Shouldn't be," Naomi muttered, munching on her apple.

I surveyed my team . . . my friends. "Then tomorrow we continue. We'll need to pack some supplies in case we have to camp along the way. I think we can all carry our share, even Sophie." Everyone nodded approval.

I glanced over to see her reaction but saw she was sound asleep on the couch. Jonni followed my gaze. He walked over, picked her up gently and quietly took her upstairs to bed.

When Jonni came downstairs again we were all lounging around and chatting quietly. He cleared his throat and looked awkward standing there. We focused our attention on him and he shifted back and forth on his feet for a few moments looking like he had something to say. He took a big breath.

"I'd like to share something with all of you . . . my friends." A pause. "When the witch cursed me, my family abandoned me with our neighbors; I was only three years old. I suppose they couldn't cope with it all." He paused again, his voice thick. "Those kind people raised me to be self-sufficient and strong and never saw me as handicapped." Another short pause. "I never saw my family again. They moved away soon after that. You have all been so patient with my affliction that I feel like you are my family, too. I want to contribute to the success of this mission as a whole person now." He stopped because he began sobbing.

We stood silent for a few moments absorbing his heart rending story. There was mist in everyone's eyes. I got up and went over to him and gave him a comforting hug and then one by one the rest of them joined in a group hug around this beautiful hulk of a man.

When we had all regained our composure, we went around the cabin gathering the necessary supplies needed for this last part of our journey. This place was stocked to the gills with everything you could ever want. If Dax is watching us right now, I hope he hears my grateful thanks.

It was late afternoon when we finished getting our gear and supplies ready and packed in the backpacks we found in a closet. Convenient. It's as though this stuff appears when we need it most and someone knew exactly what we would need. I found this a little unnerving.

As I stuffed my backpack I glanced over to where Hector was standing filling his pack with food. Naomi was facing away from him so she couldn't see his face. I could and the look he gave her was so adoring, I had to avert my eyes. I felt intrusive.

Against my better judgment I sidled over to Hector's side. He gave me a quick smile and went back to looking at Naomi.

"Maybe it's none of my business, but you like her don't you?" I whispered close to his ear and gave him a little nudge. "A lot."

"Who? Oh, yeah," he said, trying hard to act casual.

"You need to let her know how you feel. Don't let it go on as long as Eric and I did."

He thought about this for a few moments.

"Hmmm. What would a newbie want with a three hundred year old immortal like me?" he muttered, glancing again at Naomi. At that moment she chose to look our way and smile.

"Oh, I don't know . . . companionship . . . giggles . . . love," I replied. "Besides, you don't look a day over thirty five."

He grimaced as he gave a noisy snort and shook his head. "You playing matchmaker now?" he asked.

I didn't answer, smiled and walked away. I heard Hector singing softly behind me; it sounded like something from Fiddler on the Roof.

I tried out my pack and found I could carry a lot more weight than when I'd been mortal. Hector laughed when I went outside and leaped onto the roof and strutted around. He had followed me and stood there with his beefy arms folded across his chest, grinning.

"Wow, I can see a long ways off from up here H," I teased.

"Show off," he called back. I stuck my tongue out at him mockingly.

Eric's reaction to this exchange took me by surprise. He and Jonni had come outside and after seeing me cavort around were laughing too. This complete turnabout made me feel relieved that Eric was enjoying Hector's comment instead of wanting to throttle him. They must have had an interesting talk. I gracefully leaped to the ground at Eric's feet.

"I like this new Eric," I breathed against his lips. He pulled back and looked at me questioningly and then gave me a long kiss. Out of the corner of my eye I saw Hector and Jonni avert their eyes and smirk. It's good to be me.

Sophie woke in time for dinner and bounded down the stairs to Jonni's side. He picked her up like a sack of potatoes and ran around the room to her extreme delight. His return to a fully functioning individual was a sight to see . . . pardon the pun.

Dinner was steak, potatoes, salad and some very good wine Hector had found in the pantry. His culinary arts were fabulous.

After we cleaned up, everyone went off by themselves. I saw Hector talking quietly to Naomi in a corner of the room. I wondered if he was taking my advice. She seemed shy but very absorbed in what he was saying; she never took her eyes off his. I'm pretty sure I'll hear about the outcome soon.

The light was fading in the sky as I went out to the porch and sat down to enjoy the solitude. My mind was racing again with all sorts of weird scenarios about this next couple of days; I let it wander a bit and closed my eyes. Birds were singing their last songs of the day and crickets made a cacophony of noise all around me.

You're very close, my daughter. I can feel your fears now. Don't lose focus and all will be well.

"Dax," I whispered to myself. I heard soft footsteps come out of the cabin and someone sat down next to me.

"What are you thinking about, Molly?" Eric murmured.

I didn't open my eyes. "Oh, life, death; all the wonderful issues in my life right now. You?"

"I've been thinking about our conversation this morning," he said hesitating. "I really need you Molly. And . . . I need to stop acting like a schoolboy whenever someone pays you any attention." He sighed softly.

"Does this come from your talk with Hector? Or from your heart?" I asked tenderly. I opened my eyes to see him looking at me contritely.

"He did chew me out pretty badly," he said with a chuckle. "But yes, it's from my heart."

I closed my eyes again. I heard him shift around in his chair.

"I need you beside me Molly when I go home to be with my family. There's nothing I want more than to have you by my side forever and that's why this next question is so important to that end." My eyes snapped open when I felt him in front of me on his knees. I had to control my breathing, slow my fluttering heart as I realized what he meant.

"Molly, when all this is over and we're all safe, will you . . . will you marry this stupid, maniacal man kneeling before you?" He was looking at me expectantly.

Tears filled my eyes as I knelt down in front of him. I took his hands in mine and gazed for a long moment into his dazzling blue eyes, my face very serious.

"No." He startled and his face vacillated between surprise and anguish; he looked away and then back at me, crushed, but then I smiled and put up my finger to indicate *wait*.

"I can't marry that stupid, maniacal man; but . . . I will marry the man I love with all my heart who kneels before me."

A look of relief crossed his face and he let out a big breath as if he'd been holding it all this time. Our arms were around each other instantly and the kiss he gave me took my breath away. When we finally pulled apart, I knew this was where I would spend the rest of my life.

Assuming, of course, I survived my encounter with Arnos. I try not to be pessimistic but life undoubtedly was an uncertainty at this point. I was not going to let this bother my euphoric moment however.

Eric gave me his smoldering look and dropped his gaze to our hands.

"I don't have a ring I can give you," he stated, rubbing my left ring finger.

"That doesn't matter right now," I said. "We have plenty of time."

He gave a quick snuff through his nose and looked me in the eye. "I will defend you to the death, my love."

I hoped that wasn't a prophetic statement because I believed every word.

Chapter 28

In our room Eric and I lay side by side in our bed just holding each other. I gently rubbed my hand up his arm and felt him shiver. He sighed and drew me closer; one more breath and we could melt into each other. He kissed me tenderly and as usual I couldn't breathe for a moment.

"What are your parents like?" I asked, stroking his face. He sighed and closed his eyes.

"My father acts very stern but really has a kind heart. If and when he becomes the Keeper, I know his benevolence will benefit the region greatly," he said with admiration. "He enjoys riding his prize horses and playing chess. He always beats me."

"And your mother?" I asked dreamily. I could feel the tingle as I touched his face. He shivered.

"She is very tolerant of my father's moods and keeps him calm and focused, somewhat like you do to me," he said seriously looking me in the eye. "Her interests are writing and gardening. We have a beautiful garden at home with hundreds of flowers. You'll love it."

"Peonies?" I asked.

"Loads of them," he said quickly. "Funny, I never realized you both love them." He was playing with a wisp of my hair.

"Your sister, you said she was younger," I continued my inquiries moving my hand to make lazy circles on his chest.

"Yes, she is," he said sleepily. "She plays the piano and reads . . . a lot. If she could absorb books by osmosis I think she would. And then there's her gift of reading and manipulating minds. I don't know how she can think straight with all the noise in her head, but she takes it all in stride. I admire her greatly."

"I think I like them already," I said yawning. I snuggled closer to him and nestled my head against his chest. He held me tighter and eventually we drifted off to sleep.

A loud thumping noise down the hall woke me, my heart pounding. I sat straight up in bed in a daze.

"Eric, Molly, wake up!" Hector shouted, pounding on our door.

"What is it?" Eric called sleepily.

"Soldiers . . . we're surrounded," Hector shouted back. "Get out here."

We were both instantly alert and jumped out of bed.

I dressed quickly and opened the door. "Who's soldiers? Not Nolin I hope."

"No, but they're armed to the teeth with real weapons. Not like the farmers from the village," Hector said racing for the stairs.

We ran around frantically getting dressed and grabbing weapons. Running into the hall I nearly knocked Jonni over the railing. "Sorry," I cried plaintively. I leaped into the air and landed in the great room before I realized what I'd done. Eric jumped right behind me. Now that was new.

He grinned at me.

"Let's go," he said.

Down in the great room we hid Sophie again under a table, shushing her whiny protests. "You need to be safe," I whispered.

A gruff voice called from outside the cabin. "You, there. Come out where we can see you."

I peeked out through the curtains. It was almost light outside and there must have been thirty or forty soldiers that I could see; Hector had said we were surrounded. I felt a hand on my shoulder.

"You go, we all go," Eric stated quietly.

I nodded my head. "No weapons showing," I warned everyone.

Hector started to open the door.

"Wait," I said abruptly. "I have an idea." I turned to Naomi. "Do you know who these men are?"

She nodded. "Yes, they're from the next village. The farmers must have told them about us."

"Do they know who you are?" I asked.

"They might. The last time I came through I stole some bread. I got caught," she said sheepishly. I saw Hector shake his head and grin.

"Sophie, can you turn into anything you want? If I needed you to shift into an animal, could you do it?" I asked hurriedly.

"Sure, I can shift to whatever you need. I've never been an animal before. What do you want me to be?" She sounded excited.

"Could you both become dogs?" I paused when I saw Naomi rubbing her hands together in anticipation and a silly grin on her face. "Something non-menacing would be nice," I chuckled.

"So I can't be a teeth-baring German Shepard?" quipped Naomi.

"No, I don't think that would fit my plan. Go behind the stairs so your flashes won't be visible." They ran to the alcove under the stairs. I heard them whispering and two slight flashes of light appeared.

Out trotted two beautiful collies; one dark, one light. They ambled over and licked my hand. "Bark if you can understand me," I commanded. Two sharp barks hit the air. "Which one of you is Naomi?" The lighter colored dog yipped softly.

"Cute," Hector chortled, and bent down to scratch her ears.

I turned to the men who were laughing quietly. I tried to be serious, but it wasn't working; I had to smile.

"Very nice, ladies. Now here's my plan." I spelled it out to everyone.

The voice called again loudly, only this time we filed out to the porch, the four of us and our 'dogs'.

The man standing alone in front of all the soldiers was quite impressive. He was average height and built stocky with a shock of golden hair. He stared at us and motioned for us to come off the porch. We didn't move.

"I am Michael Gorman, captain of these troops. Come down here so we can talk," he said gruffly.

"I think we'll stay here if you don't mind."

I put on my best defiant face my hands on my hips. I hoped it didn't get us shot. The men closed in around me and the dogs sat in front of us all.

"The villagers said there were six of you. I only see four. Where are the others?" he asked.

He eyed the dogs cautiously. "I'm not sure what you mean," I said, stalling. "The men who came yesterday must have misunderstood me. I only said there were six, which included our dogs. I'm sorry, I should have been more specific," I answered truthfully.

"Why are you here?" he continued his interrogation. "This land belongs to Dax Fyre."

I was getting a little irritated. "We have permission to stay here and will be leaving today to continue our journey. Dax is awaiting our arrival." Okay, maybe that was too much information. I didn't want to make things worse by telling him where we were going.

He eyed me suspiciously. I began to wonder if this was such a good idea.

"Strange you should say that. I've not heard of any visitors that are expected. We are Dax's guardians on this end of his land. Perhaps I should check with Dax before we allow you to continue. My men will remain here while I ride to Dax's home and inquire as to your arrival. Do not attempt to leave before I return or you will be taken into custody."

Michael turned on his heel, spoke to a red-haired man and mounted his horse and rode off into the forest at a gallop.

The red haired man stood his ground waiting for us to do something stupid. None of the soldiers moved a muscle.

Chapter 29

I stared back nervously at them standing in the field. I decided to go into the house; it looked like we had no choice but to wait for this man to return. There was no sense in provoking these men if it meant we'd be hauled off to who knows where.

When we were all inside I told the dogs to stay in that form just in case someone took a look inside. They went and lay down on the rug in the living room. We huddled in the kitchen to decide what to do.

"Anyone have a suggestion as to what our next move should be?" I whispered. Hector leaned across the counter.

"I do. We need to get out of here . . . and damn fast," he said wryly.

"And how do you suppose we can accomplish that? We're surrounded," said Eric, looking a little perturbed.

Hector gave him a frustrated look. "You don't know, do you?" He shook his head. "Your special ability of course."

"And that would be . . . ?" Eric countered.

"My man, *you* are a shield," Hector said slapping him on the back.

"Okay, you know something I don't. How can I be a shield?" Eric replied.

Hector sighed and looked at me.

"Why do you think Molly can't read you? You block her. I can't even read you. Believe it or not you are a very strong blocker. If you try real hard you can hide us all under your shield and we can sneak out without anyone seeing us. We'll be invisible."

"How come you've never known about this?" I asked Eric, who stood there silent, thinking about this disclosure. This was the first time I'd heard anything about his gift. It explained a lot. I wondered if Arnos was even aware of it.

"No one ever told me; not even my parents," Eric said quietly.

"How does it work?" I asked turning to Hector.

"He has to concentrate just like you do . . . and say some magic words."

"We don't have a week to work on this, H. Can we speed it up a bit?" I reminded him. "Can you help him, please?" Patience wasn't something I had right now.

Hector took Eric into the alcove and put his hands on Eric's shoulders. He mumbled something in Eric's ear and I could see them nodding. Eric had his eyes closed and it looked like he was saying the same words, talking faster and faster until suddenly . . . they weren't there anymore!

I ran over to the alcove with Jonni right behind me. The dogs were yipping. I couldn't believe my eyes. I'd heard about shields but never had I seen it done.

"Where are you?" I asked as I waved my hands around in the air. Suddenly I felt a pressure on my shoulder and yelped. Then a laugh erupted from the other side of the room.

"Catch us if you can!" Hector said as his head popped up from behind the couch. I stood there with my hands on my hips.

"All right, that was awesome and you've had your fun. Let's get out of here," I muttered. They reappeared right next to me. I jumped and gasped; I'd never heard them move. "Stop that you two." They were both grinning like idiots.

"Here's how we do this," Hector started. "We need to be fairly close together, at least two feet apart. Naomi and Sophie can shift back to human form so we can all move in unison. We'll actually be able to see each other so it's not like anyone will be blind. Sorry Jonni," he said apologetically. Jonni shrugged his shoulders and nodded.

My mind was going in ten different directions at once. What if this didn't work and we were seen sneaking off into the forest? I shivered at the thought.

"What's wrong, Moll?" Eric whispered. "You look skeptical."

"Just thinking of the consequences of getting caught," I replied. No plan seemed foolproof.

"Trust me, this is going to work," Hector said. "You never heard us move around, did you?"

"No."

"His shield muffles noise and movement while we can see and hear everything outside the shield. There's no way these soldiers will detect anything unusual."

"I could cause a diversion," said Naomi behind me. She must have shifted back without me noticing. "They'd notice the door opening. I could go out as a dog, steal some food and run for the forest. Hopefully the soldiers would chase me and you could slip out the door unnoticed. How many are in the back, Hector?"

"About a half dozen," he said hesitantly. "I don't know about this plan. You could get caught or worse, shot."

"I'm very fast," she said brazenly. Hector gave a heavy sigh as he gazed at her tenderly.

"What do you all think?" he asked.

Jonni was leaning against the kitchen counter and spoke first. "I think it's our best bet. One way or the other we are likely to get caught. I say let her go."

"Me too," said Eric. I nodded my agreement.

Hector conceded defeat. "Okay, Naomi, it's your ballgame." He went and gave her a hug that lasted way longer than it should. I saw him whisper in her ear. She nodded, a wistful look on her face.

"We first have to see if Eric's shield works with all of us together," I said. I noticed Sophie was back to human. "Grab your packs and let's try it before Naomi leaves. She can confirm our camouflage."

We were all in a loose group holding hands, our packs on our backs when Eric did his thing. It was so weird, being able to see out through a slight haze but not be seen by Naomi.

"That is so freaky," she squealed. "I don't see a thing, not even a shimmer. I'm going to shift now." I saw the flash and her dog stood in her place.

"Someone needs to open the door for her," I said.

"Just reach out and do it," Hector said as we approached the door. Naomi yipped quietly as my disembodied arm reached out to turn the knob. She quickly darted out the door and headed for the men sitting a few feet away. I quietly closed the door and watched.

Our faithful dog trotted over to the men's camp and I could see them playing with her. Then she made her move and snatched what looked like a chicken they were cooking on a spit. I laughed as she ran round and round with the grown men after her. When they all seemed to be occupied with catching the dog we stole out the back door and calmly walked into the trees a few feet away. When we were into the forest a ways, Hector took out a whistle and blew a silent tweet.

Naomi the dog came rushing into the trees and vanished under the shield. The men came running after her and stopped abruptly when they couldn't see her. "Damn dog, ran off with our supper," one of them complained.

We all tried to stifle laughs but soon we were in hysterics in our little cocoon.

"Did you see me snatch that chicken?" Naomi said through her giggles. She brought her hand up and displayed a perfectly cooked chicken. "Dinner!"

"That was awesome, Naomi," laughed Sophie. "You should have seen their faces."

"I hate to break up the merriment, but we need to move. We have a limited amount of daylight left and I want to be far away from here when they discover we're gone." I steered us toward the stream. We followed its serpentine path for a while and finally came to the road. I was a little leery of being on the road at all, but with the shield around us we moved along fairly quickly. Eric was able to extend it so we didn't have to walk so close together.

Eric stayed close by my side and we held hands. I smiled at him and he started to whistle a tune I was familiar with. Of course Hector had to chime in with his perfect harmony. Then Sophie started to sing the melody; we had our own little concert going.

The sun was setting as we reached the first village and walking into it invisible was surreal. The townsfolk just passed us by without a flicker of recognition. I watched for soldiers and not seeing any I suggested we uncloak in a concealed area.

"Are you sure you want to do that?" Eric asked. "This could be the village that alerted the militia."

I thought about it for a moment. "You're probably right," I said. "Maybe we should camp in the forest tonight. Is everyone agreed?" They all nodded. "Lead on, my love."

We found a small cleared spot far into the trees where Eric dropped the shield and we set up our tents. It was decided not to have a fire so we wouldn't draw attention. The air was balmy and a slight breeze rustled the leaves overhead. Naomi brought out the chicken and we had dinner by flashlight courtesy of the soldiers.

"How much farther do you think?" I asked Naomi.

"At least another day's walk. We'll probably be through the worst part by noon tomorrow, if we keep to the road. The next village is about ten miles from here. There won't be anything else until Dax's property." She took a big bite out of a chicken leg.

"We need to be mindful of any soldiers on the way. They're going to be very pissed that we got away," said Hector.

"I'd loved to have seen their faces when they went into the cabin and we weren't there," Eric laughed. "We just vanished into thin air."

"I think we need to post a guard tonight, just in case," I said seriously.

"I have something better," Eric announced. "Watch." He concentrated and sent his shield out so far this time it surrounded the whole camp area and then some.

"Impressive, my man," Jonni exclaimed.

I looked at Eric with wide eyed wonder. He was amazing. He looked at us with a self-satisfied smirk. "Piece of cake," he muttered.

Hector stood up and stretched. "I guess we better get some sleep. You girls are in the tent by that tree and we gents will take the other one. Sweet dreams." I saw him wink at Naomi.

As we walked to our tents I had the feeling someone was in the woods with us. I really hated these niggling thoughts. Fortunately I couldn't feel Arnos' emotions so I went to bed somewhat relieved. I was both wary and excited about what was in store for us tomorrow.

Chapter 30

In our tent we three girls settled down for sleep. Sophie leaned on her elbow to face me. I watched with interest as she tried to formulate whatever it was she needed to say.

"What will happen to me when this is over? I have no family since Peter . . ." Tears welled up in her eyes and she wiped them away quickly. "Who will want me?"

I swallowed, trying to get rid of the lump in my throat; thinking of what I could say to allay her fears. She needed a home and family but I had no idea who that would be.

"We'll find a safe place for you to live. Somewhere where you'll be loved and cared for."

She thought about this for a moment. "I'd like to stay with Naomi, if it's okay with her," she said hesitantly in her tiny voice.

"S'okay with me," Naomi murmured from her sleeping bag.

"It's a big responsibility raising a child," I reminded her. *Like I knew anything about that.*

"Remember, I love a challenge," she laughed. "Besides, Sophie and I get along great. Isn't that right Soph?"

"You bet!"

"Then we'll see what happens," I said yawning. "Now, go to sleep."

We snuggled into our sleeping bags and drifted off to the noise of crickets and frogs.

Sometime in the middle of the night I awoke to rustling outside the tent. I grabbed my knife and quietly peeked out into the darkness. Hector was sprawled out in front of the tent on his sleeping bag, snoring softly. His sword was clutched tightly in his hand. I carefully receded back into the tent so I wouldn't wake him. The lumps that were Naomi and Sophie were barely visible in the darkness. I drifted back to sleep.

I awoke a few hours later struggling to get my brain to work properly; I felt like I'd been drugged. The sky was just starting to lighten up and I wondered if Hector was still outside the tent.

I rolled over to find Naomi and Sophie huddled in their sleeping bags and I watched them for a few moments. Something was not right as I realized that Naomi's bag was moving up and down with the rhythm of her breathing, but Sophie's wasn't, even though a lump was apparent inside it.

Naomi stirred in her sleep and I called her name to wake her. I shook Sophie's lump and realized with horror that it wasn't her body in the bag. Frantically I opened the bag to find a rolled up blanket where Sophie should have been.

"Naomi, wake up! Sophie's gone!" I shouted. "Guys wake up!" I leaped up and scrambled out of the tent with Naomi right behind me. Eric and Jonni were running over to us and Hector was already searching the area around the tents.

"What's going on?" Eric asked.

"It's Sophie. Where could she have gone? Do you think she ran away?" I said anxiously.

"Where would she go and more importantly . . . why would she leave? She was happy with us. Didn't she say last night that she wanted to live with me?" said Naomi.

"She's right. There's no reason for Sophie to take off by herself," I agreed. "There's something wrong here. Who could have gotten through your shield, Eric?" I remembered the feeling I had last night that someone was watching us.

"No one should have been able to see us or penetrate the shield," he said.

Hector was in the back of our tent. "Look here," he called. We walked around to where he stood, running his hand along a line on the back wall.

"Someone found a way in, cut the tent and then somehow repaired it," he said shaking his head. He looked at me questioningly.

"Didn't you hear or see anything last night? If someone took her, surely you would have woken up," he said harshly. He had never spoken to me like that . . . ever.

I didn't know what to say at first I was so surprised. I saw him react to my startled expression. He looked quickly at the others.

"I woke up once and saw you sleeping in front of the tent," I said. "And then fell back to sleep. As far as I know, Sophie was still in her sleeping bag. I didn't check. We need to find her," I cried, in a panic now. Eric came to my rescue.

"Why are you attacking Molly, Hector? This is clearly the handiwork of Arnos or others working for him. Not humans, they would have made more noise, but someone with more stealth. And why didn't you hear anything?"

Eric was furious and stood between Hector and me. "Or perhaps someone is using magic to mask themselves."

Hector's expression softened as he looked past Eric's shoulder at me. "Molly, I'm sorry. I didn't mean to imply . . ." he stammered. "Eric, I swear I never heard a thing."

Keeping his eyes on me he addressed Naomi. He had a plan; I could see it in his face.

"Naomi, darlin', how's about you go dog and see if you can catch Sophie's scent?" He looked at Naomi with a grin and she smiled at him sweetly.

"My thoughts exactly," she said and gave him a quick kiss on the cheek before flashing into a bloodhound. *Good choice.*

Eric's eyebrows knitted together as he raised a small portion of his shield. When Naomi found the scent she bounded off into the forest. We grabbed our weapons and Eric and I followed Hector and Jonni as they dashed after Naomi through the dense underbrush.

We saw Naomi up ahead as she took off to the left along a stream and then stopped short, sniffing in all directions, whimpering. She'd lost the trail.

Hector caught up to her and petted her head gently. "Lost the scent? They must have crossed the stream," he said. She whimpered again and leaned into him. "Let me try."

I watched him stand very still, his eyes closed. He seemed to be listening for something in the air.

His eyes popped open after several minutes and he pointed across the stream.

"There, on the other side. I can hear her essence. She's leaving us a trail," he announced. "Clever girl."

I marveled at his skills. I couldn't hear a thing or even sense her emotions. I felt inadequate.

"Now what? Do we continue on or break camp first?" I said desperately. My mind was not functioning on all cylinders right at the moment.

Hector's face became dark and he looked across the stream before speaking.

"Naomi and I will continue on. You collect our gear and meet us in the next town. Wait for us there," he said firmly.

I wanted to protest but I could see that statement was final in his mind—no questions required. I asked anyway.

"I don't think we should be separated, do you? You won't be protected by Eric's shield. I don't like this new plan of yours."

"We'll be fine, Molly," he reassured me. "Just a hunter and his dog out for a walk." Naomi yelped her agreement and danced around in front of him, anxious to get going.

I felt responsible for these people. They were my family now and the thought of losing any of them was not making me happy. Yet . . . I trusted Hector and Naomi. They were strong and clever.

I decided it was best to let them go.

"Okay, but please be careful. This is against my better judgment I want you to know. I guess we'll see you in a few hours," I said. I stepped forward and hugged Hector, whispering in his ear, "Be safe. No heroics." He nodded solemnly. Naomi got a brisk rub on the head and ran to the water's edge.

We reluctantly watched them cross the stream and disappear into the forest. It hurt to see them leave, knowing that any moment Arnos might strike. His army was still out there doing his dirty work. I had trusted Nolin; I shouldn't have. They all knew Sophie was a shape shifter. I couldn't see what use she was to them.

Eric and I shared a worried glance.

"They'll be fine, Moll. Let's get back to camp," he said taking my arm and gently leading me in that direction. Jonni was already walking away from us muttering to himself.

I wasn't certain that I agreed with Eric's confidence. I stopped short and wrenched my arm from his grip.

"Eric, you can't be serious. They're sitting ducks out there," I said. "If Arnos is doing this he could be drawing us into a trap."

We locked eyes. Mine must have been smoldering because he didn't say a word for a moment, his eyes unblinking.

"Molly, I gave them some protection. My shield can be used without me being there. I wasn't going to let them go without it." I stood there in surprise. "Oh," I said. He smiled and took my hand. "We need to be on our way."

Just then Jonni came crashing through the brush at us, a worried look on his face.

"Soldiers. Surrounding our campsite. Maybe ten," he said breathlessly.

"What," I said turning to Eric. "How do they know where it is, they can't see it?"

"I don't know but they must know something is there," Jonni puffed out. "They have some kind of detection device but I don't think they can figure out how to get past your shield, Eric."

Eric shook his head in an annoyed way, his face tense.

I glanced in the direction of the camp and suddenly realized we had a haze surrounding us. Eric's shield. Is he capable of using it this way in so many directions at once? *I guess so.* He never ceases to amaze me.

"Let's go troops," he said gleefully and took off through the forest with Jonni and me on his heels.

When we reached the edge of the forest near camp, we stopped to assess the situation. Jonni was right, the area around the camp had about ten heavily armed men milling around like they were waiting for us to come out.

"Those are Nolin's men," I whispered. "I recognize some of them. I wonder where he is."

"What do we do now?" Jonni said looking down at me. "Maybe it's time for a little Fyre power."

"Me? Use my fire balls? No problem." I glanced at Eric beside me who just gave me a quick nod and the *gogetum* sign.

"You want to surprise the hell out of them," Eric said. "I think you can throw them without me lifting the shield."

"You *think?* What if I toast the three of *us* instead?" I said.

"You won't," he said softly. I watched him as he raised his hand and extended the shield out to accommodate my throwing distance.

My aim at first was to scare them. As I calculated my first throw, Nolin came into view and angrily I shot a fire ball at his feet. He jumped back in amazement.

"What the hell was that!" he exclaimed. Before they could recover I started shooting fire at all of them in rapid succession and saw them scatter into the forest, their guns aimed at an unknown foe.

Eric nudged me on and we pursued the men into the trees, all the time I was throwing and setting the underbrush on fire. I certainly didn't want to burn down the forest so when I couldn't see them any longer I ceased my attack and we stopped.

"Well, that was fun!" I exclaimed. "How do we douse these fires I started?"

"Allow me," said Jonni. He rapidly put out the fires by creating a vacuum to smother them all. Smoke rose up into the air and quickly dissipated. I just shook my head and wondered how many more amazing skills my team would show me.

"Do you think they'll be back?" I snorted.

"Not for a while. If they're working with Arnos I'm sure he won't be happy. But maybe we should break camp as quickly as we can and get to the next town before they regroup," Eric said sensibly.

We headed back at a run.

Chapter 31

We managed to break camp quickly with Eric zooming around so fast he was a blur at times. I just couldn't muster that kind of speed, my thoughts focused on Hector, Naomi . . . and Sophie.

I couldn't stop thinking about what I had to do. My senses told me Arnos was out there somewhere laughing at us; taunting us, using Sophie as bait.

It infuriated me beyond words. Hector and Naomi were risking their lives and here I was, packing a backpack.

No, this was my fault and I had to make it right. How could anyone have taken a ten year old girl lying next to me without so much as a whimper? I remembered feeling out of it in the morning. Could we have been drugged or bewitched in some way? I wouldn't put it past Arnos to resort to magic.

A gentle breeze ruffled my hair and I felt a soft whisper in my head.

"Use your dragon, Daughter. Search." I nodded my head slowly. He was talking to me again. I knew what I had to do; a bold determination driving me.

"Eric, Jonni, I need to do something I know neither of you is going to approve." They gazed at me warily. "I have to go dragon and do an aerial search. My senses are more acute in the air and I can cover more area than we can on foot." Eric already had on his disapproving glare. I know he was concerned about my safety but there was no other way right now.

"You know what might happen if the soldiers see you?" he said. "They'll shoot you down."

He had a point and I considered that carefully. However it was a risk I was willing to take to keep my team safe and bring Sophie back safely.

I took his face in my hands. "If you love me you'll understand why I have to go." His blue eyes were blazing at my foolishness. It didn't make a difference.

"Didn't you tell me during training that I would heal fast if I was hurt? I'm sure I'll do better as a dragon," I said flippantly. His expression didn't waver.

"I'm not going to win this argument, am I?" he sighed. His hands were gripped gently around my wrists.

"Nope," I said bluntly.

"At least let me give you some shield," he pleaded. He pulled my hands away from his face.

"No, it will only cloud my vision. And don't think you're going to sneak it in either. I'll know." He was looking at me with that frustrated expression he always gets when I've set my mind to something. I fluttered my eyelashes at him and he burst into laughter.

"Okay, Miss I'll-kick-your-ass-if-you-don't-let-me-do-it."

"That's the spirit!" I exclaimed and now Jonni was laughing.

"Let's see your fierce dragon, Molly Fyre," Jonni said. "I've never seen it with these new eyes."

"You're in for a treat," I said backing away from them. "Will you be able to handle all the gear by yourselves? Or do you want to wait here for me to return?" I called out.

"We'll wait here," said Eric. "Don't take too long."

"I won't. Just a quick look around to see what I can sense," I assured him, placing myself far enough away so I didn't hit anyone.

My transformation was faster this time and when I turned to face the men, I saw Jonni grinning from ear to ear. I gave them a little roar and leaped into the sky.

I left the trees behind and climbed as high as I could, floating effortlessly on a warm current of air before coming down to survey the land in the direction Hector and Naomi had gone. It was easy to see the landmarks and the next town. Unfortunately

I was too high to make out people very well as they looked like little ants. I chuckled inwardly at the sight of them. I decided to fly lower to see if I could make out my friends.

As I came closer to the ground the people started to rush around frantically and I sensed another creature just like me high above me but I couldn't see it. The sun blinded me as I searched the sky for signs of wings or fire. Nothing revealed itself to me as I climbed higher.

Then just as quickly . . . its essence was gone.

By this time I was descending lower again. A shot zinged past my wing and I realized I'd been hit. My wing wouldn't work as I expected and I cursed myself for being seen.

Stupid. Stupid. Stupid.

Oddly, I felt no pain; just couldn't get that wing to flap. The craziest thoughts crossed my mind . . . what part of my human body did the wings come from and would I feel pain when I transformed back. I wondered if my arm was wounded, but concluded I had four legs, so probably not.

All of this thinking took only a few seconds. I knew I was healing rapidly when I felt a shifting in my wing and it was functioning again. However now I had the overwhelming desire to sleep. Not good when you're soaring over the trees. My mind told me I had to get back to Eric and Jonni but my body wasn't cooperating; I started to falter.

That other creature was back as I started to fall, so weary I didn't have the strength to flap my wings. Too late I realized I was reverting back to human form, tumbling helplessly toward earth.

A huge form appeared underneath me and I felt myself hit it. Instead of a jolt I felt softness and I lay there motionless for a few moments, the sun in my eyes, listening to the wings sing in the air. I knew with certainty that I was about to die . . . and then the lights went out in my head.

Chapter 32

I came back to consciousness with a snap. I was aware of murmuring a short distance away; I paid close attention to the voices, trying to decide if they were friend or foe.

"When will she wake up, Father? It's been two hours since we retrieved her." The voice was female and young.

"Soon, little one. I didn't give her much," an older male said. I could hear him moving around the room. I figured if I was going to die they would already have done the deed.

"She's very pretty. Who do you think she is?" the little voice asked.

"I'm not sure. She's definitely not from our village. And yes she is very pretty," the man answered. There was a smile in his voice. I suppose I could count that as reassuring.

Someone had moved closer to me. I was lying on a blanket covered pallet of some sort; it wasn't at all uncomfortable. I assessed myself for injuries. None were apparent. My back was sore, I assumed where this man had shot me and it dawned on me that he had used a tranquilizer dart to shoot me out of the sky and then rescued me. But why? I wasn't sure if I should hate him or thank him.

I stirred and opened my eyes just to slits to survey my surroundings. The room was small, almost claustrophobic, with a low ceiling and brick walls. The room was sparsely furnished and a fire crackled in the fireplace across the room from where I lay. The man was standing by the hearth stirring a pot.

"Father, she's awake," the small voice said next to my ear.

I turned my head toward her and she startled, falling backward onto the floor. She was a small imp of a girl with black hair that tumbled around her face in curls and dark blue eyes.

"Hello," I said brightly. "Who are you?"

She recovered her composure and said hesitantly, "My name is Ariel Hunt. And who are you?"

"I'm Molly Fyre," I replied, raising myself up on my elbows. I felt a twinge in my upper back and winced. That answered my question about feeling pain in human form. I could feel it subsiding slowly.

The man came over to us with a steaming cup in his hand and offered it to me with a kind look. He had a weathered face, not handsome, but pleasant. His dark hair was cut short and his piercing blue eyes regarded me carefully.

I considered the cup warily.

"It's only tea," he assured me. "It will clear your head."

I accepted the cup and took a tentative sip. It was chamomile with honey. I stared at the man, willing him to tell me where I was and what he wanted from me. The little girl who I guessed was seven or eight, got up without a word and went to play with her dolls.

"You're wondering what happened. I'd like to explain," he said, sitting across from me. He leaned forward and rested his arms on his thighs.

"That would be refreshing," I muttered into my cup.

He sighed. "My name is Jonathan Hunt. I mean you no harm," he started. "But others do." His blue eyes bore into mine.

"I belong to a small group of villagers who are of a . . . certain nature . . . like you." He stared at me waiting for a reaction. I gave him a level look and he continued.

"We've learned to hide ourselves well and not call attention to our—abilities. Now you've come and stirred up the army that lurks around trying to capture one of us. Do you have any idea what they'll do to us?" I noticed his scowl but his expression quickly changed and he looked down at his hands.

"I've had contact with those same soldiers a few days ago," I admitted. "They had us surrounded but we escaped with the help of my boyfriend's shield. What do you want from me?"

"Just to leave and never come back," he said flatly.

I studied his careworn face, the face of a man who'd seen much adversity. I couldn't see adding to that my worries but I needed to leave soon and find Eric.

"I'm looking for a young girl named Sophie who was kidnapped from my tent last night. Is there any way you could find out if she is near and who has her? My friends are probably looking for me right now wondering why I didn't come back." I sat up on the edge of the bed and I grabbed my head as it spun for a few seconds. "Whoa," I said. I could feel the blood leaving my face.

"Well, looks like you'd better wait for a while, until your head clears," the man said putting his hand on my shoulder.

"I'm fine," I said.

I wasn't, but I wasn't going to let him see my weakness. Why he was concerned about me was beyond my comprehension given that he wanted me gone. I should have been afraid, but somehow I had the feeling I could trust this man.

He glanced around affectionately at his daughter playing quietly in the corner.

"I doubt anyone in this area will give you any information. They pretty much keep to themselves." He took his hand away and sat there watching me.

"Let me get you something to eat." He went to the hearth and ladled out what looked like stew from the large pot into a small bowl.

I realized we hadn't eaten breakfast this morning before all this craziness happened. My stomach growling was a dead giveaway.

Jonathan brought the bowl and a piece of bread to me and set it down on the table next to the bed. It smelled wonderful and I knew I'd need my strength so I took the bowl gratefully and dug in.

"You're a good cook, Jonathan," I said after I'd swallowed the first bite. "I guess your wife appreciates your skills."

He suddenly looked stricken. "I lost my wife a year ago. Ariel is all I have now," he said sadly. He sat down heavily on the chair.

"I'm sorry," I muttered. "Was she a . . . ?" I couldn't finish and turned my attention to my stew.

"No. She died defending me," he said softly after moments of silence. I felt for this man who was so kind and giving; yet he seemed to feel that he had a curse. I was inclined to disagree with his assessment of his situation.

I ate in silence thinking about my own mother again. She, too, had died protecting a man—my father. I thought about his whisperings in my head and how he seemed to know so much about me. Could we have some psychic connection that I wasn't aware existed?

Jonathan interrupted my musings.

"Can I get you anything else? You're starting to look a lot better now."

"No, thank you. Your stew was delicious," I said hesitating. "Can I ask you a question?"

"Yes, certainly," he replied taking my bowl to a wash area and rinsing it out.

"Do you know a man named Dax?"

I could see his profile in the glow of the fire. He got a strange intense look on his face for several moments as he wavered and didn't answer me right away. His expression faded quickly to blandness.

Finally he said, "Why do you want to know?"

Great . . . he was being evasive like everyone else on this trip.

"My team and I are trying to find him," I replied, pausing. I explained that Arnos was following us and why. "And . . . I believe Dax may be my father."

He turned to face me and stared at me with a knowing smile as he dried his hands.

"I guessed as much. You look just like him," he said and dropped his gaze to a large wooden chest on the floor. That statement caught me by surprise and confirmed my suspicions.

"Let me get you a map. His castle is hidden in the hills and you'll never find it on your own." He bent down and opened the chest. It was filled with all kinds of important looking papers and journals. I stole a peek into the chest. I was curious as to why he had all these things in his possession and in my own inimitable way asked about them.

He chuckled. "You're very direct, aren't you?" he said. "Your father, Dax, entrusted these documents to me for safe-keeping. You could say I'm his historian, keeping these records of our race. Some are extremely old and fragile."

I thought about Arnos and how he'd love to get his grubby hands on them. Fat chance!

Out of the blue he said, "Your friends, you said they were waiting for you? They must be frantic by now." I nodded. He unfolded a yellowed map of Carolan and placed it on the bed next to me.

"We are here, near the second village," he said pointing to a picture of some houses on the map.

"That's where my friends and I are supposed to meet," I said. "How far from your home is it?"

"Just about a mile. You can easily walk there from here. There's a fairly good road that runs along the stream," he said glancing at me. My attention was on the map.

"I'd like to go with you if you don't mind. The army is all over the place and I would feel bad if anything happened to you." His expression was one of concern and determination.

Arguing seemed a useless waste of time; he'd already made up his mind. He was such a good man. I didn't want to refuse him; but I also didn't want to involve him in our troubles. It would not be right if he were to get hurt trying to help me. I needed to get back to Eric and the others as soon as possible. The longer we were delayed, the farther away Sophie might be.

"I don't think that's necessary," I said my eyes wandering back to the map. "Show me how to find Dax's castle from there."

"If you're worried about my involvement, don't," he said softly. "It seems I already am. I only want to make sure you get safely to your friends." He apparently wasn't going to take no for an answer. "That army roaming around, it's not Dax's. And if Arnos attacks, he won't be alone."

"You know Arnos. How?" I asked.

"We all were acquainted in the old days unfortunately. Even then he was cruel and unforgiving. He's quite powerful, just not as strong as you will be together. When he found out about our kind he was determined to destroy every last one of us, even his brother, Dax." He lifted his eyebrows at the incredulous look on my face.

"You mean Arnos is my uncle?" I hissed. Oh crap. This can't be. My own blood is trying to kill us. He needed to be stopped at any cost . . . any.

"I believe Dax has found a way to defeat him, as much as it pains him to kill his own kin. It's you, Molly. You've been brought here for one purpose only, to help us to get rid of our enemy."

"Trust him, my daughter. You're very close to me now."

I lost my focus for a few seconds and Jonathan noticed.

"He's speaking to you, isn't he?" I nodded absently. "You have a strong connection and most likely it's always been that way. You just didn't know it as such." He sat back in his chair and regarded me thoughtfully his arms crossed over his chest.

When he continued he leaned forward again, hanging his head. "There's a whole different world out here. But he needs to tell you about it. It's not my place."

My mind was buzzing like a hive full of angry bees. What had I been thrown into? How could I be a part of this new 'world', as Jonathan had put it? At this point I was willing to believe anything was possible; a father, who spoke to me psychically, an enemy, who just happened to be my uncle, and a team of talented immortals . . . Eric. I ached for him. I would walk through my own fiery breath for him.

I shook my head and refocused my thoughts to the here and now and Jonathan.

Jonathan was distracted watching Ariel play. I wondered out loud what he would do with her if he were to come with us. He answered me without looking my way.

"I'd have my sister take her. Muria would understand." His gaze found mine.

"I don't suppose I could stop you from joining our little escapade. It's for certain we need all the help we can get finding Dax but I don't want to put you in danger."

"No, I need to go." He stood and crossed the room to where Ariel sat playing. She looked up at him with her big blue eyes and smiled. He bent down on one knee and whispered something in her ear. She frowned and whispered something back to him. He shook his head.

"But I want to go with you. You always let me go!" she protested loud enough for me to hear. I was reminded of Sophie's stubborn streak.

"Not this time little one. It's going to be too dangerous. I may have to fight," he said gently. She was crying against his shoulder. "I know what's bothering you. I swear, I will return to you."

I prayed he could keep his promise.

"If I promise to keep him safe, will you feel better?" I said attempting to sooth her.

Ariel sniffed and wiped her hand over her eyes. "Could you do that?"

"Yes." I tried to make that sound more confident than I felt. It wasn't even a done deal that any of us would survive this.

Jonathan and I exchanged guarded looks.

"We must get going soon," I said.

"Yes. Come Ariel. We need to find your Aunt Muria and have you settled in before I leave." He stood up with her in his arms, still clinging to him for dear life.

He left with her and I sat motionless on the bed until he returned and gathered a few things.

He stood in the middle of the room with a small duffle bag.

"Well then, let's go," he said quickly. And off we went.

Chapter 33

It didn't take us long to walk the mile to town. We stopped short of civilization to watch from the trees for any signs of the army. Seeing no soldiers in sight I pulled the hood of my jacket over my head to hide my face and walked toward the street with Jonathan on my heels.

"We must be mindful of the people. They have been alerted to strangers in the area," he whispered in my ear. I nodded, continuing to walk purposely but trying not to look suspicious.

There was a restaurant half the way down the street and I headed for it. If there was any place that would be a fountain of information, it was an eatery. My friends had to eat sometime, especially Hector.

Jonathan was right about the stranger danger part as all eyes turned to us when we entered the establishment. I smiled at some of them as we weaved our way to a table in the back and sat down. A pretty waitress named Helen brought us a menu and eyed Jonathan warmly. He smiled back rather shyly I thought. Hmmmm.

"And who is this?" she said indicating me.

"This is my cousin . . . Mona. Just visiting us for a day or two," he said awkwardly. I raised one eyebrow at him. She didn't look convinced. I gave her my best smile and ordered.

When she left to get our drinks I glanced at him amused.

"What? Helen and I are old friends." He returned his attention to the menu. I couldn't get the smirk off my face.

Uh, huh.

"I'm really not hungry after the stew," I said putting the menu on the table. I looked around the room casually trying not to seem obvious.

"I'm not either," he said. "What we need is information." His eyes scanned the patrons. They'd lost interest in the stranger and had gone back to devouring their food.

Helen brought our drinks and made a big deal of where she placed them, reaching across Jonathan to give me mine. He was positively radiating male hormones. I had to stifle another grin.

He cleared his throat. "Um, Helen, have you seen any strangers in here lately?" he asked.

She looked at him questioningly. "Why?"

"Because . . . Mona . . . has misplaced her friends and we need to find them," he said taking a sip of his drink.

She gave me an uneasy look before answering. "There were four people in here last evening asking the same question. Could they be your friends perhaps?"

"What did they look like, if I might ask," I said.

"Let's see, one was a huge guy with a bald head and weird eyes, a really good looking guy, one tiny woman and another dandy looking fellow who laughed a lot." I could have kissed her.

"That's them," I said excitedly. "Would you have any idea where they might have gone?" My hopes rested on them staying in town.

"I believe they asked for someplace to rest so I sent them to the inn." She didn't seem happy about giving me this information but I thanked her profusely and decided to leave a good tip. Her eyes were constantly flicking to Jonathan.

As I stood up I glanced toward the door at the people entering the restaurant. It didn't register right away who they were until one turned around and our eyes met. I think we both had looks of surprise on our faces for a brief moment and then I ran across the room into Eric's arms and he smothered me in kisses. The patrons who were left were suddenly intent on our reunion.

"Damn, Molly, I thought the soldiers had caught you and dragged you away," he murmured into my hair. "Are you all right?" He pushed me away and looked me up and down.

"I'm fine, love," I said breathlessly. "Eric this is Jonathan Hunt. He . . . rescued me when I started to fall. I'll explain all about it when we're in a less public place." No sense making Eric angry. We needed Jonathan's help.

A flicker of a smile crossed Jonathan's face as he listened to my half-truths. "I'm honored to meet you," he said. He held his hand out to Eric who shook it warily and gave me a '*what the heck is going on*' look.

I was so anxious to steer everyone out of the restaurant and get to the inn that I took Eric's hand and herded them all toward the door and into the street before I'd answer any questions.

The rest of the team just looked confused and led the way to their rooms at the inn.

Once inside I began telling them my story. Jonathan filled in his part to their disbelief. I watched Eric for signs of animosity. He just sat listening to Jonathan admitting that he had shot me out of the sky and scooped me up before I hit the dirt. Eric's eyebrows went up at that picture.

There was complete silence for a moment.

"So what you're saying is that there are more dragon shifters around this town? Why haven't you done something about it before now?" asked Hector. "And thanks for saving Molly by the way."

Eric was unusually quiet, and unreadable; that worried me.

"This part of the land still has superstitions that go back many generations," Jonathan said. "It's very ingrained in their culture and they still try and hunt us if anyone forgets and gets a fancy to soar around. Dax holds the key to our living in peace, the Krystal, but he can't use it without his daughter's help." Jonathan looked at me and then all the other eyes were on me as well.

The air in the room suddenly got a lot warmer, or so it seemed to me. Just think, me, little ole Molly Fyre, was about to change the world. I felt dizzy and lightheaded. Good thing I was sitting down.

It scared me to death.

"I knew it. I knew you were special!" Hector yelped. "So what does this Krystal do?"

"I'm sorry but I can't reveal that myself. It's for Dax to tell you. I can take you to him as soon as you are ready," Jonathan said.

Though Eric had stayed silent throughout this conversation, I could see the dam about to burst. And so it did. He leaned forward and took a breath before standing.

"Let me get this straight," he said talking directly to Jonathan, "This Krystal is *not* a weapon as we were led to believe but some magical key to a better life for dragons. And . . . the love of my life has to be a part of this or what . . . you get hunted to extinction? Arnos knows this or he wouldn't have sent us here to retrieve it so he could destroy it. My wife-to-be shares this ability. There's no way I'm going to let that bastard hurt her!" He pounded his fist into his other hand.

Okaaay. *Not what I was expecting.* Go Eric, baby! I beamed at him in adoration. I wish that his father could see him now.

Everyone sat in awe of his little speech for a moment and then they all started to talk at once.

"Let's get that mean bastard," said Jonni, clapping Eric on the back so hard he nearly fell down.

"I'm in," said Naomi fiercely. She grabbed Hector's hand.

"There's no better day than one in which you can defeat your enemy," Hector said with alacrity. "Wait a minute. Did you say wife-to-be? When did this happen?"

"Two days ago, but that's another conversation, Hector. Not now, please," I said seriously. He just stared at me with a goofy grin. I turned my thoughts back to the matter at hand.

Then I had a sudden dreadful thought. What about Sophie? We'd been so enthused about this newest development that we'd forgotten she was still missing.

"Wait. We've forgotten something," I reminded everyone. "Did you find any sign of Sophie?"

Hector winced and spoke up. "We lost her trail about a mile from the stream. Whoever has her must have used a vehicle to take her away. I'm sorry." He looked heartbroken. Naomi came over and gave me a hug.

Tears welled in my eyes and I thought about her being all alone and scared.

"I may be able to help with that," Jonathan said. "The only person in the area that owns a vehicle is Samuel Bone. He's sympathetic to Arnos and may be involved. I can take you to his place."

I couldn't put into words what relief I felt. I was sure Dax had sent him to us knowing he would help.

"Do you think there are soldiers helping him?" I asked wiping my tears.

"Most likely," Jonathan said. "They seem to be everywhere lately. It's like they've been alerted to something."

"It's us, I'm sure," I said relating our recent escape.

"We'll use my shield. It can hide our presence until we're close enough to attack," Eric announced. "We should leave right before sunrise. They won't be ready at that hour. How far Jonathan?"

"Not far at all. Should only take an hour to get there."

"And I want to thank you also for keeping Molly safe and bringing her back to me," Eric said meekly and put his hand out as a polite gesture. Jonathan shook it strongly. I put my arms around Eric's waist and kissed him on the cheek.

"Jonathan has a young daughter, Ariel. We need to return him safely to her also," I added, hoping to keep my promise to her.

Hector suddenly stood and stretched his arms over his head. He gave Naomi a wink and she giggled softly.

"I don't know about any of you warriors but I'm tired. See you bright and early in the morning," Hector yawned. He grabbed Naomi's hand and laid his other on Jonathan's shoulder. "Thanks again, brother."

Jonathan nodded solemnly.

We disassembled to our respective rooms, me of course going with Eric. Jonni invited Jonathan to bunk with him since Hector and Naomi were . . . you know . . . together.

I couldn't stop thinking about the day's events as I got ready for bed and what lay ahead of me when I finally get to meet my father. Would he be the benevolent immortal I hoped he'd be or would my hopes be dashed by another enemy? It was mystifying to think I would be able to save our kind from a death sentence.

Our kind. It sounded so foreign to think of myself as another species. And yet I wasn't exactly; I was immortal, going to live a long time. Most importantly, how would Eric fit in to my new world? I was going nowhere without him. The thought of losing him made me queasy or maybe it was the stew. I couldn't tell.

Eric cuddled me close, my head against his chest and I listened to his heartbeat and easy breathing.

"Do you think Hector and Naomi are hooked up?" he said.

"You're just noticing this?" I chided and looked up at him. "I've known for days." I was idly tracing circles on his chest. "In fact, I encouraged Hector to tell Naomi his true feelings. Looks like he did. Now, kiss me and do what you do best." He made a face at me and rolled me on top of him with a wicked chuckle.

Oh, this is going to be a great night.

Chapter 34

Dear Journal,

I haven't written in what seems like a hundred years, when in actuality it's only been a few days. So much has happened I don't know where to begin. Let me just say we haven't been idle sitting on our butts.

I've discovered my main skill is as a dragon; go figure. And not just a small one either. I can fill up a whole field with my wingspan.

Eric and I became engaged two days ago and I can't stop thinking about it. Hector will tease the hell out of that. Let him. I'm so happy I could burst.

I found out I have family in the oddest places; a father, maybe a sister and—an uncle I despise. Guess who that is. No idea? Arnos, of course. Yep, my dear, evil uncle.

Hector and Naomi are together, finally. Naomi has demonstrated her shape shifter thing many times; she's a great asset to the team. And ... I think she may be that above mentioned sister. We haven't had the time to confirm that just yet but I'm pretty certain.

I've seen a vision of my mother recently. She looks the same. She gave me a cryptic message about a new ability and a surprise, but I've already figured that one out.

My father is communicating with me nonverbally which freaks me out sometimes. I'm very anxious to actually see him, since he's supposed to be dead. He is probably not the villain in our little drama. And he apparently holds the key to a secret dragon world ... whatever that is.

Arnos has been following us this whole time and murdered Peter for no reason I can think of. The man is totally without morals. I've been thinking of ways I want to harm him.

A new friend has joined our happy troupe. Jonathan Hunt is my connection to Dax and has offered to bring us to him. Oh, and he shot me out of the sky and then saved me from eating dirt. 'Nough said.

We are now preparing to go and get Sophie who was kidnapped last night by persons unknown. I suspect that Arnos is behind this also; he's really getting on my nerves.

Somehow all this strife has hardened my resolve to do what I was destined to do; defeat a man who threatens to destroy a complete group of beings who only want to live in peace, yours truly being one of them.

Eric woke me before it was light and we hastily dressed and met the others in the inn's lobby. As we talked in whispers about the upcoming raid to find Sophie, I noticed the innkeeper was behind the desk busy with some papers he was sorting. His eyes kept flicking to me nervously. He seemed to find the one he was looking for and strolled over to us with an envelope in his hand.

"Are you Molly Fyre?" he asked me. He waved the envelope at me when I nodded and acknowledged that fact.

"A man left this for you this morning. I didn't get a name, sorry." He returned to his desk and eyeing me suspiciously, fussed with more papers.

I took the envelope and stared at it for a few moments. The handwriting was unfamiliar and very flowery, almost like a woman had written it.

"Who do you think would send me a note at this very moment?" I questioned no one in particular. "And—who even knows we're here besides you know who?" I looked at Eric who looked as puzzled as I was. No, it couldn't be.

"Open it and see," he said. So obvious.

I ripped open the envelope slowly and slipped out the handwritten note reading it carefully. A feeling of dread passed through me and must have shown on my face because Eric took the note from my shaking hand and read it. His expression was one of surprise and then disgust.

"This is a sick joke," he snarled. "Listen to this." He read the poem written in that beautiful handwriting.

> Sweet little Sophie
> Hanging from a tree,
> You'll never find her
> The same goes for me!

"What does it mean?" Naomi said angrily. "Is she dead?"

The look of horror on everyone's face made me sick. I felt like throwing up; my head swam. Eric caught me before I hit the floor.

"No, no, no!" I sobbed and clung to Eric's shirt as he held me up.

It wasn't right to fall apart like this. I'm supposed to be the leader of this band but this made it way too horrible to think straight. When I dared to look at Eric, he looked as stricken as I felt.

"Surely Arnos is behind this," Jonni said, his face disgusted. Naomi had her hand to her mouth, tears in her eyes.

"This can't be true. It has to be a trick," Hector said solemnly. "We need to proceed with our plans. Something's not right here."

When I glanced at Jonathan he was quiet and his face was a smooth and unreadable mask. He had taken the note to read.

"What is it?" I asked my voice thick.

"I know this handwriting. There's a woman in town who writes letters for those who can't. This is her handwriting, I'm sure of it. And . . . Sam Bone can't read or write." He gazed at the note again. "I sure hope he hasn't done something stupider than kidnapping a little girl."

I studied his face. He had a pained look on it and I wondered what was on his mind that would cause this distress. I extricated myself from Eric's arms and went to stand in front of him.

"What's bothering you, Jonathan?" I asked. His face was conflicted. He kept his gaze on the note shaking his head.

"You're not going to believe who it is," he sighed. "Follow me." He walked toward the door the note still clutched in his hand. Now he had a grim expression as we followed him across the street to the restaurant.

Helen greeted us warmly until she saw Jonathan's doleful look and spied the note in his hand. She motioned for us to go to a secluded table at the back of the room.

We arranged ourselves around the table and Helen sat down slowly beside Jonathan, wincing when he glared at her.

"What's this all about, Helen?" he said sternly.

Tears started to well up in her eyes and she dropped her gaze to her lap, her hands trembling. She took a shaky breath and glanced around the table before speaking.

"A man came to me yesterday, after you had left the restaurant and asked if I'd write a note for him. I got my writing tablet and an envelope and we sat down at a table. When he started to dictate what I should write I was appalled and told him so, but he insisted I write exactly what he said or something bad would happen to my mom and dad. He scared me so much I could hardly write those awful words. I'm so sorry. I didn't mean any harm." With that said she started to cry into her hands.

Jonathan placed his arm around her shoulders and held her tenderly. "What did this man look like? Can you describe him?" he asked stroking her hair.

I gave her a tissue and she blew her nose before answering.

"He was not very tall, long black hair that needed a good wash and he was dressed all in black, very handsome. His voice was kind at first then his tone changed to something I'd never heard before, deep and menacing. Am I in trouble?" she questioned.

Jonathan and I exchanged a glance and I shook my head. My stomach lurched.

"No, you're not. You've helped us a lot. Now get back to your customers and we'll talk later." She smiled at him a look of relief on her face and he kissed the back of her hand lightly. She stood and wiped her face of tears before walking back to her tables.

"Arnos!" three of us said at the same time.

"He's here but I can't feel anything," I hissed, my eyes burning and I think glowing. Jonathan picked up on this but said nothing.

"You're right, Molly," Hector said. "He's hiding himself well. I think he's only taunting us again; trying to draw us out in the open. Now would be a good time for your gift, Eric."

I wanted to move; needed to move. So why were we standing here in discussion when Sophie's life was in danger from some sick person.

"We have to go . . . now!" I pleaded. "Eric?"

"We'll be less conspicuous in the forest. Let's take the road out of town and then I'll shield us from there. I don't think anyone will bother us. Jonathan, what do you think?"

"Sounds good to me. The way to Sam's place is just up the road," he said, standing. "I trust you have weapons?"

Hector opened his coat and revealed a very menacing knife so no one but us could see. "We're ready," he said gloating.

The few patrons in the restaurant were getting edgy as we all marched out of the door. I suppose to them we looked pretty intimidating. So much for trying to be inconspicuous.

Once we were outside the town Eric surrounded us in his shield and we walked along the road until Jonathan indicated a rutted dirt path to the left.

"Sam's house is a few hundred yards up this road," he said. "By the way Eric, sure wish I had this skill of yours. I could move faster and without danger of detection when I visit Dax."

Beside me, Eric beamed at the compliment.

"Let's go," I said urgently, tugging Eric out of his reverie. We started down the path and our destination came into view as we stopped in the trees before approaching the house.

It seemed to be a normal abode . . . with about four to five soldiers standing around the house with weapons drawn trying to look intimidating except they all seemed a little bored. Our advantage.

I had a strong sense of where Sophie was being held and I knew she was definitely alive.

"Wait," I whispered. With my eyes closed I concentrated on her emotions; she was so scared, terrified in fact that I shivered in response. It made me angry that Arnos would kidnap a child to torment me. He obviously didn't know me as well as he thought he did. *Surprise!* My resolve was stronger than ever.

I tried to pick up on his emotional signature but came up blank. For certain he was nearby enjoying the show.

"She's there," I said pointing to the last window on the right. "She's frightened but unharmed. Eric, tell me your shield can cover multiple people going in all directions."

"Of course. What did you have in mind?" he said rubbing his hands together in anticipation. I smiled at him.

"I'd like each of you to target a soldier, looks like only four or five out here. I'm guessing more will be inside. Eric will build a shield around each of us to conceal our advance. They'll never know what hit them." I saw Hector get a murderous glint in his eye.

"Do not kill them. Hector wipe that bloodthirsty look off your face right now!" I scolded. "Do I need to throw you raw meat?" He gave me his best pouty face. I rolled my eyes.

"To continue," I said ignoring him, "After the soldiers are subdued, I'll go get Sophie and take her to safety. Are we all agreed? By the way, none of us will be able to see the others so pick your targets now before the shields are in place so you're not bumping into each other." They discussed their strategy and I gave Eric the signal to start.

Eric closed his eyes and I could feel the shield constrict around me, a bit claustrophobic at first, then it loosened. I had a moment of panic when I couldn't see anyone. I stuck my head out of my cocoon and muttered "go".

In a matter of seconds the soldiers were handled without a sound. Impressive. Their looks of surprise when they were grabbed and whacked were priceless. I reminded myself to give my team *Atta boys* when this was done.

Hopefully Arnos wasn't in the house now that I could affect my rescue. His emotional signature was hidden from me and I could very possibly be going into an ambush. My deep breathing did nothing to calm my nerves. As insurance I produced a fireball in my left hand . . . just in case.

I approached the window behind which I was sure Sophie was hidden and peeked in. She was lying on a bed apparently asleep and beside the bed was a female soldier sitting and reading a magazine. I surveyed the room for other bodies and saw no one else.

As I pondered my next move I noticed a phantom arm reaching toward me and suddenly I found myself in the bubble with Eric.

"Nice move," I said smiling and extinguishing the fire. He wrapped his arms around my waist.

"Hey, love. I thought you might need some help." He kissed my nose.

"Well, we have a slight problem. There's a female soldier in the room with her."

"We're waiting by the front door. I'll inform everyone and take care of the rest of the troops inside. Then you can take Sophie and run. Take her into the woods and we'll meet you there."

He kissed me and pushed me back into my bubble again. In a few moments I heard a commotion as Eric and the team stormed the door. When I couldn't hear any more noise I looked into the room and the soldier was dragging Sophie in the opposite direction!

I ran around the corner of the building and saw the soldier pushing Sophie toward a vehicle. We'd forgotten the back door.

Chapter 35

My running speed had improved considerably so I quickly caught up with them and grabbed Sophie's free arm. The woman tugged back in bewilderment as my fist came out of the blue and struck her face. She went down like a rock.

"Come on Sophie, it's me Molly," I shouted, only my head and arm sticking out.

"Molly?" she said astonished. I took her hand and pulled her into the bubble with me. "I'm so glad you're all right." As I turned around to head for the trees a pair of very large hands grabbed me from behind and put a knife to my throat.

Crap. *This can't be good.* A familiar voice whispered in my ear.

"Fancy meeting you here." *Arnos.* He tightened his grip practically taking my feet off the ground.

"Now my dear, we have much to talk about. Let's disappear shall we. These shields are so handy but a bit restrictive," he hissed.

"I don't want to go anywhere with you—*uncle.* Where is Sophie?" I croaked.

He loosened his grip for a nanosecond in surprise but recovered quickly. It was getting hard to breathe.

"So, you know. A pity. We could have had a wonderful reunion, you—me—my brother." He struggled to get me into the trees. I wasn't going willingly.

"Where is Sophie?" I repeated breathlessly.

He laughed hysterically. This man was seriously crazy.

"Why do you care? Didn't you get my note? It was metaphorical, of course. She's not exactly hanging from a tree but I'm guessing she wishes she was," he said coldly. It sent cold shivers down my back.

My mind was racing as I twisted in his grip, trying to assess my precarious state of affairs. Should I go dragon on him or not. I was furious with myself that I'd fallen for his trap; but how was I to know he could shift into Sophie's likeness? He sure was full of surprises.

I hoped that Eric would see us before Arnos pulled me too far into the forest. Apparently he can detect each of us in our bubbles even though we can't see each other. Out of the corner of my eye I saw flickers of light in the direction of the house. Was that Morse code? Yes, it sure was. Eric was sending me a message. I prayed that Arnos was too preoccupied to notice.

We'll be right behind you. Oh, thank god.

I needed to keep Arnos distracted until they caught up.

"Where is Sophie?" I managed to gasp.

"You are *very* persistent. We're going to her right now. I can take care of both of you at the same time and then concentrate on the others. Very convenient."

Oh yeah, crazier than a bedbug!

"You know, this means you won't get what you want—the Krystal," I reminded him.

"I'll obtain it all right. Your father will come to avenge you and I'll have him, too. It's way too simple really." He was ranting now.

We stumbled through the forest until we reached a small clearing. The sun shone down in streaks of gold through the trees. It was way too beautiful for this insanity.

I was wondering how we would get out of the shield when it suddenly disappeared. Arnos threw me to the ground in front of him; the crazed look on his face had me cringing where I lay. I'd never seen this darkness on him . . . ever; even when he was angry. His eyes were onyx and wild. When had he finally snapped?

"You are weak, little girl!" he spit out, pacing around like a panther eyeing its prey.

Oh, I'm not that girl any more.

I stared at him, feeling myself warm up, my eyes glowing. My blood boiled, itching to go dragon and tear him apart. He didn't seem to notice me quivering.

Not yet, daughter. Conserve your strength.

Father, help me.

My gaze held firm on Arnos as he walked back and forth in front of me. All this was building up to something I really didn't want to be part of.

I searched the clearing for any sign of Sophie. If she was here he had hidden her well. Off to the left of where I lay, I saw a quick glint of something shiny. I risked a peek.

There it was again. It was as if that shiny object was rotating in the breeze like a mobile. I didn't dare chance a good look for fear that Arnos would see.

Your friends are near. Trust them.

Great. How do we handle this crazy man, Father?

All is not as it seems.

Again with the riddles. What does that mean?

I felt the need to distract Arnos until Eric and the others arrived.

"Why did you kill Peter?" I blurted.

Arnos stopped his pacing and glared at me. "He was expendable. His loyalties changed abruptly and I no longer needed his services," he spit out.

"Peter was a child. You used him and his sister. How heartless," I taunted. He fumed. Behind him Hector and Eric stuck their arms out with thumbs up. Fighting the urge to smile I bit my lip and kept my face smooth, my gaze glued to Arnos.

He was now ranting in some ancient language.

"Where is Sophie? You told me she'd be here, but I don't see her," I said letting my eyes look around. That shiny glint had stopped.

Arnos glanced in that direction with a look of confusion. Had we found her hiding place? He had his knife in hand glaring at me in that crazed way. I saw that Eric and Hector were out in the open, no longer shielded. Arnos took a step toward me not even noticing them behind him. He was much sharper than this and should have heard their movement. I wrinkled my brow. This was too strange. In my hand behind my back I had a fireball ready.

Seeing Eric nod at me I hurled the fire at Arnos and hit him square in the forehead, knocking him senseless. He staggered back into Hector's waiting arms. Hector's grip was strong and had Arnos' arms pinned. The knife fell to the ground with a soft thud and I rushed to grab it.

"Be careful. He can shift," I warned Hector.

"No problem," he grunted. He tightened his grip until Arnos gasped and collapsed unconscious in his arms. As Hector threw the man unceremoniously into the dirt, I kept a fireball handy just in case he was faking. He didn't move.

"You okay, Moll?" Eric asked rushing to my side. I wasn't.

"Just a little shaken," I lied. "That was awesome, guys. But a little strange don't you think, that Arnos was so easy to subdue?"

Hector flexed his bicep and laughed. Oh, brother!

Just then Naomi and Jonni came out of the trees; Jonni was carrying Sophie who clung to him like a little monkey. He gently placed her on the ground and sat with her. Her eyes were closed tight and she was shaking. I could truly empathize with her emotions at this moment. I walked over to where they sat and knelt down.

"Sophie," I said gently. "You're safe now." She slowly opened her eyes and tears trickled down leaving tracks in her dirt covered cheeks.

"Molly, he's nuts!" she cried. *She had my vote.*

"I know. But we have him now." I stayed in a position that shielded her from a view of Arnos.

"He had her in a metal cage with holes so small she couldn't shift and escape," Hector said. He looked down at Arnos, disgusted.

"So, what do we do with him now that we have him?" Eric said scowling at the body. I could see he wanted to kick the shit out of him right now.

"Are you sure this is really Arnos? I don't remember him being a shape shifter. True he has great powers but not this ability," Hector said giving the body a nudge with his foot. It moaned.

I considered this. He may be right. Arnos had never exhibited any shifter tendencies that I could remember; I'd known him a long time and the fact that he hadn't fought harder, like throwing his energy out, was puzzling. I can't believe I'd been so naïve.

"You're right but shouldn't this person have changed back to true form after we knocked him out?" I asked. "Now that I think about it, this can't be Arnos. His powers are too great to not have noticed you guys behind him. He would have heard you. Who is this guy? He knew an awful lot about me."

Naomi came over to the body and knelt down. "He may be a very powerful shifter. I've heard they can hold their forms for long periods of time even if unconscious." She touched his head lightly. The form slowly changed before our eyes and he moaned.

Eric was at my side in an instant, his arms around me in a protective stance. "Could this be Sam Bone?" I said.

"Could be," Hector snickered. "I have some *really* strong rope in my sack and I know exactly where to put this guy."

"You'd better be fast so he doesn't change into a fly and get away," Jonni said laughing.

Hector moved so fast he was blurred. That guy was trussed up and deposited in the cage before we could take two breaths.

Eric relaxed beside me. I took a deep breath myself to calm my nerves. My father was right about my not going dragon on this guy and about trusting my friends. Eric especially is my sun in this crazy darkness we face. I leaned on his shoulder.

"It's no wonder I couldn't sense Arnos. He wasn't here at all," I said staring into the woods in a complete funk. "He's still out there . . . waiting."

"We'll get him, Moll. It's just a matter of time," Eric said resolutely.

"Yeah, time." I looked up at him realizing something. "Where's Jonathan?"

"Oh, yeah, he went on ahead to talk to Dax. Don't worry; I have the directions to Dax's castle," he said patting his pocket. He gave me a quick kiss and we gathered the others for a meeting before taking off.

Chapter 36

At last I will be meeting my daughter and her team of warriors. They're progress throughout this journey has been fraught with many obstacles and I hope my help has been received willingly.

Molly has learned to communicate with me as well as I'd expected since we share the same affinity for fire and flying in the clouds. I look forward to sharing that ride with her if it pleases her. Her mother would be very proud of her accomplishments and I pray she is looking down on us all giving her blessing.

Our common enemy has taken to playing silly games and I am sure the last game he chooses will be his downfall. He underestimates my power and the ability of my daughters; together we will defeat him once and for all. Our very survival depends on it.

Until they arrive, which will be soon, I occupy my time trying to locate Arnos and planning our reception for him. I was very close once but he alludes my probing again and again. Somehow he has a barrier to hide his comings and goings. Two can play at that game for I also have ways to play hide and seek.

Come and find me, Brother!

Chapter 37

As we gathered in a circle I watched Sophie. Now she was clinging to Naomi but seemed to be less fearful and was smiling and joking with Hector.

"We need to do some more hiking to find Dax. Sophie, are you up for that?" I said putting a hand on her arm.

"I'm fine, Molly. It was pretty scary thinking that was Arnos. That guy was crazy," she said shivering. Naomi gave her a reassuring hug.

"I can certainly agree with that," I said, turning to the guys who were gathering our belongings. "Do you think we could go back to that house and commandeer the SUV? It would make our trip a bit more comfortable than all this walking," I asked hopefully.

"We can't be sure those soldiers haven't left in it already," Hector answered. He was hefting a large backpack onto his shoulders.

Jonni stepped up to help him. "I'd be willing to go and check it out," he offered. "With Eric's shield I could get in and out quickly without being seen."

"I'll go with you. No telling what's happened to the troops since we left them with massive headaches. They're going to be really pissed; if they're still there," Eric said chuckling.

I was dubious of this adventure but I knew the shield would protect them. "I wonder why they haven't come looking for us," I mused to myself. "Isn't it strange? I would have thought they'd be crashing through the trees after us."

"So, Jonni let's go and find out," Eric said clapping him on the back. The shield went up in a flash and off they went.

It was agonizing waiting; what was probably only a few minutes felt like hours. Naomi and I couldn't sit still. We paced back and forth crossing paths until Hector got tired of it and shouted for us to sit down.

Suddenly I heard footfalls in the brush and Jonni came rushing at us.

"There's nothing left of the house or the soldiers. They must have torched it after they came to. The wind carried the smoke away from us so we never saw it. For some unknown reason they left the SUV. Eric is checking it for explosives and will meet us on the road. Why they didn't take it is a mystery," he wheezed out.

"I'll just bet you there's a tracking device on it. Why else would they leave it there? Is he checking for that as well?" I asked.

"Good point. Hope so," Jonni said his breathing better. He took a long swig of water from the bottle Naomi offered him.

"I suppose we ought to proceed to the road then," I said hoisting my duffel.

We didn't have far to go; only a few hundred yards to the south to meet up with Eric. Sophie walked close beside Naomi and Hector; Jonni and I in the rear. There was a flicker of someone's amusement in my head. I glanced at Hector and saw him wince ever so slightly before he turned to look at me.

"You felt it too, didn't you?" I said tensely. He gave me a quick nod. "He's following us." I was sure he wouldn't show himself until he was certain we were with Dax but it made me uneasy just the same.

Hector dropped back to stride next to me with a pensive look on his face. "Tell me Molly, when you were around Nolin could you feel his emotional state?" he inquired.

I thought back to the day he left with his soldiers. I hadn't been probing him that day but nothing about deception in his head came across to me.

"Not at all. What are you thinking; that he's Arnos' shield?" I considered.

"I'm sure of it. His army is still with him. Hopefully we won't see any more of his tricks until we reach Dax." His thinking matched mine. I was anxious to get to Eric.

The day was beautiful with singing birds and insects buzzing around our heads, fluffy clouds in the sky . . . but I felt a power building up inside me, propelling me on. My legs moved faster and I overtook Naomi, who looked at me questioningly as I sailed past her.

"Where's the fire, Fyre?" she called laughingly.

I ignored her and walked faster yet until I fairly flew through the trees with the others right behind me. When I finally burst out of the forest edge, there stood Eric leaning against the SUV, a grin on his face. I flew to his side.

"Damn, she's like a bloody cheetah!" Hector panted.

"What's the matter old man, can't keep up?" I laughed. I wasn't even winded. He gave me a nasty look.

"HA, HA!" he retorted. "I'll get you for that." I'm sure he will.

"Quit whining. We have to be at Dax's before dark. Let's get going before I decide to run all the way," I said opening the vehicle door. "By the way," I said to Eric, "Did you search for tracking devices?"

He held up a small black box with the wires dangling off of it and threw it into the bushes. "Not very inventive are they?" he quipped. I hoped he was right.

After that we piled into the SUV and took off for Carolan. It was hard to put my feelings into words right now. I was anxious to see Dax and sort out this mess. In my head I reasoned that I needed to know him better and considered the fact that I actually had blood relatives. My mother though no longer around would have loved Eric. Maybe she'll make an ethereal visit while I'm here. Who knows, stranger things have been happening already.

We traveled carefully along the road out of town, ever mindful of danger with Arnos still lurking about. Hector seemed to be directing his energy, his face in utter concentration.

I had the window down and felt the soft breeze blow my flaming hair around my face. The sun was warm as it streamed through the windshield and I watched the changing scenery with interest. Naomi was right about how the environment switched gears every now and then. The road started to climb into the mountain ahead of us. I consulted the map Jonathan had given us and it seemed like we were going the right way; I hoped that he'd made it all right to Dax's castle.

As we wound our way through yet another change in forest my anticipation grew. Would Dax appear as the person in my vision or would he be someone I couldn't recognize? I concluded that I was overthinking this whole encounter and just needed to stay calm before my body warmed up and my dragon decided to show up. Not too much room in here for that to happen.

The road abruptly ended as we rounded a curve and before us loomed a wall of swirling . . . something. Eric stopped the vehicle and we stared at this barrier for a long time. Finally Hector spoke what was on all our minds.

"What the hell is that?" he said leaning out the window.

"Awesome!" cried Sophie and Naomi together leaning forward to see it better.

This barrier was so high I couldn't see the top from inside the SUV. It completely covered the road and seemed to wind around in both directions. It looked as if it were alive.

"Okay, who's the lucky person going out there to check it out?" Jonni said jokingly.

No one said a word. I would have procrastinated but I had to find out what this was. I could hardly contain my excitement and curiosity.

"I'm the leader. I guess I go," I said confidently my hand on the handle. Eric grabbed my arm.

"No you don't. We all go." He had that protector expression on his face again. "This may or may not be Arnos' doing. We need to be cautious." He was right of course. Again.

Just then a stray thought passed across my mind. *It's safe. Go ahead.* I smiled at my father's diligence.

"No. This is Dax's barrier. He just told me so." I looked at Eric as I pulled the handle and opened the door. Eric was at my side in a flash of movement so quick and fluid I almost gasped. I took the hand he offered and exited the SUV.

"It looks like a living thing," I muttered to myself in wonder gazing at it in all directions. I approached it cautiously. It was a magnificent structure, alive but not in the physiological sense. I could feel the energy emanating off it even before I got close—it was humming softly.

Chapter 38

"**W**asn't there only supposed to be three barriers?" I asked over my shoulder, testing the wall with my hand. No one answered, they were too busy exploring, pushing on the exterior but unable to go through it. I felt along the skin of the wall with my palm until my hand melted into it with no effort at all.

"Wow, look what I can do," I said as my whole arm went through the barrier like a knife into butter. I felt a tingling sensation; then suddenly Eric was pulling my arm backwards.

"Be careful," he cautioned. "It could be a trick."

"Don't be silly, my father conjured this as a deterrent to marauders. Please don't ask me how I know; I just do. Why I can penetrate it and no one else can is the mystery."

There was something familiar here even though I couldn't see beyond the barrier. I suddenly felt odd, like I was outside my body. A vision was forming, in broad daylight—*a brilliant light—a voice—a dragon.*

Hector's shout brought me back to reality.

"Over here everyone," he called waving his hand for us to come quick.

We all ran along the barrier to where he stood. I looked around at the others but someone was noticeably missing. I counted heads. There were only five bodies present.

"Okay, where's Naomi?" I asked searching the area.

Sophie looked stricken. "She was right next to me a minute ago. You don't think Arnos got her?" Her eyes started to fill with tears.

"That's what I'm trying to tell you," Hector said. "It's like she vanished into thin air, right here." He was pointing to the barrier.

"How far does this thing go?" Eric asked looking one way then the other along the length of the wall. All of a sudden I could feel his worry and concerned emotion overwhelming me. Finally he'd let down his guard. What a relief.

Hector spoke again, his hand running along its smooth surface. "I've followed it pretty much all the way around in a circle. It's impenetrable."

He poked at the misty wall which only reacted like a balloon to his touch. "That's why I couldn't believe it when Naomi just stepped through the wall. I can't even get my finger to penetrate it." He poked at it again.

"There has to be a reason she can get in," I pondered. "It's obvious I can too." I glanced at Eric, he wasn't happy about that idea. "Don't worry. I have no intention of charging through this until I know more."

Before I even consider going into the unknown to encounter who knows what, I put my senses out to try and detect Arnos. I don't know why I'm even making the effort because he's most likely cloaked anyway. My only hope is he doesn't hurt my team while I'm on the other side of this barrier meeting my father.

Just as I've made the decision to risk it, out of the corner of my eye I see a figure emerging from the mist of the wall to my right. Eric was at my side instantly shielding my body. We both recognized the man at once.

"Jonathan!"

"Welcome to Carolan, Molly. Eric you can stand down now. There's no need for caution here," he said smiling and coming to our side. I saw Eric relax and step aside as Jonathan approached.

"No doubt you have plenty of questions, Molly. Dax awaits you on the other side of this wall and will answer any and all of them," Jonathan said as he clasped my hands and gazed at me fondly. Any fear I had vanished at his touch.

"It's good to see you, Jonathan. I worried about you and prayed you arrived here safely," I said.

"The skies were very friendly. Thank you for your concern. Now, Dax always leaves an opening for those he wants to enter. I noticed your arm found its way through. Find that spot again and enter. He's anxious to see you. I'll stay here with your team and keep them safe since Arnos is lurking out here somewhere; I can feel it." He looked around warily.

I felt Eric behind me as he wrapped his arms around my waist and whispered in my ear.

"Should I be worried or just stand out here being a good guardian while you disappear into the mist?" I turned to face him.

"Well . . . since it won't allow you to come with me just yet, I guess you'll just have to wait with the others, my love. Trust me." I kissed him playfully and gazed into his blazing blues for a few seconds before I stepped backwards, melting into the misty wall.

I felt oddly composed as I stepped through the hazy curtain of Dax's barrier. Emerging onto the other side I found my heart beating wildly at the sight. It was beautiful.

The ground was carpeted in a perfectly manicured lawn that lead up a hill to the most glorious castle I'd ever seen. Along the edges of the trees were a profusion of flowers in every color and hue you could imagine. Believe me, I could imagine a lot. The sky was a brilliant blue with not a cloud in sight; I wondered if this was another of Dax's illusions.

I twirled around to take it all in. As my gaze went back to the hill I saw him. Dax was standing with his arms folded over his chest, smiling at me. My vision exactly. Well without the strange voice . . . so far.

I looked at him in wonder and whispered, "Father?"

The instant I said it he was right there, a few feet in front of me, surveying me up and down, drinking me in. I couldn't take my eyes off of his face; it was my face—my red hair, my emerald green eyes—staring back at me. He was dressed all in black, just like the lord of a manor. My stomach churned, a jellied mass of indecision. What should I do? Should I run and hug him? Or just stand here frozen until he approached. What? I was not thinking clearly at all. I could see his hesitation as well.

Then he spoke. "Hello, Molly," he almost whispered. My heart was pounding in my ears and I felt like I might faint. He came to me and enfolded me with his arms. "Don't be frightened, daughter. I love you. I'll never leave you again. Ever." Without a second thought I wrapped my arms around him and hugged hard, never wanting to let go. This was my father. I'd waited what seemed like an eternity to meet him and here he was.

We stood like that for what seemed like hours, just clinging to each other for dear life. All the longing, all the need to know this man flooded my heart until I couldn't breathe.

He sensed my emotional state and pulled back long enough to look into my already tearing eyes. Grabbing me to his chest again he shuddered.

"I'm sorry for leaving you and your mother when you needed me the most. For a few brief moments I was able to hold your tiny form after your birth but it was never enough. Arnos was the reason I had to flee, to save you and Lidia." He paused and drew back again cupping my face in his hands. There were tears in his eyes. "I miss her so much.

"As do I," I sobbed. I fought to gain control of myself. "I understand now why my mother told me you were dead; to protect me. Mom knew where you were, didn't she?" He nodded as he wiped away my tears. "She never revealed where that was to Arnos. She never gave you up to him no matter how he threatened her. I'm certain he had her killed." He looked over my shoulder thinking.

"He did. My spies in his household informed me of her 'accident' and I almost ran to kill him right then," he said his tone frightening at first, then softening as he looked at me. "But I had to bide my time until you were sent to me and I was sure he would follow you and your team into my trap." He walked a few feet from me and gazed off into the distance toward the castle.

I followed his gaze and saw a tiny figure appear on the crest of the hill. From this distance I couldn't make out who it was at first and then I realized it was Naomi. She stood there a few moments then waved and raced down the hill to us, changing into her collie half way.

I laughed when she came to our father and licked his hand. He scratched her ears and said, "Good dog," playfully. At that she flashed back to Naomi.

"Hey, Sis," she said brightly and gave me a hug. I just flicked a look back and forth between the two of them and shook my head. "I knew it! I knew it! Who is your mother?" I blurted. I was more than curious at this point.

"My mother is Ali. You'll meet her soon. I'd say it's time to show her our home, huh, Father?"

He nodded and took both our hands in his strong ones and we made our way up the hill. As we proceeded I thought about Eric, my team and Jonathan still outside the barrier. I needed to have them here with me where I knew they were safe.

"What about my friends? When will they be allowed through the barrier?" I asked cautiously. I wasn't sure what Dax had in store for us.

He gave me a harsh look and then smiled. "I'm sorry. I didn't mean to frighten you like that, but I just want some time alone with my children before we get down to the business of what to do about Arnos. Your friends are being attended to at this very moment. We'll see them at dinner." That was final. I had to laugh inwardly—it was him—being a father.

As we approached the castle I couldn't help but wonder how old this place was. The rough stone façade was reminiscent of the medieval castles of Europe I'd only seen in books. It looked like it had been here for centuries and yet it was well kept and . . . beautiful. There was even a drawbridge and a moat. Very medieval indeed.

My curiosity peaked I asked, "Did you build this?" I got an amused expression from him.

"Of course. Two hundred years ago to be exact," he said matter-of-factly watching for my reaction out of the corner of his eye. He didn't get the one he expected.

"Oh. It's very impressive," I remarked glancing up at the battlements. "It suits you."

His face exploded into a big grin and he caught me around the waist. We had arrived at the front entrance of what was probably the main hall, the heavy wooden door swung open by a very beautiful woman—who looked exactly like Naomi—her mother. I felt a pang of jealousy that Naomi had her mother and I didn't. I shook the feeling away. Arnos was at fault, not Naomi.

Ali greeted me warmly in a big hug. "Welcome. You must be tired and hungry after that rather long journey. Come inside and I'll have food brought to Dax's study. I know he's anxious to sit and talk with you." She glanced at Dax who smiled affectionately at her. Did I detect some tender connection between them? I'll need to explore this with my father later.

Dax led us down a long hall to his study. Along the way I couldn't help noticing how grand the front entrance hall was with tapestries and shields of all kinds hanging on display. The floor was black marble and a wide staircase loomed up to the next level on the right.

A very large chandelier of crystal hung over a round table with the biggest vase of flowers I'd ever seen. I found myself gaping open mouthed at it as my eyes wandered around to take it all in. And I thought Arnos' home was great.

I heard Naomi giggle behind me. "Neat, huh?"

"What an understatement," I muttered. "That's your mother, right?" I whispered conspiratorially. She nodded cautiously and tensed a little. "She's beautiful, Naomi." She relaxed and took my hand again and we entered the study behind Dax.

This room was just as grand as the hall. Dark wood was everywhere and the walls were painted a rich blue. There were shelves upon shelves of very old books and some rather new ones in a space of their own. His huge, impressive desk stood at an angle in the middle of the room with several chairs, tables and a couch scattered about. This was a man's room.

"Please ladies, have a seat," he said pleasantly as he plunked himself into a chair. Naomi and I made ourselves comfortable on the couch across from him.

Just then Ali returned with servants carrying wine and cheeses, crackers and assorted fruit on silver platters which they set down on the table between us. One of the servants poured the wine and left quietly.

Ali went to stand behind Dax placing her hands on his shoulders. He looked up at her and smiled. I saw the corners of Naomi's mouth flicker slightly. She'd noticed the move as well. Maybe she knows something I don't. We'll see.

"Ali, my love, please leave us alone for a while," he said softly, patting her hand.

"Of course. See you later at dinner." And she left the room and closed the doors gently behind her.

Let the interrogation begin.

Chapter 39

I sat back in my chair and gave him the once over, gathering the courage to ask the one question that had been plaguing me since we started. He raised one eyebrow and silently urged me to say what was on my mind.

"I've been wondering . . . Father . . . hmmm, that still sounds foreign to me. This is very hard, I'm sorry, but something has been bugging me from the beginning when I found out Arnos was keeping secrets." I stumbled and stammered and swallowed the lump in my throat.

"Just say it Molly. We need to be honest with each other. No more secrets," he said calmly taking a sip of his wine.

Naomi was sitting quietly beside me holding my hand. I swallowed and smiled at my sister's intimate gesture. Much different from the first time we'd met at Arnos'. That was creepy. This felt—good.

I faced Dax again. "Okay. I'd like to know what happened between you and Arnos that made you leave us. It must have been something horrible to make you run away from your family. And tell me about the Krystal and its story. No secrets." I was almost breathless at this point. My mouth felt pasty and I grabbed my glass and took a drink.

Dax had been staring at me attentively, seeming to hang on to every word I'd said. Sadness crossed his face and he didn't speak for a few moments gazing at the floor between our chairs.

"When Arnos and I were boys we were very competitive, in everything. As the time approached for our eighteenth birthday, we had to decide who would be the first to go immortal." He noticed my surprised expression.

"Oh, you don't know do you. Arnos and I are fraternal twins. I'm the oldest by several minutes so of course I insisted on going first; he agreed reluctantly and clearly had other plans. On the appointed day my father was the one to administer the Elixir to me. We had prepared anxiously and he and I retired to a special room for the ceremony. We were very formal in those days.

"I took the Elixir and waited for the effects to come. Nothing happened for two hours and I looked at my father in horror as he shook his head sadly. 'Sometimes it doesn't work' he said setting the chalice down and leaving the room. I was mortified and stayed in my room for three days, not speaking to anyone. On the fourth day I emerged to find out that Arnos had completed the transformation. At that point I was furious. I confronted him and accused him of rigging my Elixir to fail. All I got from him was a smirk and 'Oh, well'."

He stopped for a drink of wine. His anger was still evident in the way he clenched his fists and leaned forward. He wasn't finished.

"I went to my father and pled my case. At first he wouldn't believe me and waved me off. So I went and had my cup analyzed by a local alchemist I was friendly with. He told me the liquid in the chalice was simply red wine. I dragged him home to talk to my father and *then* he was convinced of my brother's deceit. Arnos was punished and never forgot who had caused it."

He stopped and looked at us, mesmerized by his story.

"Go on. This is getting interesting," I urged him.

"I know this isn't an answer to your question. I just wanted to preface that answer to let you see what kind of man he was and continues to be. He persisted in his cruelty to me and my friends for over a century after that. I discovered my abilities as a dragon and telepath, among other things, when I finally was immortal.

"The Krystal came to me quite by accident one day when I met a sorcerer in our village. He recognized my dragon ability without me telling him and told me there were others in the world that were being persecuted and hunted for what they were. Even though no one had tried to kill me as a dragon I was intrigued by the Krystal's power. He told me it was the gateway into a land where dragons could live safely and prosper. Only I and my firstborn could handle the stone and that one day I would know what to do.

"I didn't believe him at first and thought maybe he was trying to trick me; until he took me into that land and showed me otherwise. This is why I had to leave with the Krystal. Arnos found out about it and was determined to have it so he could destroy the gateway forever, trapping us all here to be hunted to extinction. Your mother understood, Molly. She told me to go, that you'd be safe." He stopped and took a sip of wine.

I looked at him questioningly.

"I know you're skeptical about this, I can see it in your eyes, but I assure you I speak the truth," he added.

I had been on the edge of my seat listening to his tale with Naomi gripping my hand tightly and sat back pondering what this meant for us.

He had sacrificed to save my mother and me.

"You and Mom communicated telepathically, didn't you? I know now that some of the times I thought she was having a vision she was talking to you because she would laugh and reassure me everything was going to be all right."

He sat back and looked at me knowingly. "Yes, we did. It was the only safe way, what with Arnos nosing around and harassing her all the time. As you've seen I can talk quite nicely with you as well. It comes with the dragon ability."

Naomi and I looked at each other but neither of us said a word. Finally I got up and wandered around the room running my fingers lightly over the spines of his books and gazing at the paintings on the walls, all the while feeling his eyes following me.

"Can I see the Krystal?" I inquired. I hoped he wouldn't be angry at me for asking so bluntly.

He chuckled. "You're very direct; I like that. It's in this room. See if you can find it."

I turned and frowned at him. "Really? In this room? In plain sight?" I said incredulously. I glanced at Naomi who just shrugged her shoulders and gave me a 'heck if I know' look.

"Obviously I'm not going to leave it out on a table for all to see. It's hidden away in a safe place. Use your senses and you'll feel its power." He sat back in his chair with an air of amusement.

I closed my eyes and concentrated on what I thought it might look like. A faint buzzing started in my head as a vision began to form and crystallize. I was still in this room but my father and Naomi weren't here. A blue light was emanating from one of the book shelves high up on my right. It seemed to be pulsating in the same rhythm as the buzzing.

I walked slowly toward the light; it was getting brighter. Since it was on a shelf higher than I could reach I looked around for a ladder or chair to stand on so I could get to it. A library ladder was a few feet from where I stood and I pushed it along so it was under the area of the blue light.

My anticipation grew as I climbed quickly to the shelf that was aglow; there before me was a plain wooden box with the image of a dragon on top that pulsated with the blue light. I stared at it fascinated. I touched it tentatively and when I didn't get shocked and it felt cool to touch, I lifted it gently and descended the ladder.

"Well done, Molly!" brought me out of the vision and I nearly dropped the box as I startled.

"Boy, that was fast!" cried Naomi. I stood holding the box away from my body like it was a nasty animal.

"What do I do with it now?" I asked Dax who sat there like a proud papa. He stood up and took the box from me and laid it on the table between us.

"Have a look, but don't touch the Krystal. There's no telling where you'd end up if you did," he said a wicked smirk on his face. He seemed to love playing games. Reminded me of Hector.

The object was throwing off light from a dozen or so tiny holes in the sides and top. I gingerly unlatched the lid and opened the box slowly, half expecting something to jump out at me. If someone had said BOO! I would have been on the ceiling.

Inside was the Krystal in all its glory, an oblong piece of blue stone about the size of my hand that appeared to have no power source except its own and glowed like a crystal vase in the sun.

"How can you leave this where it could be easily stolen?" I said. I really wanted to touch it; the stone seemed to call to me it was so mesmerizing.

"No one can touch it except you and me. When the time is right we'll lead our kind into the new land." He looked reverently at the Krystal and then at me. I now knew why I was here.

I thought about this next question before asking it. "Could someone gain entrance without us knowing once the portal is opened?" Dax gave a slight shudder.

"It's very possible that could happen. That's why Arnos must not gain access to this Krystal. With his ability for high energy bursts he could destroy the dragon world and close the portal forever . . . without regret. He's that jealous."

I looked questioningly at my father. "What would happen if someone else touches it?"

"You don't want to know."

Okaaay, we'll leave it at that. I heaved a heavy sigh and closed the box. Outside in the hall there was a heated argument going on.

"I'm sorry but you can't go in there right now. Master Dax is talking to his daughters." The voice was unfamiliar, a servant perhaps.

"I need to see Molly right now!" It was Eric's voice.

"Calm down, Eric. They'll only be a little longer, and then you'll see her and we can all go to supper," I heard Hector say soothingly.

Seconds later the door to the study flew open and Eric stomped in and stopped dead in the middle of the room when he saw us sitting staring at him.

"Oh, I'm sorry sir, but I needed to see that Molly was safe." He gave a little head bow. Now that was unusual for him; very formal and respectful.

"And why wouldn't she be safe with me?" Dax said.

I stood up and went to Eric's side. I placed my hand on his chest. His heart was pounding. "I'm fine as you can see, my love," I said gently. "Father, this is Eric McGuire, my protector and fiancé."

"A pleasure to meet you sir. My father says great things about you in the council. Of course Arnos doesn't." This was a side of Eric I'd never seen before. He fairly oozed adoration.

"You've made quite an entrance, young man. I should be annoyed at the intrusion but I guess I can't be since you are apparently betrothed to my daughter." He gave me a quick glance. "Molly never mentioned that." He eyed Eric warily.

"The subject never came up. I'm sorry," I said.

He looked at us sternly and held his hand out to shake Eric's. "I do hope you're sincere about this. I'd be very disappointed if you hurt her." It sounded like a feeble threat and I saw the corners of his mouth curl into a smile. Eric stood tall and shook Dax's hand firmly.

"I've never been surer about anything in my life." He gave me a sly smile and winked.

"Hmmm. Well then, shall we go ready ourselves for dinner? I'm famished," Dax said after a few awkward moments as he started to herd us out the door. "I'm anxious to meet the rest of your team."

"Uh, Father, have you forgotten something? The Krystal?" I reminded him. With a flick of his hand the box disappeared back onto the shelf, the glow gone. I raised my eyebrows and he just chuckled.

Chapter 40

After being shown to our rooms, we freshened up and dressed in more formal clothes our hosts provided. Mine was a pale green gown with matching sandals that fit me perfectly. I wondered how they knew our sizes. I wore my hair down flowing over my shoulders.

When I emerged from my room, there stood Eric in a black suit, his crisp, white shirt unbuttoned at the neck, the coat long and fitted. He took my breath away he was so handsome. His face lit up when he saw me.

"You're gorgeous, Moll," he said almost in a whisper. His eyes wandered over every inch of me and brought back those tingles I loved so much. My body was vibrating when he came and touched my cheek. A soft kiss followed and I fought the urge to drag him back into the room and have my way with him. That would have to wait until later; my stomach growled in protest and we both laughed at the interruption of our Moment.

He took my arm in his, "Shall we?"

We descended the long staircase and entered the formal dining room to find our friends already seated at the very long table. It was as opulent as Arnos' but I felt a whole lot safer here in the company of friends and family. Everyone looked so elegant in their formal wear . . . even Hector who squirmed and looked uncomfortable as hell. He was most comfortable in fighting leathers and knives. I smirked his way.

Dinner was . . . interesting. The food was fabulous and plentiful. Ali proved to an excellent hostess, making everyone comfortable and ensuring we were well fed. I started to introduced Hector and Jonni to Dax and surprise, surprise they just happened to be old friends from eons ago; something they had failed to tell me, on purpose I'm sure.

They had fought together in many battles and chattered on and on about those glorious days. Hector regaled us with such riotous stories, I thought I'd split my dress laughing. Dax was amazed with Jonni's miraculous recovery; he praised Naomi for her skill until I could see she wanted to change the subject. She was a woman of mystery and humility sometimes.

Dax was taken with Sophie's story. I had introduced her as Sophie Barger but she quickly corrected me. "I'm Sophie Simpole, my real name." He gave her a smile and told her how pretty she was and how brave she had been. She blushed and giggled.

"Tell us about the Krystal, Dax. Why is Arnos so hell bent on having it?" Hector asked over after-dinner drinks. We had retired into his study, making ourselves comfy.

Dax sat quietly for a few moments savoring his brandy.

"It's a gateway into a world where those of us with dragon tendencies can live in peace. It controls the entrance and hides that entrance from evildoers like my brother. He's been trying to gain control of it for decades. He hated me so much. He eliminates those who pose a threat to his mission or who are inconsequential, without a bit of conscience. It was with regret that I had to leave my family and safeguard the Krystal." He looked at me sadly. "Arnos found out that Molly and I were the only ones with the ability to open that portal and help the others to enter."

"Why didn't you take us with you?" I asked him quietly. It was important for me to know.

I saw him hesitate for a moment to consider his answer. "I thought it best to leave you behind so he wouldn't pursue me for a while. He needed to see how vulnerable you were to his plans. There's no way I would have left you and your mother otherwise. I was sure you'd be safe, with Lidia and me communicating regularly. Little did I know that he would kill her as a vengeful means to get to me."

He gazed at his glass and I saw a mist in his eyes.

"Father, Arnos chose this fight and I intend to give him a good one. He thinks he knows me and assumes I'm some weak little girl, incapable of his kind of violence. He's wrong. My friends will attest to my ability to scare him, even if it was only a moments warning. I felt his angry emotions. I can defeat him, with your assistance, of course." I was standing in my best defiant mode. I could feel my eyes glowing.

"You're your father's daughter," said Hector. "I myself love a good fight. So what's the plan?"

"First can we show them the Krystal they've risked their lives for?" I said to Dax.

"Absolutely. Do you want to do the honors?" He gestured for me to go ahead.

I concentrated hard on the box containing the Krystal so I could retrieve it. Instead of it glowing like it did before, it slowly floated down to my waiting hands.

"Did I do that?" I said my eyes aglow.

"I believe you did," said Dax grinning broadly. "It wasn't me this time."

I laid the box on the table between us again and opened it. A crowd formed around me as everyone stood to gaze at the object of our journey. Right on cue the Krystal started to glow a soft blue and I heard a gasp or two from my team. Then . . .

"This is what all the fuss is about, this tiny rock?" Hector chided from behind Dax.

Dax's jaw tightened.

"This 'rock' as you've so aptly put it Hector, is the key to the dragons' existence. You should be glad I'm not going to kill you for that comment, my friend." He turned and glared at Hector.

"Whoa, I'm only kidding," Hector replied holding his hands up in front of him. He looked at Naomi who gave him a scowl.

Eric had been unusually quiet throughout dinner and even now after my eloquent speech and Hector's faux-pas. I looked at him when Hector was finished getting his foot out of his mouth. He stood apart from the others looking out the window at the darkness and seemed sullen and distant again. I moved to his side.

"What's bothering you Eric?" I said touching his arm lightly. He flinched but didn't move his arm, his eyes far away.

"I need to know where my family is Moll and if they're still alive. If you and Dax kill Arnos how will we ever find out?" he said, his eyes pleading.

Big girls don't cry, but I sure wanted to. How could I ever face him if his family perished? I did not want to find out.

Dax saw our exchange and came over and placed his hand on Eric's shoulder. "I can guarantee you Eric that nothing will happen to your family. My spies will find them and keep them safe."

That didn't seem to convince Eric.

Though he gave Dax a nod, I could see the doubt in his face. His emotions were hidden from me again; the wall was up and solid. I leaned my head against his shoulder.

I sighed. It was getting late and I could feel the fatigue taking over after the wine and anxiety. I found myself yawning.

"Maybe it's best if we get some rest and gather for a strategy meeting in the morning," I said stretching.

Everyone else agreed and said their goodnights. I floated the Krystal back to its resting place and took Eric's hand. Dax gave me a hug and whispered in my ear.

"Meet me outside the main doors at first light. There's something I need to show you."

My head nodded. His warmth lit me up as he held me longer than he should. I didn't know why but I felt safe. Eric still had my hand in his and I could feel him tense. I pushed away from my father and smiled at him. He turned and disappeared into the hall without another word.

Eric and I stood gazing at each other for a moment more before ascending the stairs to his room.

"I don't care if your father doesn't approve of us sleeping together, I need you here with me tonight," he said gathering me to his chest. We both sighed as another kind of warmth surrounded us.

"I'm sure he's not that old fashioned," I whispered against his lips. "Kiss me."

Somehow the lights turned out . . . and well, you know what happens next.

Chapter 41

In the morning I arose quietly and left Eric sleeping soundly. He looked more peaceful than he'd been in a long time. He needed the rest so I tiptoed out the door and back to my room to change clothes having no idea what my father had in mind today.

It looked like no one else was awake yet, the place was so quiet. The front doors were bolted shut and I had some difficulty opening them to get out. You'd think Dax would have left them open for me. Oh, no. Make me work.

Once outside I didn't see him anywhere near the front of the castle. The structure was so massive I wasn't going to run around trying to find him. Maybe he wasn't even out of bed yet. There's a thought.

I was just thinking of going back inside when a great shadow appeared against the building. I whirled around to see a huge red dragon float lightly to the ground in front of me. In a blinding flash my father transformed back into human form.

"Good morning, Molly," he said boldly. "Hope I didn't startle you too much."

"It's the first time I've seen you in dragon form in the flesh," I said wide-eyed. "My visions didn't do you justice. You're magnificent. I have no idea what I look like when I transform but I'm sure I'm not half as grand."

"Oh, yes you are." He gave me a wicked grin.

"So you've seen me before?" I said. He gave no reply but whistled sharply.

Two beautiful black horses came galloping over the hill and stopped in front of their master. He rubbed their noses and cooed at them like they were children giving each of them a sugar cube treat. They were both saddled and raring to go.

"Do you ride?" he asked eyeing me closely.

"A little," I answered still watching the horses. I was glad I'd worn my jeans and boots because before I knew it I was in the saddle and we were trotting into the countryside.

The rolling hills around the castle were covered in wildflowers and colorful bushes I'd never seen before. I lifted my face to the rising sun and sniffed the air. It had a heavenly fragrance. We headed into the forest, the horses moving knowingly along a well-worn path until coming upon an open area the size and shape of an arena.

It was bordered on all sides by tall cedars except for two entrances on the ends. There was a carpet of mowed grass over the entire area, a low lying mist covering it. It was peaceful right now. We moved through the trees to stop at the periphery.

"I use this as a fighting field for my men to practice. This is where you and I will meet Arnos," Dax said throwing his arms out wide in a grandiose gesture. "We even have rules."

I really didn't think Arnos was going to play by the rules.

"And where will my team be during this encounter?" I asked pointedly and looking sideways at Dax.

"Very close. They can be at our side in an instant. It's me he wants, you know?" he said.

"Oh, I disagree. He definitely wants to destroy us all; to have no one in his way. We're all toast," I answered.

I glanced around the arena getting my bearings. There was plenty of room to maneuver as far as I could see if I was to transform. A plan was developing in my head. It had to work.

I kicked the horse into a cantor to the center of the field. Dax watched me for a minute or two before riding to my side.

"I need to get the rest of my team out here so we can figure out where they'll be able to hide."

Dax chuckled. "You're over thinking this. Your Eric has the perfect hiding place within himself. Arnos cannot see through

Eric's shield. Your team can be in the middle of the field and he won't suspect a thing."

"How do you know about his shield? Wait, don't answer that. I'll bet Jonathan told you." He didn't answer me but took off galloping across the field toward the trees at the far end.

"Wait!" I shouted and kicked my horse into action after him. When I caught up to him he was slowing down and turned the horse to face me.

"You have a great gift Molly. Eric has a special ability that he hasn't even fully tapped into yet. Your team is powerful. We cannot fail," he said emphatically. "Let's go home. I could eat a horse." His horse shook its head. "Sorry Balco. I would never eat you or Miklo." The horses threw their heads back and whinnied.

He gave a war whoop and we took off through the forest.

Chapter 42

I found out later that Jonathan had returned to his home and daughter. Apparently he was not staying to face Arnos with us. I was grateful for his help and glad he was safe. My only regret was not having said goodbye.

After breakfast I felt the need to gather my team together for a strategy meeting. I hadn't seen much of Hector, Jonni or Sophie since arriving here and wanted to spend as much time as I could with all of them before the big day. They had been lively and fun at the meal but I could feel the tension simmering in the air around us.

We retired to the sunny atrium I had discovered the night before.

They all stared at me standing there like I was some sort of magic act about to begin. I gave them a flourish of a bow which made them burst into laughter. Tension relieved.

"Okay, enough. Let's get down to business," I started. "I've been to the area where we'll be facing Arnos. It's a humongous field the size of the training facility we had at Arnos' house. Maybe bigger. Anyway, it's lined with tall cedars on all sides with two distinct entrances at either end. I've devised a plan . . ."

"Ahem. Does this involve bloody fighting?" Hector said seriously. "Because I'm more than ready."

"Let me continue please, H, before you get your sword in a twist." His mouth twitched at the corners trying not to smile.

Before I had a chance to say anything else Dax came dashing into the room, took hold of my shoulders and looked me straight in the eye. The fierceness in his eyes scared me.

"What is it?" I squeaked. He relaxed and loosened his grip.

"Sorry, I didn't mean to alarm you. But Arnos is here and camped outside the barrier. My men inform me there are more than fifty troops with him. Game on."

I laughed despite my fear because I'd never heard him use modern slang before. He didn't even have TV.

"Well, that changes things doesn't it?" I huffed. He let me go.

I looked at the others and sat down next to Jonni. He put his arm around me and lightly kissed my temple. "Like he said—Game on!"

We sat and I outlined my plan. Hector and Jonni shared an evil grin and snickers as I talked while Naomi rubbed her hands together in delight. Dax approved of my strategy and said his men, who numbered eighty or more, would be available to supplement our numbers.

Eric was . . . well . . . Eric, skeptical as ever.

"I'm not sure I can do that, Moll," he said. "It's not like the small operations I've been doing."

"Eric, Dax told me you haven't even tapped into your true power yet. Think about what you've achieved so far in a relatively short time. You've managed to get us here safely, I know you can stretch much farther than any of us can imagine. I have total faith in you." I tried to sound encouraging.

Dax was nodding his head. "She's right Eric. I've felt a great power surge since you've come and I know it's your ability that's causing it. Your father has it and now you do."

Eric gave Dax a surprised look. I assume he had no idea his father was so talented.

"Practice, man. I'll help you," Hector said.

We all will," added Jonni.

I could feel Eric's mind opening up to me. He was finally excited. I felt the glee jumping around inside me.

"All right. When do we start?" he said finally.

"Hot damn, gonna be fun!" Hector whooped as he picked up Naomi, kissed her and spun her around.

Dax glared at him. Boy, he was way too protective of his progeny. Did he even know that they were together? I guessed not; maybe I should tell him so he doesn't go and kill H.

"Father," I said quietly. "They've been seeing a lot of each other these last few weeks. Wish them well . . . please. You have to let us be happy."

He gave me a look that said *I know, but let me play my fatherly part and protest*. At least that would be my interpretation. A hint of a smile crossed his face.

"I've only had my daughters around for less than two days and I find you both have found men I admire. How is that possible?" he said shaking his head.

"Get used to it. We may have more surprises up our sleeves for you," I answered and added, "Would it be all right if I spoke to you privately later?"

"Of course. I'll be out in the field for a while confirming the reports of Arnos. Find me this evening." He kissed my cheek and excused himself, leaving as abruptly as he'd entered.

Hector came up to me after Dax left and whispered in my ear.

"Was he mad at me for my flagrant display of affection?"

"Furious," I lied trying to keep a straight face. "You'd better watch yourself. He has a very big sword." I tried unsuccessfully to stifle a laugh.

"Aaargh! Don't do that to me, you little imp." He playfully pushed me and walked away.

We finished discussing how Eric was going to protect us all in our confrontation with Arnos and the boys went out to practice with Dax's soldiers.

Naomi, Sophie and I decided we needed some girly time and headed to my room for that. Not having had a sister growing up it was so much fun to gossip and do the sisterly things I'd missed.

Naomi and I found ourselves laughing over stupid stuff as if we'd known each other forever. Sophie was the little sister and was so animated and silly we couldn't stop laughing at her antics. I was surprised when Naomi confided in me about her feelings for Hector. She doesn't often share.

"I really like Hector, Molly," She asked shyly. "Do you think he's too old for me?"

"Hector is old only by immortal standards. In his heart he's young and that's what counts. Dax has kind of given his stamp of approval since H so blatantly showed how he feels about you. If I were you, I'd have Hector tell Father his intentions."

"Do you think he'll approve. He can be pretty stubborn sometimes and still views things from his old perspective."

"It certainly couldn't hurt to try. I believe he's trying hard not to color his decisions with old world ideas. He's only had me around for a short time and Eric and I will keep him busy for a while."

Sophie was sitting quietly listening to our conversation intently and suddenly had a sad look on her face.

"What's the matter Soph?" I said.

"Does this mean I won't be able to live with you Naomi? I mean if you and Hector were to get married, what will happen to me?" she pleaded quietly.

"Oh, no, Sophie. You'll stay with us," Naomi said hugging her tight. "No one will ever take you away."

"That's a relief!" Sophie sighed.

Just then there was a sharp knock on the door. When I opened it there stood the three boys with the best looking ice cream cones ever dripping on the floor.

"Oooh, ice cream," cried Sophie.

"Thought you girls would like some afternoon refreshments," said Jonni handing us each a cone and a napkin.

We sat and chatted as we ate, ice cream dribbling down our chins. Eric was excited to show me some new tricks he'd learned after we'd finished and Hector regaled us with the exciting things Eric came up with to deal with the opposing army. Their tricks seemed to be something I was sure would work when the time came to confront Arnos and should scare the pants off the soldiers.

The rest of the afternoon went pretty fast. Eric practiced some more and surprised me by coming from behind and pulling me into the shield bubble, covering me with kisses on the neck. I wondered out loud if this is what he intended to do to the soldier he'd capture. He laughed and whispered, "It surely wouldn't be as exciting as this, my love", and dissolved the bubble in a pop.

That evening I searched for my father and found him in his study writing furiously in a journal.

"I see you keep a journal too," I said absently as I wandered around the room. "I've tried to keep a record of this journey myself."

"It helps to clear my head to write down my observations and thoughts." He looked up from his scribbling.

I stopped in front of his desk. "Do you think Arnos will play by the rules?" I asked staring into his gorgeous green eyes.

His eyes tightened and the disgusted smile said a lot. "I doubt my brother has ever played by the rules. He makes his own as he goes along and mows down anything or anyone in his way," he answered staring back at me. "He needs to be stopped."

I went quiet, measuring his words.

"What's going to happen once Arnos is no longer a threat?" I asked gazing at a small statue on his desk. I recognized who it was immediately . . . Hector in full battle dress.

He considered my question for a heartbeat or two.

"Hopefully we'll be able to live peacefully in our own world. The people—mortals—of this world are backward in their ways, always assuming that the supernatural beings are the enemy. I wish we could show them otherwise; let them see we pose no threat to their lives or way of life. There are hundreds of us who live amongst them and share their everyday lives and they are unaware of our presence."

He paused to take a breath and sigh. "It's difficult to change hundreds of years of fear when immortals like Arnos kill without remorse and keep the image of threat alive."

"He's a Keeper. Hasn't any other council member done anything about his activities? Surely someone must know something," I said.

"Many have tried, including Eric's father, to no avail. Arnos has many of the members fooled into believing his way is the right way. As you can see he has unsavory methods to silence the ones who get in his way."

I thought about Peter and Eric's family locked away somewhere by my uncle and wanted to spit nails.

My dragon was rolling around inside me, warming me, wanting release.

"Eric has his shield ready for the fight. He's anxious to use it," I said suddenly. Dax gave me a curious look.

"That was an abrupt change of subject," he said.

"My dragon self is angry. It was the only way to curb the urge to fill your study with it."

"Then let's take flight and let it have its way." He stood up and came around the desk to my side taking my hand.

He urged me out the door and into the waning daylight. I could hardly contain my excitement. We transformed into our carbon copy dragons and flew high above the clouds, dipping and soaring like two sparrows playing tag.

Dax talked to me as we wandered in and out the clouds, saying soothing things and reassuring me that all would be resolved soon. I wanted to believe it . . . needed to believe it. We discussed many things—my mother, his attraction to Ali, Eric and I, Hector's attraction to Naomi. No secrets.

The warmth of the air on my wings gave me peace again and I knew I'd be able to face my upcoming challenge with renewed energy and awareness.

Soon it was time to go back to the castle and rest, to see Eric. We lightly touched down outside the castle walls and after transforming, walked inside hand in hand.

Hector was waiting in the front hall for Dax a serious look on his face and the two of them disappeared into the study and closed the door. He was actually taking my advice. I'd have to tease him later. I headed off to find Eric.

Chapter 43

Two days went by without a word passing between the two opposing camps, them and us. We busied ourselves with practice and strategy meetings; I could see the tension was rising in all of us, yet my father remained cool and calm. Where were all these rules Dax had spoken of? I would have thought one side or the other would have made the first move. What did I know?

Then on the morning of the third day I woke up with a pounding headache. I stumbled to the bathroom, turned on the cold water and splashed my face. I felt like my head was going to explode.

Suddenly the pain vanished and a vision replaced it.

I was standing in a large field, alone, in full battle dress. A few yards from me stood Arnos grinning ridiculously, his arm raised toward me. A bolt of red energy emanated from his fingertips.

"Prepare to die, Molly Fyre!" he shouted in a voice so terrifying I cringed.

Out of the corner of my eye I caught sight of a figure moving toward me in a blur of movement.

"Eric, no!" I cried watching the scene unfold in slow motion.

Eric leaped in front of me just as Arnos let loose with lightening. The energy hit Eric square in the chest and he fell on the ground in front of me with a sickening thud.

I couldn't speak or even scream. Eric lay there unconscious at my feet. I heard a ferocious growl and then realized it was my own voice; my dragon was about to be unleashed.

I was standing at the bathroom sink, my hands gripping the edge of the counter, sweating and breathing hard. My heart was pounding in my chest. At least the headache was gone. Thank goodness.

That scenario was not going to happen.

I ran back to the bedroom to make sure Eric was where I'd left him . . . in my bed. He was. My heart was still beating fast. Was I seeing the future or just something that possibly could happen? How could I change the outcome? These visions were perplexing and again I wished that my mother was here to guide me.

I needed to talk to Dax. Dressing as quietly as I could, I crept downstairs to find him. The light was on in his study and I saw him sitting on the couch with a book in his hand through the half open door.

"Father?" I said quietly, "Can we talk?"

He turned around to look at me where I stood just inside the door.

His face was passive, his eyes moist and he didn't seem to know what to say.

"Is everything all right?" I said. I moved into the room closer to where he sat. He turned back to the book and flipped the page.

"I'm not sure," he replied slowly. "I had the strangest dream last night. Your mother came to me and told me to be tolerant. I have no idea what that means." He looked puzzled.

"I had a dream about her too, about a week ago. She was very vague to me also; but then she was always talking in riddles and never answered my questions directly." I inched closer to him gazing over his shoulder.

It was then I saw he was looking through an album of pictures. Most were of Naomi but there were some of me and Mom. She must have sent those to him showing me growing up.

I sat down next to him and we gazed at each other sadly.

"We mustn't grieve for her anymore Molly. She wouldn't want us to cloud our minds with sorrow." He ran a hand over a picture of my mother.

"I know. These pictures show us all laughing and having fun. It's how I want to remember her." My tears dripped down my face and into my lap.

Dax put his arm around my shoulders and we sat in silence for a long time, each in our own thoughts.

"Now, what did you want to talk about?" he said placing the album on the table.

I wiped the tears from my face and cleared my throat.

"Just now I had another vision after waking up with a throbbing headache. In it Arnos knocks Eric out with one of his energy bolts right in front of me. He was aiming at me." I paused. "Am I going to be that vulnerable? And do I have to worry about Eric getting zapped, or worse, killed?"

He stood and sighed as he walked to the window, his hands clasped behind him. "No to both." He turned to face me.

"It's time you knew the truth, Molly." He took a breath. "My brother doesn't know this but you are the fifth generation of dragons. A prophesy written centuries ago states that the female dragon will defeat the male sorcerer in the fifth generation of our line . . . 'And she shall eat the sorcerer's lightning'. My father knew this and left the documents for me to find after his death.

"You . . . my lovely daughter, are that dragon and Arnos is the sorcerer. It has been put into motion with your immortality change."

My head was spinning. I had no words to express my astonishment at this latest disclosure; this explained so much. Suddenly my headache was back, big time. What was happening to me? I rubbed my temples and closed my eyes against the pain.

I felt Dax's warm hands on my shoulders, massaging. The headache eased slightly.

"The time is drawing near to confront our foe. Your headache is a sign that the dragon senses this. I'll teach you a technique to help you cope," he whispered.

His voice was hypnotic as he talked me through the technique. My headache was gone in a few minutes and I had a new clarity to my thinking. It was as if I was coming out of a dream state into reality and I was seeing the world through new eyes. It felt . . . liberating.

I found my voice and stood to face my father.

"That's amazing. All of it is amazing. I never dreamed my life would be so important. Mother never mentioned any of this to me, I'm guessing to keep me from confronting Arnos too soon," I said.

"She and I agreed that would be the best course of action. I needed to make sure you were ready. Now you are."

"Are you sure Arnos knows nothing of this prophesy? His actions so far indicate he might not, but what if he's testing us? What if he thinks we won't follow through with what it says?" I asked.

"I'm very sure. He wasn't living at home when I found the papers. I hid them immediately in this castle and never let him know. His attention centers on obtaining the Krystal now and he won't stop until he destroys it."

I wandered over to the window and gazed out. The sky was Robin's egg blue and a soft breeze blew gently against the curtains, the fragrance of flowers wafting in. It looked so peaceful I didn't want to think of what I was about to do to my uncle. The question that had brought me here this morning seemed trivial now. I asked it anyway.

"About these rules you mentioned. What exactly are they and how do we proceed?" I was really pumped for action now.

"The rules are simple actually," he began. "The one to make the first move is the aggressor. The playing field is the choice of the other party. And—there simply are no more rules. I've ordered the barrier to dissolve and that should make Arnos happy. I'm certain my brother will contact us soon; he always enjoyed being the first to attack."

Did I detect a bit of sarcasm in that remark?

His face betrayed the conflict inside him. Even though Dax said he hated Arnos, I knew it pained him to think of ending his life. His next remark confirmed that.

"I won't enjoy destroying my brother," he said unhappily. "If only he had chosen a different path in life, we wouldn't be here like this, planning his execution."

"Something evil must have been festering inside him for centuries to make him so bitter and hateful," I said. "Hector had the same feelings of regret when he had to confront his brother. That encounter ended badly."

"I remember him telling me about it decades ago. You will have the same emotions. Don't let it consume you."

I didn't plan on it.

We gathered ourselves to join the others for breakfast.

"May I inform my team of my new status as executioner?" I said cheekily.

He gave me a grim look. "I do believe you're relishing this a bit too much Daughter. However I do think they need to know the truth of your role in this event," he said taking my arm in his and ushering me to the outdoor terrace.

Chapter 44

As Dax and I walked outside onto the terrace the atmosphere changed from laughter to serious looks at us. Eric stood up and pulled out the empty chair next to him. Dax actually escorted me around the table and handed me off to Eric.

They exchanged nods and Dax strode off to sit at the head of the table just like the lord of the manor he was. When he was seated I gave him a devious smile and winked.

A servant served our meal of poached eggs, crisp bacon, toast and tea.

Hector sat across the table from me and was watching me and Dax closely, swiveling his head back and forth. I smiled my best Cheshire cat smile at him as I chewed and he kept looking quizzically at the two of us as we exchanged sly glances.

I was really having fun with this when Dax made an announcement.

"I believe Molly has something to tell you all. Molly?" he said seriously.

I looked surprised. "What?" I said innocently. "Oh, yes."

Allowing the suspense to build up a little I paused. Adjusting my napkin in my lap I decided to just blurt out the story.

"It appears that I'm prophesied to be Arnos' executioner. As the fifth generation dragon I've been chosen to carry this out. Don't get me wrong, I truly don't want this role, but something has to be done about Arnos' reign of terror my father says has been going on for centuries. He kills for no other reason than to gain power. He killed my mother because she wouldn't give away Dax's location and now thinks I am willingly going to hand over the Krystal so he can destroy it as well.

"I wish there was another way to deal with him that would be less . . . final but there isn't. As Dax has told us, Arnos carries grudges way too long. Our confrontation is fast approaching. Dax has lowered the barrier to lure Arnos to us so we should be hearing from him very soon according to rule number one."

I gazed around at my team. Some had their mouths open, Hector sat with a satisfied smirk. He was so ready for a fight.

"About time," he muttered.

Sophie sat solemnly beside Naomi thinking about Peter most likely. I guessed she would love to be in the midst of the fray to exact her revenge but in reality she would be nowhere near it, safely tucked away here in the castle with Ali.

Next to me Eric took my hand and squeezed it firmly. "Well said, Molly." I glanced at Dax and he gave me a pleased nod.

In my heart I was afraid of my feelings. Being angry and vindictive was not in my nature; so where was all this coming from? How had I come to be vengeful and hateful?

I needed my mom. I suddenly felt the need to be somewhere else and try and raise her in a vision. Why couldn't I do that spontaneously, like just think of her and there she was.

"Father, can I borrow Miklo for a while? I need to clear my head," I said standing and pushing my chair back.

"Of course, anything you want," he said. "I'll have him saddled immediately. You should have someone go with you though. It's too dangerous to go alone."

I looked down at Eric. "I'll take my protector," I said. Eric stood beside me and we left to go change clothes.

"Thank you, father," I called over my shoulder.

Eric and I mounted the horses outside the front gate and sped off to the east of the estate. The air was warming up and I let the breeze flip my hair around behind me. Eric rode silently beside me stealing glances every now and then. I'm sure he was wondering why I was so distant. I couldn't tell him I wanted to conjure my mother, not yet.

We rode for about half an hour and reached a stand of oak trees where I stopped and dismounted. I could feel the energy in this area like static on my arms. The wind whispered through the trees and they swayed gently back and forth. Eric tied the horses close to some tall grasses so they could graze.

This was the place. There was magic here.

"Eric, I need to talk to my mother. I know that sounds crazy but I believe I can make her appear in this spot."

"It doesn't sound crazy at all. How about I wait over there by that tree and give you some room," he said walking a few yards away and sitting on the ground under the tree.

"Thanks," I replied, finding my own spot on the ground and sitting cross-legged, my hands on my knees.

Closing my eyes I cleared my mind, concentrating on the sound of birdsong and crickets chirping. I envisioned my mother's face in front of me with her beautiful golden hair and blue eyes.

"Mom, if you're out there can you reveal yourself to me. I really need your help right now," I murmured softly.

The energy in the air started to swirl and felt like pins and needles on my arms. I felt light and spaced out and then . . . there she was in my head.

"Open your eyes, Molly," she said. "I'm here."

When I did, she was kneeling in front of me, her hands raised to my face. Her soft touch on my cheeks brought tears to my eyes.

"What's so urgent my child?" she whispered wiping the tears away.

I reached out to touch her and she was solid. We embraced and I wept into her hair.

"How can you be so real? In my other vision you were misty."

"Sometimes I just can. But I'm more concerned with what's bothering you, my love." She pulled back to look at me.

I struggled to gain control and stop crying long enough to ask her advice.

"Mother, I'm in the middle of a conflict I never started and I'm confused. I need your help to get through this."

Her face softened into a gentle smile and she stroked my hair and held me close like she used to do when I was a frightened child.

"You know exactly what to do, my love. You always have, even as a child. I have no doubts that you'll figure this out on your own." I wanted her to stop being vague and tell me what to do but I couldn't find my voice.

She turned to look at Eric who seemed totally oblivious to our encounter. He was looking straight ahead throwing rocks into the dirt.

"He's handsome, your protector," she sighed, "And brave like your father—intense and determined to do their job no matter what the consequences. I miss his touch." A tear trickled down her cheek. "They'll both assist you in this very sad and necessary task that's been thrust on you. Trust them."

And then . . . she was gone.

I felt myself shudder and Eric's arms were around me, holding me upright.

"Molly, are you all right? You were in some kind of a trance and then you started shaking," he said worriedly.

"No, I'm fine, really. I saw her Eric. I held her, she was so real. It was my hope that she'd give me advice but as usual she left me with one thought . . . to trust you and my father."

Eric held me to his chest and rocked and said soothing words in my ear. "Shhh. It's going to be all right. You'll see. I know how hard this has been for you and I've promised to keep you safe and I will."

I wanted nothing more than to stay like this with him and not have to face Arnos, but there was a sudden blast of a horn in the direction of the castle. We both reacted at the same time, jumping up and onto the horses in one swift motion, racing back to Dax. Something was finally happening. There was no more time to think about it; I had a dirty job to do.

We arrived at the gates to the castle just as Dax and several of his men, including Hector and Jonni, were exiting in long black riding coats, about to mount their horses.

"What's happening?" I shouted jumping from Miklo's back. Eric was already on the ground, handing off his horse to a stable boy. I ran to Dax's side.

"Arnos' men have attacked my soldiers near his camp. We needed some more hands so Hector and Jonni have volunteered to go with us. Eric, if you would, stay here and guard the ladies. We won't be long."

Eric nodded.

"Don't look so worried, Molly, it's only a minor skirmish. The main confrontation will be soon. Arnos means this to be a distraction so be alert," Dax said turning toward the horses.

"Be careful," I said.

"Always," he replied.

They mounted their horses and rode west toward Arnos' camp. I gave Eric a quick glance and we ran inside and bolted the door.

Naomi and Sophie were waiting in the elegant living room on a huge couch, huddled together. Ali was gazing out the window with her arms wrapped around her waist, body tense.

An uncomfortable feeling enveloped me. I couldn't just sit here and wait for them to return. If this diversion was meant to divide our forces then Arnos might be planning on attacking the castle.

That was against the rules. But wouldn't that be just like Arnos to cheat and fight dirty. The man had no honor.

"Eric, we can't just stand here and do nothing. Aren't there some soldiers left to defend the castle? What if Arnos decides to catch us unawares?" I pleaded.

"She has a point," Naomi said looking at her mother.

"Molly, your father isn't going leave us without men to defend the castle," Eric replied.

"Then where are they?" I asked. "Did you see anyone in the courtyard?"

"They should be on the battlements. Look there," Ali murmured.

He looked like he was considering this fact and suddenly went to leave the room.

"I'll be right back," he said and closed the door behind him.

I thought about going after him but Naomi stopped me as I stood to follow him.

"I know what you're thinking of doing. That look is in your eye. Let him do his job," she said quietly.

I sighed, nodding reluctantly and sank back into my chair tapping my foot and chewing my nails. Ali came and sat next to me on the arm of the chair.

"He's a very brave young man," she said stroking my hair.

All I could do was nod my head. I wanted to scream.

Eric returned fifteen minutes later a little out of breath from running. He slumped into a vacant chair. I noticed he'd acquired a crossbow on his expedition that he set on the floor next to him. "There are twenty men along the battlements ready for an attack. We're covered."

We sat and waited.

And waited.

And waited some more. By this time we were all pacing the room in panic. Something better happen soon or I'm going to leave and find out what's going on myself.

The sound of pounding hooves brought us once more to the window in midafternoon.

Chapter 45

A horn sounded outside the castle and we rushed to see who it was. Dax and the men were back with the garrison that had been attacked. Some looked wounded and were ushered into the courtyard to be tended to in the infirmary. I saw that Hector and Jonni didn't appear to be hurt but Dax was holding his left arm close to his body and wobbled in the saddle. Naomi, Ali and I ran to help wherever we could.

Hector assisted Dax off his horse and that's when I saw he had an arrow shaft sticking out of his upper arm. Ali was at his side quickly, holding his arm gently and leading him to the infirmary.

"What happened?" I asked Hector. He was angry and his irritated expression frightened me.

"Arnos' men had the garrison pinned down at their camp. And if you can believe this; Arnos was there encouraging his men to aim carefully and shoot to kill. Dax of course had to go in all guns blazing and got caught in the crossfire. Idiot. He wouldn't listen to me," he hissed throwing his glove to the ground.

You rarely see Hector this mad. He was really pissed.

I ran into the infirmary to Dax's bed where the doctor was removing the arrow. Dax grimaced but didn't make a sound except a low grunt as the arrow came out. Ali was beside him holding tight to his hand, her eyes closed; he had his face against her arm. Naomi was standing behind her mother looking like she'd cry any second.

"Will he be all right?" I asked the doctor.

"In about two hours. He heals very quickly. He's lucky the arrow didn't hit the bone or an artery. You can see the wound has already closed." He had quickly applied some antibiotic ointment to the wound after pulling out the arrow.

I stood in awe of the healing powers of being an immortal and a dragon, remembering my own recovery when Jonathan had shot me down.

"We can't lose sight of our goal, Molly," Dax said weakly, wincing. "He was reveling in our attack. I believe now he is insane with power and we must at all costs confront him tomorrow and end this. Are you ready?"

I thought about that. It was the eleventh hour. Was I? I gazed around at my team as we surrounded his bed. Dax looked at me steadily, eyes questioning. *Decision time.*

"Yes, I am," I said so confidently even I believed it. "And before he regroups and decides to attack us here, we should be on our toes?" I laid my hand on his arm.

"My men will man the battlements in shifts throughout the night in case he's stupid enough to do that tonight." He attempted to sit up and then winced and lay back down. "In the morning we'll meet him on the field. Courage my love. You can do this."

"You'd best rest, my lord," said the doctor as he went to tend to another casualty. "I'll check on you later. It looks like you have three lovely ladies to take care of you now." He chuckled and indicated Naomi, Ali and myself.

Hector and Jonni had gone off to assist with the other injured. Eric stayed by my side.

Unexpectedly I had a riot of butterflies doing the tango in my stomach. Trying to maintain some semblance of calm I smiled, but Eric saw the fear in it and put his arms around me and hugged tight kissing my hair over and over. The unnerving realization that Arnos would be eliminated soon overwhelmed me. I was feeling his anger and insanity growing.

Hector's intense stare from across the room told me he'd felt it too.

"I'll be fine. I think I need to rest and maybe eat something. All this stress is getting to me big time." I smiled halfheartedly.

Molly, you do need to do those things and prepare for tomorrow. As soon as I am well I'll help you. Dax's soothing voice in my head added to Eric's touch and my mind cleared and calmed at once. My mother was right; I needed to trust these two important men in my life.

Eric and I said our goodbyes when we saw there wasn't anything more we could do here and headed to the main house, my face buried against his chest.

I couldn't fall asleep and lay staring at the ceiling. Eric lay beside me fast asleep, emitting soft moans every now and then; probably dreaming about our recent lovemaking. I glanced at his face in the dark; he was smiling.

This was the man I planned on spending the rest of my life with and it scares me to think about the possibility of losing him in this battle, if my dream proves true. My father is so confident that all will be well. Maybe he knows something I don't. We'll see.

I had some questions for Arnos when we were finally face to face; the important one being where Eric's family was being held captive and were they still alive. I needed to know this before I fry his *you know what.*

Eric moaned again and turned over toward me, plunking his arm across my stomach. I turned away from him and spooned as close as I could get against him feeling the warmth of his body. Tonight I wanted the world to go away and leave us alone.

I eventually drifted off to a dreamless sleep.

Chapter 46

The next morning it was barely light when I woke up searching for Eric beside me. His side was empty. I remembered him saying something about going out early to practice his new shield technique so I'm guessing he must have slipped out before dawn.

Eric had learned how to fashion individual shields that were flat, like a knight's shield, which could move with the person and allow them to reach out to grab someone or something they held before they realized it was happening. Pretty slick and clever; he was so talented.

After I was sufficiently awake I took a long leisurely shower and dried my hair, putting it into a ponytail on top of my head. It needed to be out of the way today.

Debating whether to wear any makeup I decided I might as well go all out for this auspicious occasion so my paint went on carefully and tastefully.

In the closet I found a great outfit—tight black pants, black sleeveless top and a gorgeous black leather jacket. Tall black boots rounded out my ensemble.

As I regarded my image in the mirror, I wondered if I was sufficiently intimidating. I did that growly thing again.

A sharp wolf whistle behind me confirmed my assessment. I saw Hector's leering reflection in the mirror and smiled. I sure hope Naomi appreciates him; he is yummy.

"Girl, you look great . . . but then you always do," he said coming up behind me. He flashed his mischievous grin.

"Be careful H, Eric may be nearby. I don't need him mad and distracted by your attentions today of all days," I warned adjusting my jacket. "Did you need something?"

"Just checking to see if you were awake and ready. Your father's orders. We'll be leaving soon."

My stomach lurched. Then the headache hit me. Hector caught me before I hit the floor.

"Molly!"

"Give me a minute, H," I murmured, struggling to collect myself and calm the pain. Hector helped me to a chair and I sat down with a thud. Not a good move. "Ow!"

"What was that?" he said worriedly. "Your eyes are glowing."

"I've been getting these headaches lately. Dax says it's because my dragon knows what's going on and wants out. If I don't let it out soon the headaches will get worse. Oh boy, this one's a doozy," I cried, my head in my hands. "Hector get my father, quick!"

Hector ran out and shouted for Dax. A second later Dax came bounding through the door and to my side.

"This is worse," I sobbed, the pain was so bad.

Without a word he knelt before me and placed his hands on either side of my head and closed his eyes. The warmth radiating from his hands was absorbed by my skin and I felt the pain slowly dissipate as if he was pulling it back into his fingers. The relief was heaven. My body went limp and sagged against him.

"We need to let her rest for a few minutes," Dax said to the crowd that had gathered in the room. He picked me up and laid me on the bed. I felt Eric's hand take mine and I gave him a wan smile and fell asleep.

When I woke up it felt like hours had passed.

"How long did I sleep?" I asked Eric. He was lying next to me stroking my hair with a placid look on his face.

"Only a few minutes really," he replied, twisting a tendril of hair between his fingers, a faint smile on his lips.

I turned to face him. He continued to play with my hair until I leaned over and kissed him.

"I'm glad you stayed with me," I whispered. "Is everyone ready?"

"Ready and waiting. The question of the day is are *you* ready?"

I touched his face. He needed a shave. "Yes. Let's go."

I sat up and swung my legs off the side of the bed; no dizziness or headache. Yea.

Eric followed me downstairs where we met up with the assembled teams—mine, Dax's and some I'd never seen before. Dax explained that these men were his household guards and would stay behind with Ali, Sophie and the servants. There was no telling what Arnos was planning. Dax stood before us.

"Eric will form our shields when we are closer to the field. My scouts tell me Arnos has arrived at the field with about forty soldiers. We have your team of four, Molly and my eighty men. We have our plan."

He moved to stand in front of me. We stared at each other for a moment, his hands on my shoulders. He never said a word out loud only pressed his forehead to mine and whispered in my head.

I love you daughter. Let's end this tyranny.

To the rest of our company he ordered everyone outside. I saw him give Ali and Naomi hugs and pat Sophie's cheek, and then he walked out the door with the stride of a proud warrior and mounted his horse, Balco.

The ride to meet Arnos took half an hour. I rode between Dax and Eric, my eyes straight ahead and I could see them steal glances at me; waiting to see if I'd freak out I guess. Hector and Jonni were behind us, oddly quiet, especially for Hector.

The butterflies were back but strangely enough they weren't rioting, just fluttery. I had a sense of detachment from all this craziness we were about to rush into and suddenly felt sorry for Arnos. He had brought all this on himself and I wondered if he realized what was going to happen today and why.

We reached the edge of the forest near the far end of the field and stopped, using the trees for cover. The morning mist was starting to rise off the grass. I could see Arnos and his men on the other side standing still as statues, some holding weapons, some with their hands clasped in front of them, crossbows dangling.

I threw my leg over the horse's head and dismounted and went to stand behind a nearby tree to observe them. My existence, all our existence, depended on how I performed here today. No pressure there.

Eric came to stand next to me. We stared at each other for what seemed like an eternity; I laid my head against his chest and felt his heartbeat speed up.

"I love you with all my being," he murmured taking a deep breath.

"And I love you with all my heart," I replied trying to hide the emotion in my voice. I caressed his face lightly. I heard my father's footsteps behind me.

"Molly, it's time," Dax said. "Eric, if you would."

"How will I know what's happening if I can't see anyone?" I asked him.

"Remember what I taught you about your senses. You and I can talk telepathically and if you have trouble I'll be right behind you to fill in the gaps. Fortunately I can see through the shields so I'll know where everyone is at all times. Your sister is out there too. I don't plan on anything happening to her either."

That was comforting. I think. Like I said—no pressure.

I readied myself mentally, my dragon rumbling around inside, replacing the butterflies with warm stirrings, reminding me I needed to maintain control.

Eric raised shield after shield, surrounding each person with a soundproof bubble to muffle their advance. He would alter the shields when everyone was in place. Hector and Jonni gave me grins and thumbs up before vanishing. Eric threw me a quick smile and disappeared. I never saw Naomi or Dax before they too disappeared.

It was eerie standing here alone all of a sudden even though I knew Dax was close behind me.

I'm here Molly, his voice a soft whisper in my head. I felt his light touch on my shoulder.

When Dax assured me everyone was in place I started my walk onto the playing field, heading for the middle. I saw Arnos react to the sight of me coming out of the trees . . . alone. The soldiers fanned out in a backward V formation on either side of Arnos—much like a bunch of geese—leaving him at the tip of the formation. Good, right where we want them. Surprise!

I could feel the full impact of Arnos' emotions and it jarred my senses for a few seconds. My pulse was throbbing in my temples and I stopped abruptly to calm my dragon before continuing my advance across the field.

The tricks Dax had taught me about expanding my range were working beautifully, much to my relief. I could feel each person's position without much effort. Those soldiers wouldn't know what hit them in a few minutes.

I stopped when Arnos started across the field, his men in tow. He halted a few yards away from me.

Neither of us spoke for what seemed like hours, just stared.

"Hello . . . *uncle*," I said finally, the sarcasm dripping off the emphasis. "Or are you just another shape shifter phony sent to front for Arnos? That would prove him to be such a coward."

His eyes narrowed and his energy reeked of anger.

"Shall I demonstrate my ability for you as proof?" he said scowling.

"That would make me feel *so* much better," I replied. I leveled my gaze at him, waiting.

He gave a quick flick of his left arm and a tree exploded in a blinding flash of light. I felt the charge ripple through my body; my hair stood on end. I never even flinched.

Hmmm. All that bluster and energy show back at his house was just the prelude. This was the real thing. Proof enough.

"I see you're alone. How convenient. Where are your protectors? Ran off I suppose," he said, his voice like black velvet.

"They're . . . around," I replied stifling a smile. It took great effort not to laugh when I saw each of his men disappear behind him without a sound. I could sense my team moving their victims off to the side of the field so they could watch the proceedings.

Now it was only him and me.

Chapter 47

"You're an intriguing woman Molly Fyre, much like your mother. It's a pity your life is about to end," he said menacingly across the expanse between us. "I could have used your talents."

I glared at him and felt my body heating up with anger at his remarks. I needed to ask my questions.

"Why did you kill my mother?"

He gave me a surprised look. "So you figured it out. Well. My brother took my wife so I took his woman," he said flatly with no hint of remorse.

My hands were clenched at my sides and I forced my dragon back. *What does that mean, Father?*

Be still, daughter. Ali came to me of her own free will after he banished her for our indiscretion. He was cruel to her all their married life and I comforted her. Naomi was the result. I'm sorry.

I don't blame you or Ali. Do you love her?

Yes.

That's all that matters.

A few deep breaths settled the dragon for now.

Next question.

"Where are you holding Eric's family? Surely you can tell me now that I'm about to die." I smiled back darkly.

He heaved a bored sigh. "I suppose it doesn't matter anymore," he said casually. "You're all going to die here today." He hesitated for effect, calmly adjusting his sleeves. "Actually

217

you were sleeping above them the whole time and didn't know it."

A dungeon in the basement. Figures.

I noticed he was inching his way forward, the energy building inside him. Then he stopped and quickly glanced left, then right, and to his dismay, discovered he too was alone.

"What have you done!" he screamed at me, his face purple with rage.

"The playing field is even now, Arnos. Feeling a bit grumpy?" There was no way I was going to take this crap any longer.

We started to circle around like two gladiators in the arena, eyes locked together. I felt the energy crackling in the air; it made the hair on my arms stand up. One of us had to make the first move. I knew it wasn't going to be me.

Arnos stopped and closed his eyes both arms held out in front of him. His hands started to glow red and I heard him muttering some incantation; I knew I had to act quickly or get blown apart.

The air around me began to vibrate and swirl and I could feel the heat of the energy pressing against me. My ponytail whipped around behind me in the wind.

Movement on either side of me made me jump and I heard Dax's voice in my head.

It's only Eric and me. We need to do it now.

There was a sudden burst of emotion in the air around us; it was protective. It felt like Eric. He threw up an invisible barrier in front of us just as Arnos threw an energy bolt straight at me. He looked momentarily confused when he saw I was still standing, Eric in front of me.

Then he strode forward throwing energy and lightning bolts at a furious rate, sparks flying in all directions as they hit but nothing penetrated the shield.

Eric flinched ever so slightly but remained solidly on his feet with each surge of energy; didn't even break a sweat. I peeked under Eric's arm at Arnos frantically trying to break through. The wind was furious around us.

I felt Dax's hand on my arm as he revealed himself to Arnos. Arnos froze and a sickening smirk lit up his face.

"Ah, Brother, how nice to see you," he hissed.

"Yes, Arnos, we meet again," Dax yelled and to me he added, "Molly, be ready." I knew what he meant and stepped back a few paces. The electricity in the air was getting worse.

"It's been too long. We should get together and talk over old times over a glass of wine," Arnos yelled over the fury. "Oh, wait, you'll be dead. Tsk, tsk. It would have been so much easier if you had just handed over the Krystal and been done with it."

"That's where you're wrong Arnos. Nothing would change. You'd want more and more until there was nothing left. Then what would you do? No, it has to end here and now."

Arnos advanced a few more steps. "And who's to stop me, you and your pitiful progeny?"

"That's exactly who will accomplish it. Molly is the fifth generation dragon. A prophesy made long ago is what's in play today. It's a shame you have to be eliminated like this but there's no other way. Goodbye brother."

"What are you talking about?" Arnos bellowed.

"Molly, do it now," Eric shouted over the din.

I only hesitated for a second. Anger and fury filled me and fueled the dragon. My body started to warm and vibrate as I backed farther away from Dax and Eric. Effortlessly I transformed into my red dragon much to Arnos' horror. If I could have laughed I would have at the look on his face as I unfurled my wings and blew a couple of flaming fireballs at his feet. He jumped back.

I started toward Arnos and it only took a fraction of a second for him to realize his precarious position. He rapidly began to back up hurling lightning at my chest's armor plating as fast as he could. I felt the force of it but there was only a stinging sensation. The next bolt however headed straight for my head.

And she shall eat the sorcerer's lightning.

I inhaled deeply and felt the heat of the energy as it slid down my throat. It seemed to fuel my fire. As I reared back I think he saw that as retreat. There was triumph in his eyes as he prepared to send another shot my way. I didn't give him a chance.

There was no pity in my heart for him now. He had killed my mother, Peter and countless others for the sake of his own selfish wants. Right now he wanted to destroy us all for a hunk of rock.

I looked him in the eye and took a huge breath.

He knew what was going to happen; I could see it in his face. I kept my eyes locked on his like a snake to its prey. His eyes widened and he actually cowered and dropped to his knees in front of me.

I exhaled a stream of red flame at him as he held his arms out in supplication.

In a shower of red sparks he was ash in a matter of seconds. The energy and wind ceased.

I collapsed onto the grass in a heap and stared at the charred spot where my uncle had been. I lay there huffing out long tendrils of smoke as a mind numbing silence followed and time stood still. My body was exhausted and I wasn't able to transform back just yet.

All at once there was a cacophony of noise as everyone's shields dropped and Dax and Eric ran to my side.

Eric came and cautiously stood by my gigantic head, laying his hand on me gently.

"Are you all right Moll?" he said quietly. My great eye looked at him sadly.

Father, tell him I'm fine. Just give me a minute.

"Eric she's fine. Give her time to recover."

And Father . . . I'm sorry. He stroked my neck and I saw him smile with tears in his eyes and walk to the blackened grass and kneel down.

After several minutes had passed, I felt that I could revert back to my human form. Eric was still there stroking my head. When I was myself again he grabbed me into his arms and I clung to him tightly.

Hector, Jonni, Naomi and Dax's men were herding Arnos' soldiers towards the trees to take them back to the castle. They all had stunned expressions as they passed the charred grass and I'm sure they were glad they hadn't been a part of the barbecue.

I could easily have killed them all with one fiery breath. I was glad I didn't have to do that.

After we returned to the castle everyone except Eric avoided me, not because I'd done something despicable but just to let me grieve alone. Dax had told me he was proud of me, that it took great courage to do what I'd done, and then he left me alone too. I don't know if that was such a good idea.

I moped around for days, just barely going through the motions of life. Incinerating someone will do that to you; slow you down and suck all your energy. I felt like crap. I hardly ate. Eric simply held me at night not forcing me to do something I couldn't and I thanked him for being considerate.

Just when I thought I'd sunk to a new low of despair my father summoned me to his study. I dragged myself downstairs and knocked softly on his door. He sat behind his massive desk shuffling papers and looked up as I entered.

"Good, you're here. I have something to say to you, daughter. Come let us sit over there," he said indicating the couch.

I sat at the opposite end of the couch curled into a tight ball. He was turned toward me, simply staring at the decrepit lump that was me. I fidgeted, feeling very uncomfortable with his gaze when he sighed and shook his head.

"Molly, my love, I don't want you to grieve any longer. I know this has been hard on you. God knows I feel the same, but we have to move on." His eyes were pleading with me and I could feel the pain in his heart. Tears were stinging my eyes.

"I've talked to Hector about this since he's gone through this himself. Still, I can't get the image of that blackened earth out of my head. How long will that last?" I cried burying my face in my hands.

Dax moved over to me and held me, stroking my hair. "I don't know my darling, but memories fade over time," he said gently. I sobbed against his shoulder.

We sat like that for some time until a servant interrupted with some good news for a change. I wiped the tears from my face and overheard him tell Dax that Eric's family had been found and they were on their way here.

"Does Eric know?" Dax asked the man.

"Yes sir, he's elated," the servant replied giving Dax a quick nod.

Dax held my face in his hands for a few seconds and then kissed my forehead. "Go to him," he whispered.

I needed to find Eric and started for the door. Dax waved his hand for me to go and I rushed to the stairs just as Eric was coming down. It made my heart leap to see him so happy.

"You've heard? They've found my parents and sister in a locked room in Arnos' basement and they should be here in a day or two." He scooped me up in his arms and twirled me around so fast I felt nauseous. Ooh, that shouldn't have happened. Maybe I'm tired or getting sick. I felt better when he set me down.

Dax had been watching us from the study doorway. Eric went over and shook his hand briskly.

"Thank you sir, I'm eternally grateful."

"My pleasure young man. Now, we must start making plans for a new Keeper. Since I'm still a member of the Keeper's Council, I've been in contact with the other members who unanimously endorse your father for position as the new Keeper. It's for certain that he will govern fairly and wisely. And as his protector you'll be required to be at his side. Do you intend to take my daughter with you?"

Eric glanced my way. "Oh yes, as soon as we're married."

Okay heart, stay still.

"Then a wedding will drive away the gloom hovering over us," Dax replied. "Ali will be thrilled; there has never been a wedding in this house. It's time for a celebration." He clapped Eric on the back and looked at me affectionately. "You'll make a beautiful bride my love. I must go tell Ali the good news," he said excitedly and headed up the stairs.

Eric and I stood there for a few seconds, silly grins on our faces. My gloom was lifting finally and I had a feeling things were going to move very quickly for the next few days. That queasy feeling was back. Was I coming down with something? Crap, not now. I think reality is catching up to me finally and I swallow hard.

"Are you feeling ill?" Eric said. "You're pale."

"I think I need to lie down for a bit. Things are moving pretty fast and I'm really tired." I smiled at him weakly.

He saw me to my room and I lay on my bed and was fast asleep in seconds.

Chapter 48

The next four days brought a flurry of activity to the castle. Along with Ali, Naomi and little Sophie, I prepared for the wedding. Ali had conveniently brought her wedding dress with her when she fled Arnos; surprisingly it fit me perfectly.

When I saw myself in the mirror I cried, wishing my mother was here to share this happy moment. Ali was right there comforting me, letting me know she understood and that I could call on her anytime I needed.

Eric's family arrived on the third day exhausted but thankful their ordeal was over and they were safe. I was introduced to his parents, Malick and Sarah, who, after looking me over critically, must have decided I was right for their son.

Sarah joined in the preparations as soon as she was rested and we sat down and had a nice chat about Eric and how he was as a child. Apparently he was quite mischievous. She hadn't seen him in a very long time and his seriousness took her by surprise.

"He's my protector," I told her. "He takes his duties very seriously but sometimes that little boy shows through. I love both sides of him."

"As well you should. Men sometimes forget that we need them to be one or the other as the need arises. My Malick is a good man but oftentimes I'd like to take a switch to his hide for being stupid!" she said laughing.

"Oh, I've wanted to do that to Eric many times," I agreed.

We formed a quick bond and I felt comfortable in her quiet presence. She and Malick showed an interest in my 'gift' and

I promised to show them my dragon before we all went our separate ways.

Now Fran, Eric's mindreading/manipulator sister is quite funny. She has been so busy reading everyone and then giggling; I've wondered what she's hearing. I can't get her to reveal anything. It's quite annoying really. Why can't she tell me what Eric is thinking at least? He only shakes his head when she's around, gives her warning looks and then smiles. She completely ignores him.

The Keeper's Council members arrived soon after his parents and met that evening in the huge conservatory at the back of the castle. It was dark already but moonlight shown through the ceiling high windows . . . the Blue Moon. The room glowed with candlelight and the smell of fresh flowers filled the air. I sat with the rest of the women off to the side, only observers to the council's business.

Each member in turn gave his or her endorsement of Malick's assent to the position of Keeper. He gave a splendid speech thanking everyone for their support and accepting the task and voiced regret that Arnos wasn't the leader they had expected, that his untimely death was not to be celebrated. They all solemnly nodded their heads.

Eric stood behind his father proud as a peacock dressed in his navy blue tunic—the symbol of his position as protector. He caught my eye and winked, making me smile.

Malick warmly welcomed Dax back into the council and Dax was the first to shake his hand and give his congratulations. Malick was soon surrounded by council members slapping him on the back and wishing him well.

"What are you thinking?" Eric said to me as I stood off to the side watching the well-wishers, lost in my thoughts.

"Oh, nothing in particular," I said looking him in the eye. "Does this mean you'll be leaving with your family soon?"

"Not without you," he answered his blue eyes shining. "My father can do without me for a while. This is what you want isn't it, to go back with us?"

"Of course. But I would like to stay and visit some more with Dax. We have a lot of catching up to do." I ran my hands up his sleeves and put my arms around his neck.

"We won't leave until you're ready." He gave me a peck on the nose and we went to join the crowd.

The day of the wedding arrived bright and sunny with just a hint of fall in the air. I woke earlier that I expected and turned to watch Eric sleeping. His eyes opened slowly and we gave each other a big smile.

"Good morning almost wife," he said softly, pushing back a wisp of my hair.

"Good morning almost husband," I whispered planting a kiss on his lips.

"Let's just stay here until someone sees we're missing," he laughed. Then there were footsteps outside our door.

"I'll bet you ten bucks it's going to be Hector who bangs on the door," I muttered.

"We'll ignore him."

Right on cue a loud knock sounded.

"Go away!" Eric shouted.

"Get up you lazy louts; you'll need your strength for the festivities. Come join us for breakfast," Hector boomed.

We looked at each other and burst out laughing. "Pay up, McGuire," I said jumping out of bed and racing to the bathroom.

Eric pulled on his pants and sauntered to the door opening it so fast Hector jumped back a few feet. "Can't you ever leave us alone?" he hissed.

"It's so much more fun this way," I heard H say. "You did pick me to be your best man and it's my duty to harass you."

"Point taken. Now go away. We'll be down shortly." And the door slammed shut. I could hear Hector's cackling laugh as he went away.

Breakfast was fun and took up most of the morning. It was now time to get ready for the afternoon wedding. The servants had converted the conservatory into a magnificent wedding chapel and the kitchen was busy cooking a feast.

I said goodbye to Eric and the boys and joined the ladies in my room to be pampered and dressed.

At precisely one o'clock I walked down the aisle on my father's arm and married my protector. The highlight of the ceremony was Hector's very loud snort when I said 'for better or worse'. I glanced back to see Naomi give him an elbow in the ribs as everyone else snickered.

After a very long kiss that had everyone laughing, Eric and I headed down the aisle as husband and wife to loud applause. Halfway down I glanced to my right when I saw a brilliant blue light appear. No one else reacted so I guessed I was the only one who saw her.

There stood my mother in a blue mist, tears in her eyes, smiling brightly at me. I smiled back and blew her a kiss. She slowly vanished, receding into the mist, catching the kiss I'd sent.

"Who was that for?" Eric asked, looking down at me.

"My mother," I replied wistfully, wiping away a tear.

"She's here?"

"She was, right over there," I said pointing to my right. "She's gone now."

He didn't say another word, just squeezed my hand as we were surrounded by well-wishers.

Dax gave me a huge hug and whispered in my ear, "I saw her too. She's beautiful." We exchanged teary looks.

The party lasted into the wee hours of the morning and the house was alive with laughter and song, my friends and new relatives mingling amicably. Eric quietly walked up behind me and hugged me to his chest.

"It's over, Moll. Now we can get back to normal," he whispered in my ear.

I closed my eyes and leaned into him. My body and mind were so weary I could sleep for a week. Normal—I couldn't imagine life being normal again after the events of the last few weeks.

I thought of the people we'd lost along the way and the new acquaintances that had come into our lives. My defeat of Arnos was tragic but as I've found out from Eric's father, Arnos had indeed killed several council members who had opposed him. Even though I grieved for the man he should have been, I was satisfied that we had done the right thing, as painful as it was.

My father's voice brought me out of my reverie.

"Molly, Eric, I have a wedding gift for you." He handed me a large envelope. I looked at Eric and he shrugged.

"What's this?" I inquired taking out a sheaf of papers. Eric was looking over my shoulder.

"A gift . . . a place for you and Eric to start your new life," he said fondly. "I believe everything should be in order."

We sifted through the papers in disbelief. Here was the deed to a home and land . . . a lot of land.

"We can't accept this," Eric said. "It's too much. And where is this place?"

"It lies in the land of dragons, which we will open the gate to very soon. If you don't accept I'll be very insulted." His face was stern for a brief second or two and then his expression softened, giving us a warm smile.

"Thank you, Father," I said giving him a hug and a kiss. "This will be a safe haven in times of stress. You know I'll be going with Eric so he can be with his father."

"I do. But you'll be back."

"Yes."

Later in our room Eric and I stood on the balcony overlooking the garden, gazing into the moonlit darkness, in each other's arms. He was shirtless and as always, beautiful. There was something different about him I thought; a tattoo on his left arm I had missed before. I ran my hand lightly over the red heart with our names over and under the word FOREVER. A warm glow filled me.

He smiled in amusement.

"When did you do this?" I asked.

"Two weeks ago. Hector did it."

"Before the wedding? You were that sure?

"Of course."

I continued to rub my fingers over the tattoo. He shivered and took in a breath. My eyes met his in a loving gaze.

"I have a wonderful secret to tell you," I whispered close to his ear.

His eyes got wide as I relayed my happy news.

"Are you sure?"

"Yes," I murmured. He gently placed his hand on my stomach as he kissed me.

He gave me a sly smile. "I guess I'll need another tattoo soon."

So here our story ends . . . for now.

My life was complete. I'd found my place in this world, defeated our enemy, found family and married the man I love all in the space of a few weeks. Our child would be born in the spring, a time of new beginnings.

Dax and I have opened the dragon gate in the same grove of trees where I'd seen my mother; a place I knew held great magic. I have yet to venture into it . . . but I'll be back.

Who knows what adventures lay ahead? Only time will tell.

Acknowledgements

I would like to thank Kathy, Heather and Ken for their feedback on this my first novel. It's gratifying to know that my efforts are appreciated.

Thanks also to Ivey, Hazel and the design team at AuthorHouse for their help and support in bringing my book to fruition.

A special thanks goes to Jessica Feinberg for her excellent cover art. Like I said, you're a genius and brought the image of my character to life.

Thanks to JoAnne Marino for my author photo.